Herald Angels

by

Renee Canter Johnson

Herald Angels

COPYRIGHT © 2017 by Renee Canter Johnson

Cover Art by *Rae Monet, Inc. Design*

The Wild Rose Press, Inc.
PO Box 708
Adams Basin, NY 14410-0708
Visit us at www.thewildrosepress.com

Publishing History
First Sweetheart Rose Edition, 2016
Print ISBN 978-1-5092-1224-8
Digital ISBN 978-1-5092-1225-5

Published in the United States of America

Stealing a cursory glance in her direction,
the background beyond her mom's profile was the same
as it had been the last time she'd visited. It slid by in
flashes of white saltbox houses dotting November's
gray-green landscape. Sara realized little was different
in the appropriately named Bland, Virginia.

If duller, less vibrant now, perhaps the only change
was in her perspective. Living in the city, energetic
colors intersected all views, if just from red-soled heels
entering yellow taxis beneath Broadway's flashing neon
signs. Maybe it was her current lackluster attitude or the
fact she'd previously returned to Bland only during
spring and summer when the alfalfa fields bloomed
with emerald brightness and the deciduous trees formed
shady canopies beneath the surrounding blue mountain
ridges.

Nor had her mother changed much. Her fluffy
hairstyle was certainly the same as it had been for
years. It had only paled, growing lighter and lighter
until now it was nearly white. She had accumulated
more wrinkles around the eyes, weakening their
sparkle—or was the duress Sara's presence caused the
more likely culprit to their reduced shine? She knew
better than to mistake diminishing appearance for
waning resilience.

While Sadie Goode might look fragile to the eye,
her fortitude was as sturdy as Bland Chapel's
foundation—built on rock, circa 1819.

Dedication

To my husband, Tony Johnson,
who understands my desires to travel and write.
~*~
To my sister, Lisa Canter Blevins,
who understands our own family dynamics.
~*~
And to my editor, Maggie Johnson,
who continues to provide
wonderful guidance and opportunities.

Chapter 1

Sara Goode was the only passenger in the car driven by her mother. Well, almost. A half-dozen freshly-made wreaths, layered between old corn sacks to keep resin and sap off the rarely-driven sedan's upholstery, covered the backseat and evergreen garland filled the trunk. Preoccupied with her troubles, she didn't mind the brooding silence as they drove toward the church.

Does the entire town know? Have they heard about my failure? Sara wondered. *Is Mom about to launch a diatribe about the many disappointments I have given her since I left home?*

Despite her mother's past stinging remarks, she rarely ranted. Sadie Goode preferred a slow simmer to a rolling boil. Even now, the heat in her mother's petite, dainty-boned framework crept up gradually, pulsing with building urgency through the raised purple veins trailing her tissue-paper-thin flesh.

Stealing a cursory glance in her direction, the background beyond her mom's profile was the same as it had been the last time she'd visited. It slid by in flashes of white saltbox houses dotting November's gray-green landscape. Sara realized little was different in the appropriately named Bland, Virginia.

If duller, less vibrant now, perhaps the only change was in her perspective. Living in the city, energetic colors intersected all views, if just from red-soled heels entering yellow taxis beneath Broadway's flashing neon signs. Maybe it was her current lackluster attitude or the fact she'd previously returned to Bland only during spring and summer when the alfalfa fields bloomed with emerald brightness and the deciduous trees formed shady canopies beneath the surrounding blue mountain ridges.

Nor had her mother changed much. Her fluffy hairstyle was certainly the same as it had been for years. It had only paled, growing lighter and lighter until now it was nearly white. She had accumulated more wrinkles around the eyes, weakening their sparkle—or was the duress Sara's presence caused the more likely culprit to their reduced shine? She knew better than to mistake diminishing appearance for waning resilience.

While Sadie Goode might look fragile to the eye, her fortitude was as sturdy as Bland Chapel's foundation—built on rock, circa 1819. Her opinion of Sara was as strictly adhered to as the tenets forming the little white church her family attended. And her viewpoint of her younger daughter—Sara supposed—had been cemented a long time ago. Success in Sara's career had not altered it.

Sara had entertained the notion that her radio show's cancelation might accomplish what her achievements had not. Anticipating her mother might respond to her defeat in ways she had been unwilling or unable to during her successes, Sara now knew she'd been wrong.

Her nervous throat-clearing cough bit into the silence as Sara tested the air for its acrimony. "Isn't the

Hanging of the Greens service being held earlier than normal this year?"

Her mother's fingers tightened on the steering wheel, the effort forcing tendons and arteries to visibly lift upward on the backs of her hands. Whether the tenseness was from Sara's voice, or the impending sharp turn from White Pine Drive onto Suitor Road, her daughter couldn't be sure.

Ignoring the distress signal, Sara stared out the window onto the rise to her right. The frostbitten field was distantly speckled with dark bodies she knew indicated a deer herd was moving in to feed on the hay remnants left behind by the cattle.

After making the turn, her mother sighed. "Yes, Sara. A lot has changed while you've been gone."

Biting the soft flesh inside her left cheek, Sara tried to ignore the barb. Although she had only been in Manhattan for the past five years, college had commanded the majority of her time in the previous four, with small time blocks adding up to a year, at least, in between dedicated to traveling with student-focused opportunities.

"I'm certain it has." *Things have changed for us all*, she thought, recalling this past Halloween and the shameful way the day had progressed.

Sadie Goode exhaled, the sound of breath being squeezed from her diaphragm reminiscent of the valve on the pressure cooker she used for canning garden vegetables in the summer, and as audibly nerve-shattering to Sara. "We decided three years ago to decorate the church right before Thanksgiving. The new pastor, a real forward-thinker, is amenable to minor tweaks."

3

By *new pastor*, Sara knew her mother didn't mean *recently* hired, but the replacement for tradition-honoring Reverend Dinkins. She couldn't remember the pastor's name who had replaced him four years before, having not made time during her rare visits home to attend church functions. Her avoidance, attributed to what had happened—or rather hadn't happened—there, wasn't particularly unexpected she'd been assured by her father.

"So you like this guy, the atmosphere he has created?"

Her mother didn't speak right away. Sara wondered if she was composing a retort sarcastic enough to dig at her, without being an obvious attack demanding a response. Probably something about the wedding she'd run out on, or the family she'd deserted. When Sadie did reply, it was impossible to discern, even with her sharp tone, if there was a double meaning.

"You might be surprised, Sara, at how progressive Bland Chapel has become. We've adopted a rather all-inclusive path, respecting individual faiths, and even evolving scientific knowledge."

If Sara were dissecting the words, there was nothing untoward being spoken. But Mother's voice grated. A point was being made. She should understand they were neither simple country heathens nor Bible-thumpers, but thoughtful, smart, people who were aware of the changing environment around them.

Sara wasn't taking the bait. She wasn't going to succumb to a defensive position and say what she might otherwise have said—*I didn't say you weren't. Why would I think otherwise?* "That's…terrific."

But she wondered if it could be as wonderful as her mother made it sound. In Manhattan, she had attended a few services at different area churches, from the massive St. Patrick's Cathedral on Fifth Avenue, to the tiny St. Paul's Chapel across from the World Trade Buildings' footprint.

"There's something similar in New York," she added, thinking about All Souls Parish. She longed for some way to connect with her mother. "I remember hearing about it from an interview I had with a local poet. Maybe I'll check it out when I get back."

Her mother's head snapped in her direction, locking stormy eyes with hers. "So you're going back to your concrete kingdom?"

Wilting beneath the intense gaze, her efforts to bond were failing. Her spine straightened, yanking her upward as though a metal rod in her back had made contact with an enormous magnet attached to the roof. In her mind, responses volleyed by the dozen. All were acerbic. None were spoken, though she had to clamp down on her inner jaw with more torque than before to prevent them from spewing out.

Sara knew Sadie didn't need an answer to form an opinion. With icy demeanor she lifted one hand from the steering wheel, rotating it in the air. She appeared to be snatching words with it to hurl against Sara, who braced for her mother's verbal weapons. "Got another—what do you call them—*gigs*?" She made it sound like a distasteful comedy or musical act, something bawdy to be saved for back alleys and unsavory dives.

Why doesn't she just yell at me, tell me off, or give me a tongue-lashing? Anything would be better than the slights and digs meant to get the point across while shielding her from direct blame.

If she said anything harsh in return, Sadie would turn large, sky-colored eyes up to her with the notorious response—*What did I say?*

Sara didn't want to argue with her mother and was trying to let other insults pass, but she felt obligated to defend her profession. *Sara's Secrets* had been a well-respected show at a high-profile station in one of the most prestigious office complexes in New York's business district. There was nothing *gig-like* about it.

She wanted to tell her mother how successful it had been; about winning the Gracie Award, whose televised ceremony no one in her family had chosen to attend, about the legendary people she had had the very good luck to have face-to-face conversations with.

Yet she knew it would only bring the inevitable reminder—it had not been enough to retain her position. "I'll get something lined up. I just have to stay positive until the New Year. Nobody is hiring until then."

She once again turned her face away to stare out the window at the Jefferson National Forest's stark trees. Provided a fire or blight didn't sweep across the mountainous ridges, those trees would be here long after they were both gone.

It was something to think about when the pressure inside the car increased. It was certainly much easier to focus on the woodland than to succumb to the last three weeks' memories in New York—the unemployment agent and his dismal attitude, the successive line of doors slammed in her face as interviews bombed, the homeless lady she'd met by sheer happenstance on the bench in Rockefeller Center.

Squatting at the stairs' landing leading upward to the ritzy stores on Fifth Avenue, now surrounded by white wire angels holding trumpets to the sky in a great seasonal heralding, the bench was often overlooked. But it had called out to her on that fateful day. The conversation with the impish woman she'd met there reverberated in Sara's skull, silenced only by the recollections of the radio station manager's voice when he'd announced her show wasn't being renewed.

Shocked, staring at the wall calendar behind his head as the slow-motion auditory relay bounced between her ears before lodging in her brain, she had noticed the date and laughed—thinking it a prank. Even at this moment, far from the city, in Southwestern Virginia, the memory brought pain and embarrassment. *How could I have been so foolish? How had I not seen it coming?*

Her mother exhaled again, jolting her from the horrible moment's memory back into the current one. "Well, I hope it will be a *real* job this time. You'll soon be thirty, Sara Jane. That's a bit old to sit around in a cubicle talking to people through a microphone, isn't it?"

Sara bit more than her inner cheek this time, sinking quivering teeth into her tongue. She didn't need a reminder she'd celebrated her twenty-ninth birthday just two months before. This was the last year she'd be seeing the world through a twenty-something lens, the most valuable to be had in her industry's social circles.

And it was quickly turning into the worst year she'd ever known. Gripping her fingers toward her palms, she glanced down at her nails' ragged appearance. They hadn't looked this horrible since, as a teenager, she'd helped her dad on the farm. In the city, she'd kept her hair and nails perfectly styled and polished. Without a steady income, she was quickly turning back into the farm girl with unruly curls dangling uncontrollably and snags and chips on her self-polished fingertips.

The car slowed and Sara looked up. They were arriving at the church. In spite of her apprehensiveness at seeing it again and the memories it might dredge to the surface, it was at least a place where her mother was certain to behave with gentility. Several vehicles were parked near the entrance, two with standing trunk lids.

A long trailer attached to a dually truck had an enormous evergreen tree filling its bed. It was strapped down like a captive, all movement restrained while its branches stuck out from the tie-downs in protest.

Sara opened the car door and prepared to help her mother carry the filled bins of freshly-made roping into the church when a familiar sound wafted over to her. For a moment time ceased as Cade Norton's voice came from somewhere close by. She could hear it—*surely she wasn't hearing things*—but couldn't see him.

Her mind flashed on past reminiscences shared by the two of them: in school, cheering her on, or her rooting for him, whispering in her ear, laughing with her over silly movies. And then the awful...*no, don't think about it*, she cautioned herself, steeling for the moment when she'd come face-to-face with the man she had once loved and so horribly wronged. It seemed poetic justice for Cade to have the opportunity to adjudicate revenge at the last place they'd seen each other.

Boots hitting the asphalt resounded, the noise rising up as Cade ran the final few steps toward her—*thunk, thunk, thunk.* Her pulse careened into overdrive, racing as she thought about seeing him again. *Will he chew me out in the church's parking lot?*

If he did, she deserved and would take it. Bracing against the vehicle's sleek side, she grounded her feet and watched with trepidation as the man she'd deserted approached. He swept her into an embrace before she could protest—even if she had actually wanted to—and she flung her arms momentarily around his waist.

"Sara! Wow, how long has it been?" He released her from the hug but continued to keep an arm on her shoulders, searching her eyes with his darkly happy ones.

Taken aback by the sudden clinch, she squealed, "Cade! What a surprise!"

Nodding at her mother, he said, "Hello, Sadie."

Using the tender tone she reserved for others, Sadie replied with a sweet smile. "Hello, Cade. Nice to see you. Sara, I'm going to go ask Beverly where she wants these extra wreaths." Snatching two from the backseat, she walked toward the double doors.

"Yes, Mother, of course," Sara blurted.

Cade's unexpected appearance incited a nervous attack. Somehow she hadn't imagined seeing him again, ever. Nobody in her family spoke about him in her presence.

He shouldn't be so pleased to run into me. He should hate me.

His gaze followed hers, squarely aimed at Sadie's back, before returning to bore into her eyes once again. "I thought you might make it down to the class reunion

9

back in September," he said. "Didn't you get the invitation?"

His voice was clear and jovial, the old Cade from high school, not the brooding graduate trying to figure out his life's path. He sounded settled, comfortable, while her gut churned out butterflies like a metamorphosis caterpillar factory.

Where is the vitriol, the hatred, the accusations?

"I...I did...and I meant to come down for it...I couldn't get away..." She stuttered and sought an explanation, feeling small beneath the intense gaze from the man she had dishonored.

As though reading her mind, or feeling the twitch of anxiety in her shoulder, he dropped his arm, shoving both hands into his functional denim jeans' pockets as he rocked backwards on his heels. "You couldn't get away for many events, apparently. Must be exciting to live in the city."

Sighing, Sara realized his words never sounded sarcastic. If her mother had said the very same thing, she would have been offended. But with Cade, there was no harsh intonation.

Perhaps she had been wrong to discount their relationship. Maybe they had just needed some time apart, time to grow up and do all the things young people needed to do to purge them from their systems. Here they were, five years later, standing in the same parking lot their wedding guests would have used.

Had destiny intervened? Had the time in Manhattan been a thorough-enough lesson in the dating world? Was it meant to teach her to appreciate Cade before marrying him and forever-after succumbing to a lifetime of curiosity about what waited beyond

Jefferson National Forest's border?

Time slowed, then catapulted backwards. The pair of them darting around together, broken by a brief space hiccough, seemed like yesterday. Fate had rejoined them once again, depositing them into the world's same familiar indentation.

Her heart swelled. A smile radiated with each beat until it settled into a full grin. Turning it on, she tilted her head, softening toward him. *Cade Norton, perhaps it was always you.*

He shifted his weight and reached up to rub his chin. The gold band encircling his ring finger gave her the information she was about to ask for. *So, he's happily married. Likely the reason he isn't angry with me anymore.*

Though she was pleased he was no longer upset with her, his belonging to another woman stabbed into her chest. *How is it possible to experience so many high and low extremes in the space of hours, even minutes?*

Biting back disappointment, trying to keep it from lacing through her voice, Sara pointed to his hand. "Who's the lucky girl?" It came out a bit clipped, sharp. *Darn it.*

He looked sheepish, shuffled a foot against the smoothly-tarred surface. The unruly swath of bangs he'd referred to as a cowlick slid into his eyes and he tossed his head to send it flying backward into place. "Emily."

The single one-word answer ticked in Sara. This wasn't possible. It couldn't be. It had to be another woman with the same first name. Risking, she asked the burning question, "Emily who?"

Cade's face twisted into a frown. "Starnes. Emily

Starnes. I thought you knew. Didn't you hear?"

Sara gasped, feeling her eyes bulging in surprise. "No, I hadn't heard."

He shoved the offending hand back into its hiding place. "I'm sorry. I had no idea...I mean...I certainly assumed..." His voice trailed away, and the giant gulf existing before she had landed back in Bland returned to separate them.

A sharp pang of betrayal gutted her while a dull thud whacked into her forehead, lodging in her brain. "You married Emily?"

"Yeah. I was pretty inconsolable after you left, Sara." His voice softened. "And well...Emily...being your best friend and all...I thought you would call her. And then I thought she would tell me what I did wrong..." His mouth continued to make soundless movements. He had lost all his initial suaveness and just appeared confused. "I figured you knew..."

Guilt for the pain she had inflicted on the man standing before her overwhelmed her. It was suddenly so palpable it could have been its own entity. Simultaneously, she too felt deceived. *How and why had this been kept from her?*

"Obviously, I had no idea." Feeling both betrayed by everyone and shocked by the news, it was one more thing to join the enormous self-reproach weighing down on her. Standing outside the church where their wedding would have been, facing the man she'd hurt, shouldn't make her feel like an outcast. Yet, it did.

Cade shifted his weight again, looking behind him. If he was searching for support, it wasn't coming. Sara kept one vigilant eye on the people milling about the church's exterior. Her emotions, and Cade's, were too sacrosanct to be witnessed.

Though a few acquaintances started toward them, they appeared to smack into an invisible wall the moment they realized it was Cade standing by the car with her. Extending greetings to her could, and would have to, wait.

They all knew. Of course they did. They'd been invited to the wedding, one failing to take place due to the bride's swift and unexplained departure. Each had probably received a personal note from her mother in appreciation for the gift she was returning, in Sara's stead.

Did I ever thank my mother for that? It had to have been difficult for her, nearly as traumatic as it had been for Cade.

Turning her focus back to him and away from the would-be intruders, Sara wondered what he saw when he looked at her. *Does he see the successful radio show host, or does he know about the failure? Do I appear as a woman nearly thirty, or as he does to me, seventeen and brimming with potential and possibility?*

Cade yanked his hands free, thrusting them out to his sides, and cleared his throat. "I...I would have told you. We just...I mean...there wasn't an opportunity...until now."

Sara felt like berating herself. *How can I stand here acting appalled at not knowing about Cade's wedding when he's never been privy to what prompted my decision to walk out on ours?*

"Of course not. I...it's my fault. I meant to call. I meant to stay in contact." This time she was the one stuttering, stammering, seeking the correct word recipe to turn the bitterness she'd served up to him into something digestible, easier to chew on and swallow. But it all still tasted noxious.

"So why didn't you? What stopped you?" He was squinting at her. The casual nature their first few moments seeing each other was now over.

Emotional distress waves were eroding the soft underbelly reserved for niceties, leaving misery in its wake. She'd known him too long and too well not to recognize it.

Swallowing hard, feeling every muscle and tendon in her neck squeeze out whatever moisture was left in her mouth, she tried to find the words to eradicate her horrible past behavior. "It's just...one day led to another and pretty soon it had been a year and then..." She shrugged and frowned. There was no logical explanation.

Cade focused his dark and knowing eyes onto hers. The moment of surprise having passed, he now projected something entirely different, something resembling compassion, sympathy. His voice softened. "Are you home for good? We heard about your show."

The acknowledgment shocked her further, causing her stomach to plummet. Somehow, she hadn't expected people in Virginia would know yet, not the majority anyway, especially not her high school friends.

"Wow. Bad news travels fast, doesn't it? I should have flown down on it instead of taking that horrible flight."

He lifted an eyebrow. "It is a nationally syndicated radio show. I listened occasionally, as did more people here in Bland than would care to admit to it. So, are you moving back?"

"No, I'm only home for a visit. I've got several

things on the…" She looked into his face—a veil slid back and forth between past and present—and caught a glimpse of the internal scars from the wounds she was responsible for inflicting. Pride dissipated in her despicable behavior's pall toward a man who had once cared deeply for her.

He dropped his chin, as if aware of her scrutiny on his unshielded emotions.

Thinking he might lash into her, really let her have it, she took a deep breath and waited for a moment. The venom she knew she deserved didn't spew from him, only adding to her guilt.

Releasing her shield, Sara dared an apology, a real heartfelt explanation for something she could never repent sufficiently. "You know Cade, I'm truly sorry for hurting you. I loved you, really I did. In many ways I still do. You didn't do anything wrong and I should have had the courage to say so. I apologize."

Sara took a deep breath awaiting the onslaught she knew was warranted. Releasing the sentiments had a cleansing effect on Sara, though Cade continued to shuffle his foot, clearly uncomfortable.

"I accept your apology. We've both moved on."

Relief flooded Sara when she realized she wasn't about to be verbally assaulted in the churchyard. "Thank you, Cade. That's truly generous, much more than I deserve."

Someone calling Cade's name broke the magical spell that had led them to momentarily revisit the past and now extend olive branches. Jerked back into the present, Cade waved in the direction of the voice. "Coming," he yelled back. "Duty calls."

"Yes, of course." She watched him scurry along

the walkway, disappearing through the double doors leading from the church's portico to its vestibule.

A cold breeze bit into Sara's face and fingers, though her cheeks flushed warmly. Irritation bubbled beneath her cool exterior. Grinding her teeth together to keep them from latching onto her inner cheek's sore flesh, she wrapped her arms around her waist and paced around the car's rear. *Emily Starnes? Cade married Emily?*

Why hadn't someone warned her, told her about their marriage? Not even Beth had sent word. It should have been something her sister would have loved having the opportunity to use to take a dig at her.

Did it bother her so much because she and Emily had once known everything about each other and now knew nothing? Or was it a left-out feeling—ostracized from the friendship's cocoon she'd spent years spinning from shared confidence's rare silk and supreme trust— to now discovering she hadn't even been invited to her wedding?

During their formative years, Emily had been the sister Sara had always wished Beth to be. They pinky-swore to never date any guy the other had dated, to be each other's maids of honor, to name a child after the other, and to recite their friendship code:

We pledge to sit on the front porch,
in straw hats and gauzy dresses, in the middle of
summer,
drinking sweet iced tea from silver straws,
while the wild jasmine- and honeysuckle-scented
breeze,
ruffles our skirts, fanning them through the air like sails
blowing in the wind.

Funny how she could remember those exact words, the ones they'd written in Mr. Stewart's literature class, and for which they'd received glowing comments from him. It had become a mantra, a rope-skipping, rhythmic language cadence about their southern roots and how they viewed their friendship going into the future.

Perhaps her dejection wasn't about who Cade had married, but that he had married at all. He'd moved on, no longer anchored to her and their past. But she hadn't exactly been waiting for him either. She had dated three guys in New York, though neither seriously, nor for long.

She sensed her grimace growing into what she knew was most likely a scowl. A wide berth was still being afforded her, as if she might blow and cause a scene in the parking lot sending pine cones and evergreen garland thirty feet into the air in her wake. People whose names she had forgotten, some she had never known, took long exaggerated routes around her as she fished the never-ending roping strand from overturned bins in the trunk.

Draped in giant waxy magnolia leaves interspersed with pine tips and feathery hemlock, she realized her bruised ego was getting the best of her. Cade—and likely everyone else—knew about her show's cancelation, while she knew nothing about his life or Emily's. *How embarrassing*, she thought, wincing. Sara's pride in achieving the success she had was now little more than collateral damage. *I failed*.

Cade's voice once again swept across the churchyard and she gave a final tug on the decorative strand. Its end raced through her palm, and the effort tossed her backward, nearly causing her to fall.

Righting herself as the sound grew louder she turned away from the trunk and toward its direction.

He emerged from the opened church doors with a similarly-built man about their same age, late twenties or early thirties. There was something oddly familiar about the other man, though she couldn't quite make out his features, nor put her finger on it.

Returning from wherever she had disappeared to during Sara's short reunion with Cade, her mother, hands on hips, materialized before her. She pointed at the garland, and then to the doors Cade had just exited. "Are you still playing, or can we get that to the church's entrance now?"

Cade's and the other man's long legs were carrying them down the steps and along the walkway. Sara looked from the two of them to her mother's expectant face. "Yes, of course," she replied.

The effort to untangle herself took the wind from her irritation. With each greenery yard she managed to corral back into its bin, she peeped around at the closing gap, gathering details about the pair with each glance. As they neared, she thought they could have passed for lumberjacks—tall, lean, snug denims, beige-toned brushed calfskin jackets.

But the comparisons ended there. Everywhere Cade was dark the other man was light—blond hair, fair skin. His jaw was square where Cade's was round.

They both wore huge smiles, laughing as they jogged to the trailer housing the fallen tree.

Cade did a double take, spying Sara as if for the first time, or like he had forgotten she was in Bland at all, much less in the parking lot. He smacked the other man on the arm with the back of one hand and motioned for Sara with the other.

"Sara! Sara Goode! Come over here," he called out to her. His voice was cheerful and carefree.

Her mother jerked her head toward the men. "Go ahead. I can't do anything with the garland until that monstrous tree is past the doors anyway."

"There's someone I want you to meet," Cade said. He tossed an arm territorially around her shoulders. Whatever bitterness he may once have harbored had disappeared from his demeanor and he reacted like any person simply happy to be reuniting with an old friend.

Can it be this easy? Can we slide past the broken-hearted agony without casualties? He pointed to the other man hastening over to her from the truck's opposite side.

Sara's stomach plummeted, her blood turning cold. "Oh, no." She gasped. *Could this day get any worse?* Sara finally recognized the last person on earth she ever expected to see again.

Chapter 2

Luke Sterling, shocked beyond all measure, stared into the one face he had never thought to cross paths with again, except in prayer.

Now, here she was, standing before him in the church parking lot, and she had a name—Sara Goode. It was one he'd heard before, and often—the youngest daughter of Ben and Sadie Goode, regular church attendees and hard workers. Their older daughter, Beth, had married and stayed in Bland while Sara had taken off for more glamorous surroundings.

He'd caught parishioners' comments about the *other Goode girl*, the baby of her family. Some things were quite impressive—her popularity in school, college years traveling around the world in various study-abroad programs, the acclaimed radio show. Others were less admirable—ditching her fiancé within hours of the ceremony, rarely returning home, living a rather fast and loose life in the city.

Luke had known Cade for several years—since starting the interview process with the deacons for Bland Chapel's helm. Although happily married, with a lovely family, something had clearly broken Cade and its sting hung on his breath from time to time. It followed him, attaching itself to his body, a phantom limb he scratched at.

The wound, it turned out, had been a lost love, a

broken heart, a wedding dashed at the last minute by a disappearing bride who—if rumors could be believed—never explained her reasons. Luke admonished himself for succumbing to base gossip. As the church's pastor, he should be thinking about his parishioners' needs, not the local chitchat.

But after the airplane scene he'd witnessed, he was now having less trouble believing the whispers. Wondering if he should mention their brief encounter, he realized doing so would out his own secret mission. It could result in some explaining for him, as well.

How would I clarify what I was doing on a flight from New York? How would I explain why I hadn't told someone, especially Cade? No, Luke wasn't any more eager to reveal the contact than she would likely be, so he chose to keep it to himself.

"Sara Goode," he whispered, gazing at her while remembering their prior tense exchanges.

Cade took no notice of the change in atmosphere. He continued with the introductions.

Had Cade always been this oblivious?

"Sara, this is Luke Sterling. Luke, this is the gal I was just telling you about. We go way back."

Chapter 3

Sara, still dumbstruck, wondered how her day could get any worse; the entire past few weeks had been trashed as far as she could tell. *How did I end up on the mirror's reverse side? How did this happen?*

It seemed as if her life had teetered on a continuum line's positive axis she hadn't realized existed until something shifted the balance. Now all good things were on the seesaw's opposite end while she had been dropped, dead weight, into bad luck's bucket. This man's sudden appearance in her life, beginning onboard the plane as they settled into their seats before take-off from New York to Roanoke, was evidence the scale hadn't been tipped in her favor.

Cade's words rattled around in her brain, while his arm remained around her shoulders. *What had he meant by 'girl I was just telling you about'? What had Cade been telling him?*

His friend was apparently experiencing a similar recognition. Raking cool eyes up and down her body, he appeared to be suppressing a frown, or a jeer. She couldn't tell which.

Finally regaining composure, he extended a large hand. "I'm pleased to meet you." His voice was warm and friendly, belying the harsh undercurrent sweeping between them regarding their previous meeting.

Sara accepted his greeting, mentally assessing the

sensations his palm incited as it touched hers. An invisible cord pulled in her stomach, as fierce and sharp as an electrical current. His grip was sturdy, his fingers long and strong.

Her eyes shot up to find his. They were blue and chilly in defiance of the growing warmth. *Had he noticed it too? Had he experienced the jolt as well?*

Instinctively, she yanked her hand from his. "Likewise." Unable to look away, she wished to make some clever comment about his unappreciated interference. *But then, I'd have to admit to the scene. Maybe he won't mention it either.*

"I know your parents rather well. *They* are fine people."

Had he meant his comment as a cut? They are fine people, so what happened to me? Still stunned by her physical reaction to his touch the best she could come up with was, "Thank you."

"Sara has been keeping her distance from Bland"— Cade gestured toward her and then himself—"and me, and the rest of her friends and family down here in the South."

The man just introduced as Luke Sterling raised an eyebrow. "Oh?" His intense gaze zeroing in on her was as chastising as his words had been on the plane, commanding a response.

"I've been working in New York. It's hectic…was…anyway…" Her cheeks grew hot with embarrassment. Trying to change the subject from her recent misfortune, she craved something more interesting to talk about. "So…what business are you in?" she asked.

Before Mr. Do-gooder, the name she'd dubbed him

with on the plane, could answer, Cade dropped his arm from her. He pointed to the other man, his eyes growing large and expressive. "Why, Luke here's our preacher."

Cade's statement jolted Sara. It was the last thing she had expected to hear him say. She snapped the question. "Preacher?" It came out wrong, as if she were implying something unpleasant; something odd and unforgivable, as disagreeable as his behavior had been.

He laughed, whether at her or the shock she had been unable to keep from her voice, she couldn't decide.

"Yes, trying to be anyway."

She could tell he was assessing her reaction, but she could come up with nothing else to say. Her physical response to him was leaving her a bit shaky and at a loss for words, even more so with the information identifying him as a minister.

Leaning in, he whispered, "Does that bother you?" He appeared amused by her obvious discomfort, or perhaps it was just their shared secret, his witnessing of her meltdown.

Why is he acting as if we've never met? "No…of course not…why should I care what you do…or…" Her stuttering was interrupted by her mother.

"Reverend Sterling, Beverly wants to know which side of the sanctuary you have selected for the tree. She wants to place the podium for the service on the opposite one."

Sara couldn't help but notice the sweet tone Mom always used when addressing anyone else. They likely didn't grate on her nerves as much as her youngest daughter appeared to do, and had always done.

The reverend looked away from her in responding

to Sadie's question. "If you don't mind, please tell her we'll be right there with the tree. We can better decide on location once it's inside."

"Yes, of course." Her mother trotted off.

"Thank you, Mrs. Goode," the minister called out. He swiped at his face before turning his attention back to Sara. One finger stopped to rest against his bottom lip.

With her initial shock's heat simmering down, she found her voice and tried to sound nonchalant. "Is Beverly your wife?"

His wrist collapsed, falling away from his chin. "Heavens no," he responded. "Beverly is the choir director." He leaned close again, peering at her with thinly concealed amusement. "I'm not married." He said it like it was a secret only she was privy to. "I'm not even seeing anyone at the present time."

She blushed, feeling the heat emanating from his body. "How very…unfortunate for you…" Her voice faded as he burst into another grin.

Cade overheard. "Good luck with this one, Luke. She's like a greased pig."

Sara punched him in the ribs with her elbow and he groaned.

"Greased pig?" she squealed.

"Geez…you haven't lost your elbow strength." He gave her elbow a gentle squeeze and howled with amusement. "Hard to hold onto is all I meant."

Luke laughed. "Come on Cade. Let's get this behemoth inside before another parishioner tries to claim its rightful corner."

Sara watched them manhandle the tree, taking it in bottom first to its final destination.

As soon as it cleared the opening, Sara's mother began to haul the garland from the trunk. "Sara!" All prior sweetness in her tone was replaced by irritation. "Are you going to help me or not?"

"Coming!" She forced her eyes from the reverend's backside. *And when did they start making preachers who look like him? Too bad he's so darned handsome when he's clearly shown himself to be insulting and annoying.*

Why hadn't he mentioned their previous meeting? She didn't get it. Maybe he had a twin brother who had flown in to spend Thanksgiving with him. Smiling, she envisioned a pair of Sterling brothers with Cade positioned between, like a vanilla sandwich cookie's cinnamon filling.

"Sara!" her mother exclaimed. "You dropped your end."

"Sorry," she apologized. Grabbing onto the length of evergreen roping, she lifted it to the opened doorway's right upper corner.

Reverend Sterling turned and caught her eye. She tried to look away, but he had her entranced. Luke smiled, and warmth settled in her cheeks. She knew she was likely blushing. Glancing away and suddenly back again, she caught his non-blinking eyes returning to hers.

Twisting around, he focused on Cade and the lady who was apparently Beverly. But Sara could feel his gaze stealing back to her incrementally, and it made her clumsy and uneasy.

What is he thinking? Will he tell? Will he out me as the shrew I momentarily became in the wake of my personal disaster?

Her mother made little noises as she twined the roping around the prepositioned prongs.

"Mom, how long is this service normally?"

"Oh, it doesn't take much time. We'll mostly have everything completed beforehand. We just have a few decorations for the kids to put on the tree, and then a few more are placed in someone's memory or dedicated for whatever. The choir sings a few songs. The preacher reads a scripture or two, we throw the switch, and the lights all glitter. Everyone stands around for a minute oohing and aahing, and then we commence the coffee- and dessert-sharing in the fellowship hall."

"Sounds perfect!" Contrary to her words, Sara couldn't understand why she might find the prospect of spending an evening with the pastor and his flock so amusing.

Chapter 4

Luke Sterling watched the way Sara Goode interacted with her mother. There was an unmistakable rift between them. It was as evident to him as a crack in a precious china bowl would have been to a museum curator.

He had known Sadie Goode for four years. He'd watched her sympathetic manner in dealing with other church members during committee meetings and events. Generous of spirit, kind to all with an easiness generating from her core, he had thought her one of the sweetest women he'd met in Virginia.

But now, in her youngest daughter's presence, her slight shoulders hiked up around her ears, her tone developed an edge, even her face appeared to be drawing in on itself. The rarely-visiting daughter, whose return for Thanksgiving should have been a welcomed and cherished occurrence, had somehow managed to rankle his parishioner's nerves.

It wasn't open hostility, but a veiled irritation—a partially-knitted wound whose scab itched and burned and demanded to be picked at. Her tone caused Sara to flinch, twist, spin into action. Yet, he'd also seen an ugly side of the daughter, one without much compassion for others.

He scratched at his jaw, leaving a forefinger resting against his bottom lip. *Which came first, the cranky daughter or the unyielding mother? What had happened between them?*

Maybe the reason had to do with why Sara had reacted so poorly to the young couple and their baby. Trying to forget the rumors surrounding her, Luke watched from a distance with an open mind, absorbing information from the body language exuding from the three people forming a giant battle-wearied love-and-betrayal triangle.

Cade kept turning his head toward her, a shadow frequently crossing his brow, clouding his usually-bright face. Sara cut her eyes first at him, and then at her mother. Surely there was something beautiful about her aside from her physical appearance or Cade wouldn't have been drawn to her for such a long time. Otherwise the loss wouldn't have been felt as keenly. Her abdication from the area wouldn't have left the cavity people kept running their tongues through.

Luke watched them maneuvering as though characters in a movie whose ending might not turn out to be very happy. Unresolved anger and hurt flashed to the surface only to be forced behind gentility's façade. Cade was a gentleman, but a wounded one.

After getting the tree securely in its stand, Cade pulled Luke behind it. His face was strained, stricken with distress. "Sara didn't know I'd married Emily."

"Why would that upset her?"

Cade peeped around the branches as if to ensure Sara was still with her mother framing the doorway with the intertwined magnolia, fir, pine, and holly boughs. Snatching at Luke's jacket's shoulder, he positioned his mouth near his friend's ear. "The two of them—Sara and Emily—were best friends…always."

He nodded, punctuating the statement's truthfulness.

"Are you sure about 'always'? They couldn't have been too close or she would have told Sara at some point over the past—what is it now—four or five years?"

"Four-and-a-half." Cade released his grip and peered back out at the entrance. "And yes, I'm sure. They were inseparable"—he twisted his forefinger and middle finger together and held them up for Luke to see—"like this."

It clicked. Maybe Sara *had* known and that was the reason she hadn't returned to Bland very often. It made sense in an otherwise-nonsensical environment. "Maybe she's just telling you that. Maybe it's why she's been avoiding coming home."

Cade shook his head, his cowlick dropping down onto his forehead. He was breathing heavily, though not from wrestling with the tree. "No. She didn't know. I saw the shock in her eyes, the sheer surprise when she pointed to my ring finger and asked who the lucky girl was."

He looked down at the plain gold band. Appearing to be reliving a recent moment, he ceased talking and just stared at the ring.

Luke crept around the beastly fir and watched Sara, aware of so many things simultaneously, yet grossly unaware of their underlying causes. She looked up and caught him staring at her, and quickly turned her attention back to her mother. Something wasn't right about this whole picture.

Cade jerked on his sleeve again. His head tilted to meet the shoulder inching toward it. His elbows jutted out making winged shapes by his sides. "Emily's coming tonight. If Sara's here…what if…?"

Patting him on the back, Luke sought reassuring words. "If Sara comes she will be with her family, and Emily will be with you and the babies. All parties involved are too courteous for scenes, too cultured for outbursts."

Cade swallowed hard and nodded. "Yes, of course. You're right." His gaze swept across the pews, landed briefly in the doorway, then returned to Luke. "Thanks, pal, I'll see you this evening."

Jerking his head upward in the ubiquitous salutation he'd picked up since moving south, Luke watched his friend bustle out the back, avoiding further interface with Sara. It wasn't like Cade to be so jumpy.

The revelation that nobody had mentioned her best friend eventually marrying the man Sara had skipped out on said much about many things. *Why hadn't her family told her?* He continued to glance in her direction.

Sara reminded him of a too-tightly-wound timepiece. There were no smooth clicks in her movements, but rather sharp, jerky, and forced ones, without grace and ease, though he sensed she normally had both those things in abundance.

Someone accustomed to being cranky and stilted wouldn't draw back as if stung, wouldn't appear quite as uncomfortable. This had to be new territory for her. If she maintained this kind of attitude on her talk show, she wouldn't have been such a popular host with normally-spoiled celebrities.

But, he recalled, that engagement had fallen through as well. And then there had been the disastrous plane incident he'd witnessed. The image of her after she'd switched seats flashed in his mind—her scared eyes, trembling hands, emotions riding the edge of her nerves. If she wasn't ashamed of her behavior, if she thought it justified, why hadn't she mentioned having already met him?

Is it possible she didn't recognize me? Could she have a look-a-like, a doppelganger?

He scratched his chin and ran a fingertip across his lower lip. *No, it was definitely Sara Goode on the plane.* She'd gasped, *oh, no,* upon seeing his face in the first seconds of their meeting in the parking lot, making it obvious she'd realized who he was.

She'd likely said nothing about having previously met him on the flight because she wasn't proud of the encounter. Maybe she had interviewed for a position at another station earlier in the day and it hadn't gone well. Perhaps it was knowing how her presence in Bland would be received and dreading it.

Smiling, he looked from Sadie to Sara. One thing was certain. It was going to be an interesting Thanksgiving. The rest would all work out in time.

He now knew why he'd been allowed to witness the unguarded scene with Sara. There was something meant for him to reconcile, and it was within the two women—the mother and child—standing in his little country church's doorframe. If he handled it well, their healing might crack the window on the past wounds Cade was harboring, allowing forgiveness to patch the trio trying to pretend none was needed.

Chapter 5

When Sara and her mother returned from the church, two wild things were running around the living room, attacking her father—one with a plastic sword and the other with the inner cardboard tube from an empty paper towel roll. Their giggling voices wafted through the house and both sprang forward now, racing for their grandmother.

"Maw-maw," the five-year-old cried. Two braided, blonde pigtails dangled to her soft shoulders, a tuft of bangs sweeping across her forehead dipped into hazel eyes—a Goode family trait.

"Maw-maw," the younger-by-a-year mimicked. His words were where the similarity ended. Dark, curly hair framed his cherubic face, soft brown eyes peered quizzically at Sara.

They had both grown exponentially since her last visit home. *How many months had it been? Was it in April for Easter? Did I come home this summer?* "Can these two be Benjamin and Darla?" Sara asked.

Her mother, squatting to catch the children as they ran at her knees, confirmed. "Right on both counts."

Her father stood to stretch his back. One weathered hand poised in the curve of his spine pushing it forward. His voice rolled out, deep and rumbling, ominous, like a deity's. "Thank goodness you've returned. I thought I was going to be sacrificed at the

33

fireplace."

Sara surveyed the unusually disheveled room, suppressing a shocked gasp by swallowing hard. Pillows were scattered across the weathered leather sofa, toys littered the faded oval rug. Cups, with straws, perched on coasters on the clear-plastic-corner-covered end tables. She hadn't noticed these protective contrivances before.

Trying to remember if she'd ever seen such a mess in the house, she commented, "Looks like the living room was sacrificed instead." Expecting an outburst, she turned her attention back to her mother, completely undisturbed by the disarray, doling out hugs and kisses to her grandchildren.

As if the visual assault wasn't enough, the cantankerous voice belonging to the person Sara dreaded seeing most filled the atmosphere. "Children, do you remember your Auntie Sara?"

Caught by surprise while assessing the general melee, Sara had forgotten about her sister. "Beth," she said. Catching her breath, she offered a passively accepted hug. "I didn't see you."

She had expected a change in appearance with her niece and nephew. Children grew by leaps and bounds as a daily ritual. But Beth appeared to have aged more than she should have in the few months since Sara could actually remember returning home.

Maybe it was her new look. Sharply bobbed, dark hair was starting to sport a few grays at the touch-up-starved roots. Severe dark burgundy lipstick conflicted with her pale face. Was it the lines beginning to form around her Goode-colored eyes? Possibly it was in keeping the warp maturation speed set by her children.

For an instant, Sara had the impression of witnessing a fairy tale princess in her decline—the years after the prince sweeps her away, where life and childbirth broaden hips, and passing time brings with it a fresh wrinkle supply and sagging flesh.

Her sharp tongue though, as youthful as ever, was still lively. "Sara, it's so good of you to leave your life up north to come down and pay us all a little visit. How long do we have with you this time?" Sarcasm dripped from her wine-colored lips, its sting accurately delivered.

Sara's mind reeled, her heart plummeting into her stomach. There was no way Beth hadn't heard about the show's cancelation via their parents, other crowing residents, or from the show itself. She was baiting her, wanting to make her say the awful truth—she had failed in Manhattan. Vagueness was called for in this situation.

She took a deep breath and met Beth's bitter stare. "I'm not sure. Most likely a week."

Beth lifted an eyebrow, extended a hip, and crossed her arms over her chest. "A *whole* week?"

Their father stepped closer to Sara, placing a protective arm around her as if to make the point he would defend her against everything, including thinly-veiled mockery if the need arose. His speech slowed even more than its normal drawl dictated, taking on the air of warning only those closest to him might pick up on. "Beth"—exhaling for a long moment before finishing the sentence—"we talked about this."

Beth slumped, his drawn out words served to deflate her stance. "Right. I do recall hearing your little show didn't pan out so well. Pity."

She spun around before Sara could reply. Turning her attention to her children, Beth chattered on about them to their mother who had said nothing except to the little ones. "I got some more greenery, Mama. Can we make some garland for my house?"

Sadie patted her oldest daughter on the face in the same loving gesture Sara recalled from childhood. "You know we can. Come on out to the porch and we'll see what's still there. We can start work on it in the morning." Their mother had chosen her ally as well. With children tagging along, they slipped out the back leaving Ben and Sara alone.

It was how it had always been. She was her father's favorite and her sister was, and always had been, her mother's—neat and tidy, one child for each parent. Maybe she had feared his feelings had changed while she was away, and her father now preferred her sister as well.

Ben gave Sara's shoulder a squeeze and planted a kiss atop her head. "She's just jealous. You do know that, don't you?"

Reverting to childish pouting, Sara turned her lips downward to indicate her displeasure with her sister. "Right. Now she's just gloating."

He patted her reassuringly on the arm. "Let her. You'll come out on the other side of this. You always have."

His soothing voice made her feel as if anything was indeed possible. The comfort she received from his strength reinforced her own. She no longer wanted to talk about Beth or her mother. "Thanks, Dad. Do you mind if I tag along with you guys tomorrow for the *Hanging of the Greens* service at the church?"

"I'd love it. Hey, why don't we make our father-daughter fudge while you're here?" His eyes lit up.

Sara couldn't suppress the smile forming at the memories of something they prepared together. "I think it would be wonderful."

"It's settled. In the morning, they'll make garlands and we'll make fudge." He winked at her before darting out to make his last run to check on the cattle.

Sara's heart swelled with love for the one person who made her feel special. Perversely, she longed for the days when retaliation on her sister had been simple. All she'd had to do was climb the limbs of one of the two massive maples flanking the house and deposit Beth's books or dolls up on the highest branches she could reach.

Her mind conjured Beth's squeals and earsplitting cries for help in rescuing whatever lay beyond her reach. They both knew Beth wouldn't attempt a rescue alone. When Sara hadn't been forced by their mother to retrieve the captive items, her father usually had taken care of it.

As 1550 White Pine Drive's sole operative of the peacekeeping-mission, he had always tried to resolve border skirmishes beneath the square, red tin-roofed, chestnut-boarded, porch-wrapped house.

Slipping onto the porch in front, Sara squinted at the landscape as sunset turned winter wheat's swaying-in-the-wind beige tips into an impressionistic painting. The wheat rustled, nodding in complaint to the fading sky.

Beyond the waving stalks, and into the cattle pasture, something huge in shocking emerald moved along the slope, slicing into the orange-striped sky as it rolled up the hill. From the distance and with the fading light, it resembled a hump-backed Irish-green buffalo. Its bright yellow wheels flashed as sunlight's last ray exploded off the machine before the fireball's own color turned sallow and dull and dropped beneath the mountain peaks.

The tractor continued its path until the animal tusk-like giant forks sticking out from its front end lowered to the earth in supplication to several plastic-wrapped hay rolls. It stabbed beneath the next in line, lifting it upward. Tines tilting backward with the snagged bale, the turn toward the pasture commenced in silhouette against the darkening sky.

It was the same vision she'd seen a thousand or, more likely, ten thousand times. She filed this memory away for future retrieval along with the one of seeing him at home on the farm earlier today when she had driven through the gates and watched him in action. Images whipped through her memory, as though gathered by the same wind that now swirled the maples' leaves. They whirled into a tumbling tornado of dry crackles and were deposited hither and yon around the fields and up onto the porch.

The season's aromas caught in her nostrils; wood smoke from hearth fires, tractor exhaust, decaying leaves beneath the fresh just-fallen dry layer. She closed her eyes and recalled the moment she'd hugged her dad. She'd proceeded to glue her head to his shoulder while inhaling the scent clinging to his clothes—dried hay, old leather, and something like diesel. He had probably acquired this last odor from filling his tractor with the manual pump.

"I've missed you, Dad," she had whispered, as the

tears dropped.

The memory was one she had actually been aware at the time she was making, and it would sustain her. It had teeth, a real grasp.

His eyes had moistened, and he had chucked her under the chin. "Let's get you inside. I bet you're freezing. Where's your coat?"

Sara had ignored the cold, assuming her heart would warm her better than the expensive feeding blanket her coat had been reduced to on the plane. She had been given a welcoming moment alone with her father, wishing every minute in Bland could be as sweetly rewarding as the one they had just shared.

Just now reality assaulted her. The urge to run, to flee, whipped through her veins, being fanned by the same furious gust scattering the leaves back off the floor boards. Her heart thundered with her accelerated pulse, and her breath quickened into shallow pants.

She'd had her moment with her father, and had now borne the weight from the opposing team her mother and sister represented. Maybe she should go back to Manhattan straightaway before things worsened, as they inevitably would.

But she'd lost her job there. She began mentally listing today's disasters; her expensive coat—although she had washed and dabbed at the thing with soap and water—was likely ruined, the interfering man on the plane had turned out to be the local minister, her ex-fiancé was now married to her once-best friend, her sister was living on the hill with the view—the very spot promised to her—and if she didn't get something lined up soon, she'd have to move back home at least for a while. What could be more humiliating?

****

As soon as Sadie and Beth retreated to the back porch the following day, Ben and Sara hurried to the kitchen. Sara retrieved a large bowl from the cupboard. "How old was I the first time we made this? Six? Seven?"

"More like four. You ran to me, crying, and saying your mother wouldn't let you help her and Beth make cookies. Your grandmother was alive then and I called her up, asking for a recipe I could handle by myself. The church ladies were more surprised at my involvement than yours."

"I remember you telling them we could make anything delicious with sweetened condensed milk and some peanut butter and chocolate," Sara mused.

"That was the year we won the dessert category at the Valentine Ball. Mary Lambeth asked for our secret." Ben grabbed a jar from the cabinet. "Gotta add the salty peanuts." He began to bounce a long chef's knife through a pile he corralled with a cupped palm to prevent them from shooting away from the board every time he felled the blade into the over-sized stack.

"Finely chopped." Sara nodded toward the ever-shrinking pieces he attacked feverishly.

"Why would you have it any other way?" *Thwack, thwack, thwack.* "You get the salty sharpness with every sweet nibble."

They went back and forth, reminiscing as they melted and stirred and chopped.

Finally, the entire concoction was poured into a foil-lined pan and shoved into the refrigerator beside a clear, large bowl with little nectar dollops weeping from perfectly-browned meringue peaks and valleys sitting atop a creamy layer separating wafer disks from matching sliced banana rounds. Pointing to the concoction, Sara asked, "Is that what I think it is?"

Ben stood behind her, looking across the top of her head toward her accusation's victim. "Yep. The preacher loves your mother's banana pudding. He requests it for every occasion."

"Oh? I met him yesterday." Although she said it nonchalantly, her pulse quickened at his mention. Sara was also discovering she wanted to say his name and talk about him for some reason.

Her father snapped to attention and closed the refrigerator door. "You did? What'd ya think?"

"He's nice," she said simply. Afraid to say more, she quickly began clearing the emptied milk cans and chocolate bags.

Her father gave her his fanciful look, the one framed by raised brows and a twisted mouth. "The women love him. Our congregation has gained twenty or thirty new members since he's taken the church office—all females in his age bracket, and single." Her dad laughed. "Coincidental? I think not."

"He is quite attractive…for a preacher. I certainly don't remember us having another as handsome." Sara felt heat rush to her cheeks and knew a blush was reddening them. She hadn't meant to admit she found him attractive. With her head down, she ran a soapy cloth across the microwave and scrubbed at its handle. Leaning over the counter, she gazed down its length as though looking for a spot needing further attention, shielding her face from Ben's scrutiny.

Her father didn't speak right away. Waiting quietly, she looked up and met his twinkling eyes. He gave her a wink, clearly amused with her unspoken admission. "You find him handsome, do ya now?"

"Yeah." She laughed. "I suppose he is nice-looking, Dad."

Turning her head, she cleaned the backsplash and then the refrigerator door, wiping away fingerprints which may or may not have actually been there. What she really wanted to know she couldn't ask straight out. *Why didn't he admit our run-in?*

Leaning against the countertop's edge, both elbows resting on it, he watched her work. "Uh-huh..." His continued silence communicated he was waiting for her to verbalize the thought he could likely tell was burning in her brain.

She snagged a fleshy bit from inside her cheek with her teeth, and then released it before making it raw. "What's his story? What on earth is he doing out here in the middle of nowhere?"

Her father ran fingertips and a thumb along the marionette-like lines framing his chin and mouth. "You'd have to ask him. All I've got is hearsay, and that ain't worth a nickel."

She ached to ask for the hearsay. Gossip—even when off the mark—hinted at the truth. At least, in her profession—*do I still have a profession?*—it often led to a good story. "Maybe I will."

He jerked his chin at her then shook his head, delivering a full message without speaking a single word.

"I can't help it." She giggled. "It's still how I identify myself, you know."

"My daughter, the professional interviewer."

The door swung open and the chubby figure of

Beth's husband, Thomas Moore, plunged into the house following his booming voice. "Hey, family! Whose car is by the barn?" His chocolate eyes scanned the room, landing on Sara. "Oh! That would be Sara's." He spread his arms wide. "Come over here."

"Hi, Thomas. Good to see you." She leaned in for the expected hug. Her brother-in-law was a little too friendly and a lot too loud, but a nice man nonetheless. "We heard," he said. "Tough place to survive in—New York."

Extricating herself from his embrace, she bristled slightly. "It's just one job. I'll get something else."

Grabbing an apple from the pitted and scarred wooden bowl, Thomas rubbed the already-shiny fruit against his sleeve before biting into it. "That's the spirit! Look on the bright side, huh!"

"She's a smart young lady," her dad said. "She'll take the place by storm once again, if she wants to."

"Thanks, Dad."

Ben jerked his head toward the rear of the kitchen. "Beth's out on the back porch with her mother, making garland."

Thomas stopped nibbling at the apple. Sounding surprised, he asked, "Kids too?"

Ben nodded. "What do you think? It's wire and pine cones and magnolia leaves. What could be more entertaining?"

Thomas disappeared into the same wormhole as the others.

Listening for the door to slam against its tightly-hinged frame, Sara laid the cleaning cloth across the sink's middle divide. "I think we're done in here."

"Yep, I got a newspaper calling my name."

Retreating to the living room, her father snatched up his paper while Sara scrolled through her smartphone. She was deleting emails when the sound of the door snapping shut again cut into the quiet, followed by footsteps of varying weights. The children's bickering voices wafted forward, and then she heard the intonation that never failed to grate on her nerves, always sounding catty and biting.

"We're going to my house now," Beth announced from the doorway. Her arms were laden with strung-together evergreen tips and leaves.

Ben looked up and nodded. "All right." His gaze fell on the children, his face brightening. "Come here and give your papa a hug."

Benjamin and Darla made a beeline for their grandfather while Sara watched her sister's face. It puckered and soured, its pale countenance yellowed like ruined buttermilk.

Beth caught her looking and narrowed her lips. "Sara, do you want to come watch us decorate and see the view from my living room?"

The wiggle-worm children raced back toward their mother. "Yay. We're decorating," Darla squealed.

"Deck-o-waiting," little Benjamin mispronounced.

Sara shot her father a look and he glanced back down at the newspaper, avoiding her stare. "No Beth. I'll stay here with Dad."

"As long as you promise to come up onto the hilltop before you go back."

"I haven't been gone so long I've forgotten what the view from up there is like."

Apparently sensing she'd hit a nerve, Beth couldn't let it go. She brandished her red-hot poker taunts with skill and ease. "But it's so much better now, with the house's additional elevation. It's like sitting in a treetop looking across the valleys and mountain ridges."

Sara's face blazed hot. Fury churned in her gut. "What would you know about sitting in treetops? You were always too frightened to climb."

"Yes, well, now I don't have to dirty myself to get the best views. They are just waiting outside my window for my enjoyment."

Her father rustled the newspaper but did not look up. Sara understood she was alone in defending herself. Nobody would be coming to her aid. Her parents had given her sister the one piece of the property she had held sacred in her heart, the only section where she had imagined living.

That had been hurtful enough, but to sit and listen to Beth's taunts was simply too much. She couldn't stop herself from reacting. "The only view better is of the skyline from my apartment. Perhaps I could show it to you sometime? Of course, you'd actually have to leave this mountain in order to see it, but the invitation is there all the same."

Their mother stepped forward, dangling more roping from one elbow's crook. Throwing her other arm around Beth's waist, she interceded. "You'd better take her up on that invitation soon, Beth darling. I understand it has a short window of opportunity."

Ben bristled and sucked so much air into his lungs he resembled one of the crested grouse fluttering around the woods edge. Sadie must have noticed it, too.

She dropped her arm to retrieve a garland-filled tub and motioned for Benjamin and Darla. "These garlands are heavy. Children, come help Maw-maw before she drops them all right here."

Thomas put a hand against his wife's back and she scooted out the door with her kids in tow. "'Bye, guys," he said. Glancing over his shoulder, he was the only envoy member to give a farewell.

When the door had shut behind them and the SUV cranked up, Sara spun toward her father. The rancor had developed into a firm, seething detest of the situation. Her words stormed forth, thunderous and angry. "Why did you let her build up there on my spot? You promised it to me, Daddy, and then you gave it to Beth!"

His face crinkled up in the exact way it always did when he bit into something unsavory, mashing his lips inward against his teeth and drawing his bushy eyebrows toward each other. "Well, Sara, honey, you had made it pretty clear you didn't want to move back here. We wanted to have at least one of our daughters close by. When Beth had our first little grandbaby…I…well…I would have given up everything to keep them near me."

She tried to keep the bitterness from her voice, but failed. "You could have told me first."

"I wanted to." He nodded, admitting the error in judgment. "But I wasn't comfortable asking over the telephone. And you weren't home often enough to bring it up before she had the house plan picked out and the footings poured."

He picked up his daughter's hand and gave it a squeeze. "You'll forgive us, won't you?"

It was difficult to think one sister would want to do something simply to irritate the other, but that was the only possibility. "Beth doesn't really love it up there.

She only wanted it to hurt me. You see how she rubs my face in it."

"Let it go, Sara. She doesn't have the potential you do, nor the same ambition. It could be equally as disturbing to be her, and to have to live in your shadow. Think about that," he advised.

Though still stinging from her sister's taunts and her father's rebuke, Sara did consider his remarks. She had always been much more outgoing than Beth. Though Beth was the eldest, Sara was the one who had the spirit for adventure and the courage to go after her dreams. Beth could be a little mousy and was quite the homebody. She hadn't played sports or joined clubs, while Sara had tried everything at least once. She'd stayed with basketball and softball and the dance team.

Sara's room had practically been wallpapered with awards and ribbons, the shelves lined with trophies. Beth's stayed as simple as its occupant—never changing, painted in a nondescript pale green background which blended into the rolling hills beyond the window. Sedate. Serene.

The only time Beth had shown any spitfire was when gouging something into her sister. She didn't like to travel. She hadn't joined in the social networking craze. And her hobbies could all be accomplished without getting off the sofa: reading, knitting, crocheting, needlepoint, cross stitch. She had now apparently taken up floral design as well, which did require a move to the kitchen table.

Sara's mind clicked through her adventure roster in the form of a slideshow. Not only had she left home to go to college, she had spent one summer in Europe and another in Asia. The thought of sitting around with a yarn ball trailing off her lap made her apoplectic. There was no denying it. They were total opposites.

"She could have. She just chose not to," Sara said. Refusing to give Beth a reprieve, she added, "Nothing I have ever done was intended to hurt her. I would have supported her in any venture, but I can't force her to take one on."

"That's fair." Her father nodded. "Now tell me some more about meeting the preacher."

He had changed the topic. There would be no more talk of Beth right now.

Chapter 6

Luke prepared for the service in much the same detailed way he might have strategized a football game play when he had been on the Columbia Lions team. It was all performance art, a drama. All had been done before. Rules applied. *Sometimes people didn't abide by the rules*.

He rubbed his knee. It was sore from the trip—the plane seat had shoved against it and there were the heavy items he had dragged with him—and now handling the massive tree. He hoped his limp tonight wouldn't be noticeable.

Crooking his forefinger on his bottom lip, he wondered why it suddenly made such a difference to him. Chuckling at himself as the insight into his concern jolted into his mind, he knew it had to do with Sara Goode. It was possible Sara wouldn't even come out to Bland Chapel for the Saturday evening *Hanging of the Greens* service, but odds were she would show. After all, she had helped her mother decorate, had a niece and a nephew taking part in the children's program, and her mother and sister were singing in the choir. Luke knew Ben would be there, likely meaning Sara would come as well.

Running through his sermon once again, he wanted it committed to memory. It was more powerful to talk about bringing light into the world when not reading from notes. After all, wasn't that Christianity's core, and the reason for their religion's existence? Light? The gospels? Good news? Love?

Love. Mentioned more than three hundred times in the King James Version of the *Holy Bible*, it was given five hundred fifty-one mentions in the New International Version.

Perhaps I should dedicate an entire service to the Bible mention of love and its forms. As quickly as the thought popped into his head, three types sprang to his mind. Little words with big connotations—a*gape, phileo*, and *eros*. *Agape*—selflessness, all inclusive, for strangers even—had been turned into charity in most minds. Some organizations used it in their titles.

He *agape*-loved New York's Mission for the Homeless, the plane's young couple and their baby, the newest parishioners he'd not had a chance to become friends with as yet. But those close to him, people like Cade Norton with whom he shared a meaningful friendship, was the second kind of love, *phileo*.

Eros? Can I talk about eros from the pulpit? If so, how would I configure it? Sexual passion, fiery desire, the longing for another person's touch—that was all *eros*. Often defined as erotic love, the word *eros* didn't actually appear in the Bible, but it was discussed at length in ways that made it clear.

Song of Solomon was all about *eros* and desire, though sprinkled with euphemisms and analogies. The text was about two lovers praising each other and acknowledging their carnal yearnings. Not surprising, given King Solomon's seven hundred wives and three hundred concubines.

It was unclear how many wives King David had,

though eight were named in the Bible. What was clear was his *eros* for his friend's wife. He had placed Uriah in a battle, to be slain, just to obtain Bathsheba, the woman he'd lain with subsequent to his lusting for her while seeing her bathing.

Even the story of Boaz and Ruth described their desire for one another, though most people considered it another love type, *storge*—the love for family. Ruth cared for her disapproving mother-in-law, Naomi, left alone after losing her husband and sons. She'd taken her to live with them after she and Boaz had married.

The church bell's chiming announced the hour and brought Luke back from his mental voyage into Biblical love. *Why am I thinking about love now? Is it only because of the season?*

He knew why, though he didn't want to admit it. Luke had as many demons as Sara, as many as Cade. Watching the former couple together had been a reminder of his past mistakes, the ones made before accepting his call to preach.

Luke dropped his hand from his face, turning it over, studying the betraying palm. Swallowing hard, he recalled the very instant Sara's hand touched his. A lightning bolt couldn't have been more shocking.

She'd felt it too. He was certain she had. It was written in her startled blue-green eyes, the whites suddenly bathing them in brilliance as her eyelids jumped upward. The way she'd yanked her hand away, stuttered, searching for words was confirmation.

Stop thinking about her, he chastised himself. She's a diva, and one likely to be at tonight's program—a critic returned to her past's stage.

There was no denying she intrigued him, especially

as she hadn't mentioned the incident leading to their initial meeting or the soiled coat. It had been a long time since anyone had piqued his curiosity in such a manner. Difficult, intense, self-absorbed, and yet he sensed she had a weak spot, a tenderness her gruff exterior attempted to cover.

What was she trying so hard to prove to everyone? Why had she skipped out on the wedding to Cade when it was obvious they still had a connection? How had it happened she hadn't known he was now married to her once-best friend when the marriage had occurred in such a small town? If people were keeping secrets from her, they must have thought they needed to be kept.

And what about the once-best friend? Emily would most likely be at tonight's church service. What would happen when they came face-to-face?

Hopefully, the drama would be reserved for the *Hanging of the Greens* service and nothing more. But angst built in his chest. His forefinger returned to rest against his bottom lip as he contemplated what could happen. How would he be able to mend all the hurts suddenly bursting free from their misery cocoons into Bland Chapel's serenity?

Chapter 7

Sadie Goode returned from her oldest daughter's hilltop home just in time to get herself ready for the church service. Nothing was said about the remarks made to her younger daughter, as if all was simply forgotten, shoved under the rug with the dust bunnies.

Sara filed the earlier comments into her full-to-bursting mental filing cabinet housing such slights. They served as paper cuts across her heart, surface wounds so numerous they might be fatal. Patched with her father's attempt at stitching them closed, bleeding stemmed, she swallowed her pride. After changing into the only dress she had packed, she and her parents left for the church.

Beth and her family led the way in the SUV driven by her brother-in-law. Sara was struck by the haughtiness in Beth's posture, the way she sat a bit too straight in the car's front seat, the uncomfortable-looking tilt to her head. She wondered if this was her normal stance or only occurred when her little sister was around.

Among the first to arrive, both vehicles circled around to the lower parking lot even though it meant a longer walk. Beth and Sadie each took one child around to the back entrance to get them ready for their presentation, and to dress themselves in choir robes.

Sara ambled up the walk and stood in the empty

sanctuary with her father and Thomas. The only other people in attendance so far were choir members or behind-the-scenes volunteers doing last-minute preparations and checking sound.

"Why aren't you two singing with your wives?" she asked, in an effort to make conversation.

"You apparently haven't heard your father sing," her brother-in-law joked.

"Yeah," her father agreed. "The only sound worse comes from *his* mouth." He pointed to Thomas.

Sara's laughter reverberated in the empty vestibule separating the entry from the sanctuary.

They were not alone for very long. In a few minutes, cars swarmed into the parking lot. Old friends and acquaintances entered, extending greetings to each other, in addition to Sara, Thomas, and Ben as they filled the church. The inner door's constant opening, with accompanying cool air, assaulted the sanctuary's thermostat causing the furnace to kick into high gear.

Thomas grabbed Sara's arm. He nodded toward the sidewalk, a concrete runner fanning out from the momentarily propped-open front doors to the parking lot. "Don't look now, but your old boyfriend is headed this way."

His warning had the reverse effect. Sara immediately jerked her head in the very direction he had cautioned her against. Afterwards, all motion slowed.

Emily, long chestnut hair pulled into a ponytail, bounced along the walk with a baby in her arms. The breeze whipped her skirt softly behind her.

Cade's arm was protectively around his wife's back and his other extended downward for a toddler to grip. Their gaits were evenly matched. Though his legs were much longer, he took small steps to allow the child to waddle along. The four looked perfect together, reminding Sara of the family photos on store shelving.

For a moment she imagined her own face substituted for Emily's, the child in Emily's arms belonging to her and Cade, as would the other pattering along beside his dad. It could have been. He had wanted it. But she had wanted something more, something flashy and faster than Bland, Virginia's speed.

Now she had neither. It tore at her heart, wrenched at her gut. She and Cade had been so comfortable. *Did I think he would wait forever?*

"Why, Sara!" Emily exclaimed, seeming genuinely happy to see her old friend once again, though a nervous tinkle gargled against the words.

"Emily Starnes…Norton," she added. "I've just recently heard you guys got married. Congratulations…late…but you'll forgive me…I failed to get your invitation."

It sounded catty, and she wanted to take the words back. Sarcasm wasn't the soup du jour as it was in Manhattan.

"I'd forgive you anything," Emily replied sweetly. "Even disappearing on your old back-home friends."

"You're right, I have been out of touch," she offered. "We must catch up."

Cade reached behind him, tugging the outer doors closed.

Sara smiled as warmly as she could manage and gave Cade's arm a squeeze as he passed, aware of Emily's eyes cutting sideways at him.

"Sara." Cade acknowledged her, and then nodded

at her father and brother-in-law as he passed by them. "Thomas…Ben." He pushed against the inner swinging door, holding it open for his wife.

Sara watched him through the long glass inserts as the door swung slowly back into place while he escorted his family up the church aisle.

The heat was going full throttle now and she felt its arid industrial fan-like blast on her face. It burned her eyes. At least, she'd use that as her excuse if asked about the wet trickle down her cheeks.

"Excuse me," she said to Ben and Thomas. "I'm going to get a little air."

They both nodded. She could feel their eyes boring into her back and was sure they suspected seeing Cade with Emily had upset her. She didn't care. She just needed to cool down and catch her breath.

Sara walked to the large front doors and flung her weight against them, throwing herself outside as quickly as she could. Instead of feeling the invigorating rush of cold air, she immediately fell against something simultaneously hard and soft.

Someone grabbed her arms. The object she'd hit had a voice. "Hello again." And she knew the voice. She had met its owner twice in the two previous days.

"Excuse me," she said. To her horror, tears continued pricking her eyelids, leaking past their barricades.

"Hey." Without releasing his grip, Luke Sterling nudged her chin upward. His voice echoed concern, revealing tenderness his imposing size might have kept undiscovered. "What's the matter?"

"Oh, I'm just…it's…" She rolled her eyes upward and into the softest, clearest, sky-colored set. If possible, they were even more azure than before, competing with the bluest object she had ever seen for their heavenly perfection. *Is the shade robin's egg, or sea-along-the-Caribbean-shore?* Perhaps the color was due to his black suit and white shirt with red tie, a fierce contrast to the sheepskin and denim from the day before. More likely it was the tears just slightly blurring her vision.

"Come with me," he said. Pulling her along the walkway through a side door, they continued into the pastor's office. "We can have some privacy here, at least for about five minutes. Then the crowd up front will be expecting me." He winked, passing her a tissue-filled box.

Feeling small and childish, Sara sought to explain. "My life's a wreck right now. I'm just feeling sorry for myself. It's silly to usurp your time when you should be preparing for the service."

Luke settled against his desk's edge, neither sitting nor standing, but some combination of both. Compassion softened his square jawline as he pulled his mouth into a contemplative smile. "Listen, people come first. If you have problems we can't solve in the time I have right now, we can make an appointment for tomorrow after the Sunday service. What do you think?"

"For counseling?" Her voice went up an octave. "You think I need therapy?"

He tucked his chin and pulled his face backward as though struck by a hard smack. "No, not counseling. More like a fresh set of ears. I can be trusted, having taken an oath. I could offer you a few new ideas, and maybe lunch."

All she could do was blink and stare. An emotional kaleidoscope had her trapped inside its spiraling wheel.

He held up his hands, palms toward her, in the same surrendering gesture she'd seen before. "I'd like to be your friend, Sara."

Suspicion curled around her brain, its tentacles flailing around her mind. "Why?"

He looked stricken and at a loss for words. "Why?" He blinked a few times. "Why not?"

"Do you always answer a question with another question?"

"No, not always. Why do you ask?" The pastor laughed then, a genuine laugh recalled from childhood before life's cruelty had gotten its fangs into it, forcing it to become more respectful and dignified.

"I suppose I wasn't always this cynical," she answered, finding she rather liked his offer. "And I could use a friend right about now. Although I'm not sure it should be you." She knew time was short and the explanation for her rudeness likely longer than he had time for or she cared to give right now.

He leaned forward, closing the gap between them. "Give me a chance to prove myself. That's all I'm asking."

"Well, I suppose…"

Sara made a visual scan of the room—Bible on the desk, armoire in the corner with one door ajar, revealing varicolored raiments, and a large white-blocked wall calendar with plenty of space for notations hanging behind the desk chair. The calendar was identical to the one in James Higgins' office—the one she had stared at while he delivered the horrid news about her non-renewal.

As though hypnotized by the white space marred with black lines, she was no longer in Bland Chapel, but sitting in the radio station manager's office, staring at the number 31 on the October page—Halloween. The bad news had been a prank, a joke. Laughing maniacally from relief, she had assured him he had really gotten her.

Mr. Higgins' face had registered the shock in her disbelief. "I'm afraid this is no trick, Sara," he'd said sternly.

"Excellent." Luke Sterling's voice brought her back to the present.

Sara was lost, stuck between two worlds and their opposing time frames. "What?" she asked in her confusion.

"Tomorrow. I'll meet you after the service." He opened the door to the outside for her to exit, though he stayed behind. "I'll slip out the other way." He indicated he would use the connecting door to the sanctuary to face his congregation.

Sara walked back around the church, wondering how it happened she had agreed to meet him the following afternoon. She hadn't really finished her sentence, her thoughts interrupted by the momentary mental office inventory and the ensuing memory it kicked into gear, but it was done.

She slipped quietly through the entrance doors and into the pew beside her father. The choir director was already in place and the pianist began to play soothing music. It had an unexpected comforting effect on Sara.

The enormous tree she had witnessed being carried from the trailer was now erect and partially decorated. Clear light strands generously draped its limbs. The upper section had a plethora of ornaments, while the lower section—that in easy reach of the parishioners and their children—had been left bare for the service about to take place.

The choir door opened and a golden-robed sea swell of people surged outward. They stood at attention, all eyes on Beverly. Another door opened and Reverend Sterling, now robed in a long white vestment with a golden, embroidered-near-the-bottom stole hung around his neck, took his place at the podium. He caught Sara's eye and nodded. It was a small gesture, but it made her feel less self-conscious.

He continued to make random eye contact with her throughout the service. She suspected he was also making similar connections with every other person in his congregation. Young women, with their heads forward, appeared to be waiting for a moment of his attention.

It was less like a religious service and more like a reflective one with its purpose of festooning the church with the meaningful decorations.

Sara's mind went back to New York, to the giant toy soldiers marching across Radio City Music Hall's sign, the enormous colored light bulbs in a semi-circle in the McGraw-Hill Companies' front office complex on the Avenue of the Americas, the many-storied tree in Rockefeller Center. Even to Marge McKay, the homeless woman she had met on the bench while they watched the tree being erected in Rockefeller Center.

Marge had said she found solace in the white wire herald angels as opposed to the glitz and glamour offered by the hundreds of displays of Santa and his elves.

Every word of Bland Chapel's service held meaning. Every person hanging an ornament on the simple tree did so with emotion. The children beamed with pride in their handcrafted beaded-wire *Chrismons*—the ornaments representing Jesus Christ's name, or some part of His ministry through language or symbols.

Thomas leaned over and whispered with pride in his voice, "They made those during Bible School. Your niece and nephew now associate fish with Christ, saying over and over *Christi monogramma*."

"Latin, at their age! Nice." Sara turned to her father whose face was glued to his grandchildren. It was wonderful to see him so happy.

The lights dimmed and the switch for the tree lights was thrown as the choir sang "O Christmas Tree." After the first stanza, the congregation joined in. The choir's processional escorted the congregants down the aisle, followed by the minister.

They all filed outside to see the lights on the evergreen garland Sara had helped install the day before. It was beautiful. And the prayer said by Reverend Sterling was very moving. He ended by saying, "We are destined to be the light-bringers, the singers of the gospels, and the tellers of the good news therein. It is our duty as prescribed by our God; be the light we wish to see in the world."

"Let there be peace on earth, and let it begin with me," the choir sang, their *a capella* voices in perfect harmony.

It made goose bumps ripple on Sara's flesh. She had the sensation of being transported to the first Christmas and the scene by the manger with angels singing and giving thanks for the light just brought into the world. It left her feeling lighter and less angry.

Sara followed her father into the fellowship hall. Minutes later he proudly announced their father-daughter fudge, made possible only when his youngest daughter was home to make it with him.

Sara noticed her sister's face fall into a frown as their father made a fuss about the fudge. She wondered why he'd never made it with Beth. Perhaps, occasionally, Sara wasn't the only one to feel left out.

Although she had no idea whether or not it was true, she spoke up, "And Beth helped Mother with the banana pudding. So you can have mother-daughter pudding or father-daughter fudge."

"Or both," Reverend Sterling said, "as I intend to do." He caught her eye, lifting his chin as if to say he approved of her crediting her sister, as well.

She sensed she had done the right thing for a change.

Another blessing went forth for the food and fellowship they were about to have. And then the long wooden table was rushed by hungry children and adults eager to assuage their sugary cravings.

Sara took a fudge serving, placed it on a napkin, and grabbed a cup of steaming coffee. She could have eaten some of everything—the cheese wafers, the chocolate cake, the coconut pie piled high with meringue. It all called to her taste buds as she glanced over the sinful display including doughnuts, cupcakes, and club crackers wrapped in bacon. A gooey baklava tray, its crispy thin filo dough drenched in nuts and honey, made her mouth water. She had to look away.

People approached her compassionately. They had

all heard the news concerning her radio show. The peace she had received from the service was wrenched away with the constant reminding of her failure. At least this way the sympathy salvos were going to come to a head quickly, the swift yanking of the bandage as opposed to a slow peeling away. They all knew, and she knew they knew, so it could now be buried and laid to rest

"How are you holding up?" a familiar female voice asked.

Startled, Sara snapped her head around. "Emily," she said with surprise. "Does it show?"

She kept more distance between them than old friends normally would. "Yeah, you look a little displaced."

"It was a nice service. I really loved the children's *Chrismons*."

Sharply exhaling a deep breath as if preparing for some unforeseen danger lurking ahead, Emily blurted an arbitrary explanation, "I would have invited you to the wedding. I just didn't think you'd come…and I…wasn't sure you would be happy for us." Her hands wrung over themselves. Her ponytail jiggled behind her like a bobble-head doll perched loosely in a car's back window.

Sara turned to fully face her once-best friend. The features she would have known anywhere just a few years back looked somewhat transmuted. Her eyes were shadowed with dull rings and tiny feathery creases, both things Dr. Daniels from the radio program airing just before *Sara's Secrets* would have known how to eliminate. Her lips, with teeth pinning them inward, disappeared into a thin line.

"There was a time when we had no secrets; when we knew everything about one another," Sara said with regret.

Emily's woeful eyes met Sara's, betraying her underlying emotions. Pushing a foot forward, rocking into it as if to bolt, she stammered, "Whatever I did to lose that, it was my own great loss."

Sara grabbed her arm, recognizing there were times in life when an opportunity was given to make amends, to relinquish past wounds. Emily having captured her end of the proverbial rope compelled Sara to do likewise. "Mine as well," she offered earnestly. "I'm afraid I wasn't very good at keeping in touch once our paths unwound."

Still jittery, Emily's fingers bunched up her skirt at the hip, gathering and releasing it like a cat's kneading. "Cade was inconsolable after you left. He was in rough shape for a long time. It was several months before we started seeing each other romantically, and I think—for at least some time—he was only with me in order to feel closer to you."

Sara, heard the vulnerability and possibly a tinge of jealousy in Emily's voice. She reached forward, caressing her friend's cheek to offer reassurance. She had always been the more flamboyant of the two, the more outgoing, and the one with the most acquaintances. *Is it possible she thinks I've returned to pick up where I left off, including with her husband?*

"That's sweet of you to say, but why on earth would he want me when he has you? He chose wisely. I wish you both the best, Emily."

Emily threw her arms firmly around Sara and sobbed wildly. "I…should…have…I didn't…I'm not as confident…you…"

"It's okay," Sara soothed her. "Cade is very proud of you and your children. Cherish one another."

"They're waiting…for me," Emily said. She attempted to stem the tearful, emotional rush, though her voice still quaked and quivered. "Come…over to see…us."

"Thank you. I would love to."

Sara, humbled by Emily's confession, began the mantra and Emily soon joined in.

"Maybe we could sit on the front porch,
in straw hats and gauzy dresses."

The light of recognition sparked in Emily's eyes and she joined Sara in the next line.

"In the middle of summer,
drinking sweet iced tea from silver straws,
while the wild jasmine-and honeysuckle-scented breeze,
ruffles our skirts, fanning them through the air like sails blowing in the wind."

Both were now crying; the words they chanted took them back into their teens. Emily shook her head. "I can't believe you still remember." She blinked as she walked away.

Sara watched her leave, understanding why Emily hadn't reached out to contact her before. Her words reverberated in Sara's head. *"He was in rough shape for a long time. He was only with me in order to feel closer to you."*

Clearly, Emily had feared some unresolved emotional pull between her and Cade would draw them back together. Having witnessed Cade's trauma over her unexplained disappearance, Emily knew first-hand the extent of his heartbreak, and therefore, the depth of his love for Sara.

That explained Emily's reluctance, but what was Sara's excuse? She thought about it. *Was it as simple as having too-little time, being crazy busy in the city? Or was it something else? Did I take our friendship for granted? I guess I do have a few personal failings I need to look at.*

Sara rejoined her parents and they left without saying goodbye to Luke Sterling. She didn't want him to misunderstand her reasons for agreeing to talk with him tomorrow. And she definitely didn't want the town gossiping about them. There would likely be plenty of that after their lunch meeting tomorrow became public knowledge.

Chapter 8

Luke had more than lunch on his mind. Hearing about Sara's radio show had triggered an old desire. He wanted to bring His message in an approachable way to as many people as possible. *What better forum than a fun and exciting broadcast program?*

He wasn't enamored of stagnant taped television programming. But the immediate idea exchange of a call-in radio show—assuming there would be enough people interested in talking about faith in the world of technology and scientific exploration—would add flavor and spontaneity. *I'll have to win Sara over, of course. I'll have to convince her I'm worthy of both time and effort.*

He scratched at his chin, trying to merge Sara Goode's opposing behaviors. The professional, quick-witted, feisty Sara didn't mesh with the teary-eyed, broken, and sad woman who had smacked into his chest as she'd raced out the church doors. Luke saw the connection most people missed.

It was possible Sara hadn't left Bland because she was running from a man she didn't love or want to marry, but had left Cade because she was fleeing Bland. Something within the bowl-shaped valley comprising the land between the Big Walker Mountain and East River Tunnels had tormented her sufficiently to incite her complete abandonment of the place.

Sara had not only ditched her fiancé, but her church, her friends, and even her family. *What had happened to upset her so badly she was willing to leave and never look back?* He'd witnessed her empathy and forgiveness as she'd remarked on her sister's mother/daughter pudding.

Luke had seen the way Emily watched her husband steal glances at the woman he'd first intended as his wife. Cade's fears concerning the moment Emily and Sara would reconnect were indeed valid. Emily's knowledge of how much he had once loved Sara meant her return to Bland brought a level of unrest into their marriage. Rapid eye movement, heaving chest, hands wringing in her skirt's fabric—all signaled her anxiety.

When they'd bumped against each other in the fellowship hall, he'd been prepared for the worst. Recalling the event was enough to give him palpitations. Seeing the pair together from across the room—Emily turning to leave, Sara grabbing her arm—he'd thought Sara was about to strike out when her hand had extended to Emily's cheek.

Rolling his eyes at his own silliness, he wondered what had made him consider such foolishness. Once again, Sara had reacted with compassion, embracing Emily, whispering something meant only for her friend's ears. Luke hadn't needed to hear the words to know their effect. Emily's entire body had slackened. The breath she'd been holding released with one gasp and fingertips swiped at her eyes.

Sara had displayed a much softer side than he'd expected. It probably wouldn't hurt to show his finer qualities to her as well.

He was certain she still bristled from the incident

on the plane and his lack of sympathy with her plight. Her refusal to relinquish her aisle seat to the young couple with the baby played in his mind as one of the coldest acts he'd had the displeasure of observing. Swatting at imaginary lint on her obviously-expensive coat, she'd been reluctant to even engage in the possibility of taking a middle seat in order to help out the baby and his parents.

Interceding, though he had known even then it would be a mistake, Luke had made little headway in her steadfast denial. Only when the flight crew threatened to step into the fray did she begrudgingly oblige.

The sneers and ugly stares he had received from her afterward chilled him to the core. He'd made a mental note to add *the woman in the winter-white coat* to his prayer list.

Her reaction when the baby's nervous stomach rejected his dinner and spewed the bottle's contents onto her precious garment had offended the entire plane's occupancy, at least as far as he could discern. Taking possession of the bathroom for most of the flights' remainder, she'd exited with another huff. Water dripping from the coat's hem, she'd been allowed a wide berth to snag her bags from the overhead compartment and disappear into Roanoke's dark night.

But a baby with no seat, a young couple asking for a favor from another for their child's sake, was a little too close to Mary and Joseph's plight preceding Jesus' birth.

His parents had loved the narrative so much they had named him after the disciple whose recounting of the events was the one most often quoted. He could quote the passage from the Apostle Luke's second chapter, verses six through fourteen, by heart. Whenever he needed to be uplifted, he did.

"And so it was, that, while they were there, the days were accomplished that she should be delivered. And she brought forth her firstborn son, and wrapped him in swaddling clothes, and laid him in a manger; because there was no room for them in the inn.

"And there were in the same country shepherds abiding in the field, keeping watch over their flock by night. And, lo, the angel of the Lord came upon them, and the glory of the Lord shone round about them: and they were sore afraid.

"And the angel said unto them, Fear not: for, behold, I bring you good tidings of great joy, which shall be to all people. For unto you is born this day in the city of David a Saviour, which is Christ the Lord.

"And this shall be a sign unto you; Ye shall find the babe wrapped in swaddling clothes, lying in a manger.

"And suddenly there was with the angel a multitude of the heavenly host praising God, and saying, Glory to God in the highest, and on earth peace, good will toward men."

Chapter 9

Sara expected her parents to be upset at her accepting the pastor's lunch invitation so early during her stay with them. She searched for a polite way to bring it up, as they had begun to apologize for being caught off guard by her rare visit.

Sadie led the trio across the porch, talking as they walked. "Making the garlands and the desserts took all my time. I planned to go to the market tomorrow after Sunday service. Since it's just the two of us…well…was—"

"But you can join us," her father interrupted. Ben's long strides quickly took the lead. He reached forward, holding open the door for Sara and her mother. "We'll grab a sandwich after church and drive down to Wytheville for the week's grocery binge."

"Wytheville?" Sara asked, surprised. "Don't you have a place to shop right here in Bland?"

Her father shook his head in lamentation. "We used to always shop at Bland Grocery, but they closed after the giant superstore opened in Wytheville. Most people felt the extra twenty minute drive was worth getting more value for their dollars."

It was time—her moment to tell them her plans. "Well, as it turns out, the pastor has invited me to lunch. He wants to discuss something with me."

A thin streak of disgust, mingled with surprise,

threaded through Sadie's voice. "Already? You've barely been here a day and you're already going on a date with the county's most eligible bachelor?"

Humor danced in her father's eyes. His tone, though playful, was edged with warning. "Leave her be, Sadie. Maybe he'll talk her into staying here for a while."

Shaking her head in the same way her father had in lamenting the local market's loss, Sara protested, "It's not a date. We don't even know each other."

Sadie's displeasure registered in both body language and tone. "Yet, he'll undoubtedly be the next recipient of heartache left in the USS Sara Goode's wake."

Sara flinched. Sadie Goode could whittle joy out from the day exactly like a wood carver chiseling into an oak block—chipping away at everything bearing resemblance to self-confidence and fun. She knew the remark referenced her abrupt disappearance when she was about to marry Cade. Her actions had wounded her mother's pride, causing her embarrassment.

But Cade and I have both moved on. Why can't she? "Cade is happy now, Mother. He couldn't leave this town and I couldn't stay right then."

"Couldn't *stay*?" The word *stay* was dragged out into three syllables, partly due to her drawl and partly to the disdain dripping from it. "You just couldn't *stay*? Does the preacher know about this? I doubt he'll be eager to leave his parish and this town either."

Sara had never been disrespectful to either of her parents, but her mother had been baiting her as Beth did—likely where she learned it. "I don't know what the preacher knows. *I* didn't even know Cade had married Emily." She gestured between her mother and father. "Seems like someone might have mentioned that sometime over the past four years."

Sadie's hand shot to her hip in defiance. Her chest puffed out. "I might have if you'd been here longer than ten minutes twice each year." Her right forefinger poked forward and Sara braced for another verbal assault. Sadie was about to release another accusation stream from the guilt, blame, and disapproval river she captained. It ran fast and deep through her soul.

Ben stepped in front of Sara, his body forming a protective shield. "Setting out for a little adventure is another Goode family trait."

He cupped her chin as he had done when she was a child, though his rough calluses and dry fingertips were more recent souvenirs from the farm's demands. Yet there was something comforting about the sandpaper scratchiness along her face.

"Family traits," she repeated. *Where do I fit in? Who do I take after? I don't feel like an English Goode at all.* She turned the Claddagh around on her ring finger. Its silver hands grasped the golden heart of her O'Grady Irish ancestors. *Nor do I feel Irish. There must be another branch I don't know about, maybe Vikings, pirates, or explorers?*

Ben Goode stared into her eyes—a match for his— as though her thoughts were some text rolling across them that he could read. "Yes. Did I ever tell you about my adventures when I first left home?"

Sara mouthed, *thank you Daddy*, before turning back to face her mother. "Adventures, huh? I'd love to hear about them." Sara leaned against the doorframe.

Her mother threw her voice over one shoulder as

she walked away. "Not me. I'm going to bed. I've put fresh towels in your bath, Sara. Sleep tight."

Her mother's voice faded and Ben settled into his recliner by the fireplace. "Sit," he commanded. Obeying, Sara nestled into the sofa's soft leather while he began to spin a tall tale of jumping westward-bound trains. Too shocked to respond right away, she was content to let him talk.

"My best friend and I were right out of high school. Our fathers wanted us to follow them into the fields, while Uncle Sam wanted us for the Vietnam War. We weren't too happy with either prospect, so off we went to college and had a dickens of a time…until we realized we were both going to flunk out."

Ben chuckled. "Well, we knew our time was up. We'd be sent off to war just as soon as our transcripts had time to get to the recruiters. So we figured if we only had a few weeks, we might as well live out our dreams."

"I didn't know you went to college." Sara kicked off her shoes and pulled an afghan over her legs. The fire crackled but most of its heat, along with the smoke, disappeared up the chimney.

"Yeah, I don't talk much about it. I'm actually ashamed of doing so poorly, of not applying myself more. Well, my friend—he's dead now—had a heart attack last summer." Ben stalled, looking down. He grew quiet and appeared to become lost in thoughts known only to him.

"Tell me more," she encouraged.

"Well, we both jotted down everything we wanted to do before we died. I think you young'uns call it a 'bucket list' but we didn't know it had a name. We only knew we were likely to die or get too maimed to fulfill most of the things we wanted to do. So we made the lists, and set out to complete them."

Sara loved hearing about a side of her father she had never known existed. "What was on yours?"

"I wanted to see wild buffalo and giant elk and grizzly bears. And I wanted to see the Yellowstone geysers, ride a wild mustang, and ski through the Tetons. You know…guy-stuff."

"And did you?" Sara tried to imagine him doing those things, but it was difficult.

"I did," he said. He leaned back against the chair with the biggest grin on his face. "And then we came home and got the news we hadn't been drafted after all. The war was over."

"I know there's a moral here somewhere."

"Yes." He pointed a finger at her. "It took running from what others wanted for me in order to discover myself. You might find what you've been running from is what you truly want. It might just need to be in a different form."

The only light in the room was from the fire's glow that flickered between them. Her father's eyes sparkled, whether from the firelight or the memories Sara couldn't tell. It was hard to believe she'd never heard about this before. Yet she knew he wasn't making it up.

"Thank you, Daddy, for sharing that story. I want to see the proof you rode a wild mustang though."

She tossed the afghan aside and gave him a hug. Sara went to bed and dreamed of horses, mountaintops, and skiing through wildflowers.

****

Sara sat in the backseat of her parents' sedan that

her father had preheated before their departure for church. "Why do dreams make no sense?" she asked.

Ben glanced at her through the rear view mirror. "What do you mean?"

"I was dreaming about skiing through wildflowers. Isn't that crazy?"

Shooting her husband a dirty look, Sadie pointed a forefinger in his direction. "It was your father's nonsense. I warned you not to listen to it."

He winked at Sara through the mirror. "Anything she doesn't understand she calls nonsense."

Sara grinned at her parents' needling. They were such opposites, yet their marriage appeared to be a happy one. It had certainly withstood the test of time.

Ben pulled into a parking space as though it belonged to him, and jumped eagerly from the vehicle to assist his wife's and daughter's exits. He paused, whispering, "Perhaps your inner voice is trying to tell you that just because it hasn't been done before doesn't mean you can't do it."

Before she could respond, he turned and began his ritual of bestowing *good morning* and *hello* to whoever joined them along the walkway. Sadie extended her hand to first one and then another while Sara merely offered a smile and a nod. Her attention was on the man standing outside the church doors.

Reverend Sterling, cheerfully withstanding the cold, shook hands with the parishioners, exchanging greetings. Grinning at Sara, he leaned in. "Will you meet me in my office after the service?" The scents of peppermint and cedar wafted beneath her nose.

"Yes," she whispered, barely slowing. Continuing a steady march toward the family's pew, she hoped to prevent the color she knew was creeping into her cheeks from being seen. Like one of their horses on its way to the barn, she knew the path leading to place the Goodes always sat during service.

Families in Bland chose their seats, and kept them week after week, year after year. It was commonly joked about as *God's real estate*, which they made payments on through tithing.

Sara didn't even need to glance around to know who would be sitting to her left or behind her. She smiled as she thought about growing up on that pew, sitting beside her parents as a child, and now as an adult. The messages from the pulpit in Bland had been delivered to her in the same seat for her entire life.

Tradition, her parents called it. Yet she wondered back then if the acoustics were different from another angle. And did the pastor easily notice an absent flock member if he or she failed to return to their routine spot like a nesting bird?

The bells rang out, announcing the last call. Just as they had done during the *Hanging of the Greens* service, Reverend Sterling and the choir entered through the doors near the pulpit, facing the audience. After a round of *Blest Be the Tie That Binds,* the choir sat.

Luke Sterling flipped to the back of his Bible. "Thanksgiving. Christmas. These holidays often merge in our minds. We gather with family and friends. It's Luke's Gospel that reminds us of the importance of people in our lives. It is Luke who gives us the Herald Angels, proclaiming their knowledge, *He is the Christ Child*."

Sara's mind went instantly to Marge McKay, the

homeless woman she had met in Rockefeller Center. Marge had sworn those Herald Angels, albeit made from wire and tiny white lights, spoke to her. *Who's to say they don't?* Perhaps being without life's routine distractions made the woman more receptive to voices the rest of the world pushed aside.

Reverend Sterling continued his sermon, speaking on the blessings of people surrounding those with nothing and giving to others. "Joseph and Mary were temporarily homeless, without shelter, until blessed with the simple housing inside an animal stall. Jesus could have been born to any number of wealthy people in the Middle East. He could have had protection from the elements and the dangers of King Herod's minions. Yet God, in His wisdom, chose to give Him the gift of poverty."

Sara kept envisioning the diminutive homeless woman who had told her to "go home." Marge didn't ask for things other than warmth and food and the ability to get around. Her image reverberated inside Sara's mind as clearly as if she were sitting right on the church bench instead of the one in Rockefeller Center.

How many people walk past her without sharing a simple gift? Most fail to even notice her, choosing to ignore she, and others like her, exists. How many times did I walk by without seeing her until I was broken open?

Luke Sterling's voice mesmerized his captive audience. Even the babies seemed soothed by his melodious words, regardless of the fact their meaning was nothing to them yet. The hour went by as if only a few minutes. Sara was spellbound by his ability to bring the Word to life and to humanize the Gospel writers.

We've put the emphasis on presents and toys and the like, she thought, as he reminded her of what Christmas was supposed to be about. The gold and white glittering tree in the corner, covered in Christ symbols made by the children, oozed both meaning and spirituality.

Sara exited the service, shook Luke's hand, and excused herself to reenter the church through the side door.

Fifteen minutes later, Luke Sterling appeared, looking like an athlete in spite of his raiments. He pulled the stole from his neck in a football gesture—one she recalled seeing Cade perform as he'd tossed his shoulder pads up and over his head—and hung it and his robe in the small closet. Its cedar aroma rushed forward with the tall door's opening and closing.

Luke's voice rose and fell with a melodious lilt. "I'm so pleased you agreed to meet with me. Where would you like to have lunch?"

"Wherever you decide is fine. I don't really know what is available anymore," she ruefully admitted.

"Do you mind a twenty-minute trek? There's a place in West Virginia, just through the East River Tunnel. We can talk while we drive."

"Sure," she agreed.

They waited until the church's parking lot cleared before Luke opened the door. One straggler had hung back from the crowd. Her sports car was so tiny it hadn't been spotted during their occasional outward glances. A young lady with skinny legs—bare for a foot up the thigh—greeted them.

"Reverend Sterling, I was wondering…" She stopped speaking when Sara stepped from behind him.

"It's all right," he said. "Come in." He stood back and indicated she should enter his office.

Sara smiled and nodded.

The girl—barely seventeen, nineteen at the most—in heels and a chest-hugging sweater, though there was precious little to form around, had thin hair hugging her cheeks in long strands. It desperately begged for a serious cut. A long-leafed pine branch slithered through Sara's mind as she observed the girl.

"No...I'll come back...later..." She turned to leave.

"Stay. I'll wait outside," Sara said, excusing herself. "Take your time. We're in no hurry."

Did she imagine the girl sneering at her? Sara walked up and down the sidewalk, pulling her coat, happily washed free of the baby's yellow-stained spit-up, tightly around her. She adjusted the collar in the same manner as the morning she'd received the bad news.

Irritation swelled, though she didn't know exactly what she was irritated about. She was put out with the coat's designer. It was all style, offering little warmth. *So how does that girl refrain from freezing in a miniskirt and sweater?*

The sight of her standing at the door after everyone else had left caused Sara to suspect her intentions. Or was it her outfit? Or the disdainful look she had given as Sara motioned for her to walk inside? *Perhaps I've been in the city so long I've grown suspicious of everyone.*

She was just imagining things, irked at being outside in the frigid temperature. She had only herself to blame for that. She had volunteered to exile herself from the toasty office. She could have gone upstairs or into a back room. Instead, she had thrown herself out into the cold.

Sara blew on her fingers, and marched to the church's front, tugging on the doors. They had already been locked. Having to lock up the entrances here in the country struck Sara with a sad blow. *When had this started?* She remembered coming out to an always-open sanctuary to pray for her grandparents, set up fresh flowers, or just to be alone.

Clearly, even in the hinterlands, thieves and vandals had made door-locking necessary. Jogging down the steps, she marched back along the sidewalk. The door pushed open and the girl ran out, tears streaming down her cheeks. She didn't make eye contact as she passed Sara.

Chapter 10

Luke Sterling exited the church office less hurriedly than Cathy Tibbs. He wanted to give the young woman time to collect herself and make it out of the parking lot before she could observe him settle Sara Goode into his car. She had enough to feel badly about without adding guilt at delaying him from his lunch appointment. Toying with the keys, he finally inserted one in the deadbolt and twisted it. He turned and scanned the surroundings, locking eyes on Sara.

"There you are," he said, smiling. "Are you ready?"

Her teeth were chattering as she answered. "Yes. And I'm freezing."

He took her by the arm and escorted her to his vehicle, opened the door, and helped her inside. Scurrying to the driver's side, he jumped in beside her, cranked the engine, and let it run for a few seconds. As the heater warmed, he pointed to the sports car speeding down the road. "Sorry about the interruption."

Sara briskly rubbed her palms together. "Who is she?"

Luke backed away from the parking lot. "Cathy Tibbs, a local girl. She has a few problems right now."

She fidgeted with her coat edges. "Like what?"

Under Sara Goode's inquisitive stare, Luke regretted mentioning Cathy Tibbs. He should have said nothing. "Perhaps you are unaware that confidentiality is at my profession's core," he teased. "I'm afraid I can't tell you. Sorry."

"You brought it up," she replied defensively. "I'm an interviewer. Asking questions is what I do."

Luke sputtered. "I'm sorry," he repeated. "Of course you are only making conversation. I mentioned Cathy only to explain the delay."

She pointed an accusatory finger at him. "Then keep it to yourself. I was only continuing the discussion *you* started."

Amusement coursed through him and curled around the corners of his mouth and eyelids in upturns he couldn't force downward, though he tried. "Are you always this defensive?"

"Sometimes," she answered. "I'm a talk show host. I query people for a living…at least I used to. Not so much anymore. But that's neither here nor there." She swiped at a drooping curl over her brow. "Just know this. If you initiate a topic, I will ask follow-up questions. So if you don't want to discuss something, don't bring it up."

He lifted both hands from the steering wheel for a brief moment and laughed out loud. "Fair enough. Point made. I surrender."

Her lips cracked into a smile. Unable to stifle a laugh, though he was certain she would have liked to, Sara chuckled, too.

Luke pulled his four-wheel-drive sports utility vehicle—a necessity for the rough winters in the area— onto northbound I-77, focusing on merging into traffic.

"May I make an observation?" she asked.

"Absolutely." He grinned as their eyes met. It was

a brief moment, but one in which he held her gaze, feeling a connection penetrating beneath her icy surface.

She seemed frightened, alarmed, in this new territory of unemployment. From being around her no more than he had, he could tell her career was important to her. She'd mentioned being an interviewer several times, in one form or another, since they'd met.

His pulse quickened and he wondered if she saw through him as well.

"You aren't like any minister I've ever met before," she murmured.

Luke was used to stereotypical comments about preachers. He was equally as used to people judging him when he'd been an athlete—assuming he wasn't very smart if he played football and consequently had built up some muscle. Taking a breath in preparation of her comments, he asked, "Is that a good thing?"

"I guess." She laughed. "But, how did it happen? How did you wind up in a pulpit?"

Silence penetrated the atmosphere as Luke contemplated how much to tell her. They'd really just met. "It wasn't my first choice," he admitted.

"No? You're still quite young. What could possibly have preceded this?"

Luke subconsciously cupped his knee, circling its knobby outgrowth with his palm. "It was rather short-lived." He heard his voice crack when he spoke. *She's going to pick up on that and know it means something.*

"Oh?"

Her question was simple, yet beneath the two letters was a world of meaning. *What had it been and why wasn't he doing it now? What had called him to the ministry?* His hand lifted from his knee to his face. The other gripped the steering wheel, perhaps too firmly.

"Football. I played football." Even saying it took him back to the field. The game had been like an addiction. Back then it had taken all his time, all his energy. He had focused, with laser intensity, on keeping in shape.

Her voice housed a smile and he didn't have to take his eyes from the road to know she was assessing his physique from her passenger seat. "Now *that* I can believe. But how did you go from football to preacher?"

"It was almost the other way around. I knew all my life I was interested in the Gospels, but I fought it."

Surprise etched her words. "You knew, and yet you didn't follow this path initially?"

"I couldn't quite merge everything together. I wanted to play football. And I wanted to understand science, which I studied in college. But everywhere I went I felt compelled to do good works, help those around me, and then give God the credit."

"So why didn't you just play for the seminary team?"

Although she chuckled at her own question, the truth bared the ugly dogma he had grown up with, and had been surrounded by, as a kid.

"I saw things differently than a lot of people around me. I struggled with the strict religious order my family belonged to. At college, I found this higher-minded group who believed science explained God's handiwork."

"A perfect fit," she said.

"You would think so. But no. Not at first."

"Why?"

In a consummate interviewer's true nature, she attacked every statement with another question. But Luke didn't mind. In fact, he liked her interest in him and his newly found niche.

"I was playing football at college. Had hopes of being picked up by a professional team. When I got hurt and couldn't play ball anymore I was devastated."

Her voice became soft and low. "I know what devastation feels like."

Maneuvering through traffic, Luke couldn't respond as he wished he could. Glancing from the road to her face, once again he saw her eyes look past him into a place he had seen before. "I recognized the look in your face." He tried to assure her. "It took me right back to that time, not so long ago…" His voice faltered and cracked.

"But?" she spurred.

He turned what he hoped was a happy face toward her. "I found my real calling. The football gig was just a vehicle getting me into the right place. It took losing what I thought I wanted in order for me to find my true passion."

Her mouth dropped open. "You won't believe this, but my father said almost the exact same thing to me last night."

"It's true." He nodded. "Sometimes the waves deliver us to a different spot on the shore. Then we can discover the place we're meant to be and realize it was all part of a grand scheme."

Sara shot him a look of disbelief. "So you're telling me losing my radio program was part of some elusive great design?"

"I hope so." The sudden darkness of the East River Tunnel took a few minutes to become accustomed to.

"You hope so?"

Luke had meant to ease into the subject, bring it up slowly, maybe not at all today. But somehow the timing felt right. It blurted from his mouth of its own volition. "I've got a proposition for you."

Chapter 11

In the dim light coursing through the tunnel dividing Virginia and West Virginia, Luke's voice sounded provocative. Sara was glad for the darkness so he wouldn't see the beet coloring she knew was creeping into her cheeks. "A proposition?"

"Yes."

Her face blazed. *Obviously, he has me confused with Cathy Tibbs.* She instantly regretted thinking badly of the young woman, especially as it was based on appearances alone. "I realize I've been living in a sinful mecca but, I'm not that kind of person. Maybe you didn't understand that about me."

Luke broke into laughter as they burst from the tunnel into bright sunlight. "It's not *that* kind of proposition," he declared.

"By all means, do share the kind you have in mind."

He quickly took the first exit, focusing on the traffic before resuming the conversation. "I've been toying with the notion of starting a radio call-in show for in-depth Christian philosophy, conjoining science and faith. I have the expertise in the faith and science departments, but none in broadcasting."

His long pause left Sara wondering if he had another statement to make or if the silence was meant to allow his words to be fully digested. When it became clear he was waiting for a response, she translated what she took to be his meaning. "I see. I have the broadcasting background and no current job."

Luke shrugged. "As long as you're not busy, want to help me out?"

Things were looking up. "I'll have to think about it," she agreed.

He pulled into a parking lot near an old log house. Sara leapt from the car as soon as it stopped, before Luke could come around and open the car's door. *This isn't a date. Spare me the gentility*, she thought as she glanced around.

"Is this someone's home? Are you sure we're in the right place?"

"Yes, it used to be the home of Green Valley's founder, Uriah Green, and his wife Elizabeth. They raised eleven children here, farming the 1100 acres that make up the valley."

Their footsteps crunched against the gravel. "How did it become a restaurant, and how is it you know so much about it?"

Luke smiled, but it wasn't his usual grin. It pulled mostly to one side, and with his diverted eyes, it gave him the appearance of guilt. "I helped with the fundraising to save it."

"You? Do you own part of it?"

"Oh no. I just thought it would be a shame to lose another historically important building. The people operating the restaurant keep it authentic. And the view is…" He took two more steps upward onto the porch and motioned outward with a sweep of a hand. "Well, judge for yourself."

Sara joined him at the railing, following the

direction of both his gesture and eyes. Beyond the metal roof's overhang, a long succession of ridges in graduating blue shades filled the space between the sky and the ground. It was lovely, she'd give him that. Even the house with its weathered logs separated by chalky chinking, and its wavy glass windows, bubbled with ageless beauty.

Luke pointed toward the chalkboard hanging from a hook beside the entrance. "In spite of the place's humble beginnings and colonial feel, the menu has incredible offerings—salmon, duck, trout, bison, and elk. They also offer several great vegetarian dishes, like fried grits with tomato jelly."

Sara winced. "Fried grits? How on earth would you fry grits?"

They were laughing as they stepped inside, and a hostess immediately greeted them. "Welcome to the Log House Restaurant and Grill. How many in your party?"

Luke answered, "Only two. I wonder if we could get seating upstairs, if it's not too much trouble."

"I'll check for you. Just a minute."

Sara diverted her eyes from his while they waited, not wanting to feel another blaze of attraction for her parents' preacher. She glanced about the interior. Its walls were identical to the outer ones, wooden logs with white mortar between. The tables appeared to have been made from reclaimed wood, marred with ancient ground-in scratches and insect holes beneath the surface veneer. Ruffled curtains in the color of natural raw linen adorned the short windows.

The hostess returned, offering a warm smile as she snagged two menus and motioned for them to follow her up the stairs.

Sara ordered the grilled trout with sautéed vegetables, and Luke the filet mignon and a baked potato. Calling out in sudden remembrance, Luke snagged the waitress's attention. "Can I add something please? An order of fried grits with tomato jelly."

Sara laughed. "Couldn't resist, could you?"

"You'll thank me. Just wait." He winked.

Talking to him was easy; too easy. It made Sara nervous to think she might reveal a little too much. There was something unsettling about Luke and the way he could see right through her.

"Cade Norton thinks a lot of you still," he offered unexpectedly.

Hearing Cade's name rattled her confidence. *How much does he know about Cade and me? What had Cade said to him?* "Oh?" she asked. "How do you know this?"

Before he could answer, she pointed at him with an accusatory finger. Remembering her mother's similar habit, she dropped her hand, but finished what she wanted to say. "Just don't give me the whole privacy speech again, because I warned you. Any subject you instigate is fair game."

"No. I wasn't going to. He doesn't talk about you directly."

Sara was confused. "Then what makes you assume he still thinks about me?"

Before Luke could answer, the appetizer arrived. Two crispy planks of grits, apparently chilled so they'd stick together, had been dipped in breading and browned on all sides. They were dressed with a red, chunky relish, not actually jelly.

"Bon appetite," Luke said. He lifted his fork and she followed his lead, taking a small bite of the strange-sounding concoction.

To Sara's surprise, it was terrific. The grits were crispy on the outside, creamy on the inside. With the topping, it reminded her of bruschetta. "Perfect," she said. "Good call."

He leaned back, nodding. His shoulders commanded her line of sight, nearly as broad as the table and the dormer window above his head. He inhaled and his chest expanded to accommodate the additional oxygen. Without skipping a beat, he returned to the discussion topic before the first course had arrived.

"Cade hasn't said he dwells on you, but the fact he often brings you up in conversation proves he does, doesn't it?" His hand migrated to his face, its forefinger resting on his bottom lip, a gesture she'd seen him make before.

Sara dropped her fork and grimaced, unblinking, unflinching. Whatever it was he ached to understand, they might as well get it out in the open. "Are you trying to ask me something about Cade? Or Emily? What is it you want to know?"

Lowering his glass to the table with a *plunk*, he said, "You intrigue me. I haven't met anyone as interesting as you in a long time. Getting to know you isn't going to be easy, is it?"

"There you go again, ending your statement with a question." In spite of herself, Sara was amused. He wasn't like any other man she'd met in a long time either. Though he expressed interest in her prior connection to Cade, he didn't follow up with the expected questions.

Dropping the subject, he talked about the restaurant and its history, the area in general, and the fine people he'd met here.

Following his lead, she didn't pry either. Despite how much she wanted to ask questions about him, she didn't proceed with them.

When their meal was over and they were in the car headed back to Bland, he took her hand in his and lifted it to plant a kiss on its back. His lips didn't linger, but simply fluttered across her flesh, causing her veins to burst with urgency, like water racing to the falls.

"Thank you," he said.

Her stomach quivered. A thousand butterflies danced inside and she had a desire to kiss him. His lips had felt soft and demanding simultaneously. Time stood still. He quickly jerked his head up, looking in the direction they were traveling.

They were quiet for the remainder of the ride home. Luke kept one hand wrapped securely around hers. Sara liked the way his big palm and long fingers housed hers, making it feel small and delicate. She wondered if he could feel her racing pulse thump across her wrist and into the meaty space behind her thumb and first finger. Though she could have withdrawn her hand at any time, she left it there.

The steep mountain passes, stark in their winter contrast to the bare fields, streams, and creeks rushing through the valley, commanded attention. Somehow she had expected he would drive back to the church. Instead, he veered onto the exit toward White Pine Drive.

With consternation, she realized he would have to

drive her home. "That's right," she said aloud. "I didn't drive to church. I rode with my parents. You've got to take me to their house."

"It's okay," he assured her. "I know how to get to your parents' house."

Sara gasped in horror. "People will think we're dating."

"Would that be a bad thing?" His thumb caressed the side of her hand, stroking it effortlessly.

She found it easy to imagine the same effort applied on other body areas, then remembered his profession and flushed with guilt. "Which part—what people are thinking or that we're dating?"

"Pick one." He chuckled.

"I've had enough of small-town gossip. But dating you could be fun, I suppose." She looked away.

"You suppose?" He feigned insult. "I'll have you know I am an excellent date."

Continuing to stare out her window, she hoped to hide the grin she could feel spreading across her face. "So you say."

"You've just had lunch with me," he pointed out.

"And you offered me a job without pay. Not the best of first impressions," she teased.

"Some toil is for its own reward."

Sara shook her head. She liked the banter. In radio land, playful discourse between interviewer and interviewee, when smart and swift, indicated high intelligence. "There better be some kind of fringe benefits. I'm not used to working for free."

"We could make it a partnership. You'd get half of everything." His eyebrows were raised and he had dropped his chin.

Looking hopeful, he was impossible to refuse. "I'll think about it," she said.

He smiled. "I do like you, Sara Jane Goode."

With indignation, she asked, "How did you know my middle name?"

"Because your mother talked about Sara Jane for so long I thought it was one word."

My mother's been talking about me? To the preacher? It likely wasn't good, probably a prayer request. "I like you too, Reverend Sterling," she replied.

"Just Luke, please." He entwined his long, sinewy fingers with hers and squeezed his palm tightly against hers.

"Then it's just Sara." She ran a fingertip against the back of his hand.

Luke took a sharp inhale and let it out slowly. He stared at the road, glancing at her with regularity. His voice sounded thick and dreamy, as if he were waking from a long nap. "Just so you know, I'm a man complete with all human emotions and sensations. Please don't forget that."

She had to avert her eyes to keep the sultry expression she knew she was wearing from being visible to him. Every part of her longed for him suddenly, but she couldn't let him know it. "Forget you're a man? Not likely!"

He took the road into her parents' property with the ease of someone who had been there before. He insisted on opening the car door for her and helping her exit the vehicle.

She could see her parents peeping out the window through a gap in the curtain they thought wouldn't give them away.

Luke walked inside with her, greeted Ben and Sadie, and turned back to Sara. "Can you meet me at the church office at ten in the morning?"

"Sure." She smiled.

He turned to leave, offering goodbyes as quickly as he had offered greetings.

Sara watched his car go through the gate and disappear into the curving tree-lined, forested drive.

So did her parents, and the explanations were torturous. "That was a date," her father declared. Poking her on the shoulder with his forefinger, he seemed to be saying, *I told you so*. Ben kept staring at her with suspicion in his eyes.

"Absolutely not," she tried to explain. "We are planning a little business venture."

"Men don't open car doors for women they are just in business with," he reasoned.

"And when did you become the expert on what men do for women?" her mother asked.

Sara doubted her mother really cared about the conversation, more likely choosing to join in for the sake of arguing with him.

She would never admit to feeling attracted to the preacher to her parents, regardless of the sensations he awoke within her. All she wanted to do was change the subject. "Do we have Internet here?"

"No, but your sister does." Her mother pointed up the hill. "You can go up there if you'd like."

Sara wouldn't have walked up the hill to her sister's house for the speediest Internet service known to mankind. "I'll use my phone. It will transmit what I need. Thanks you two. And don't say anything to anyone about this project just yet. I don't want it to get out unless we are actually able to get something off the ground."

Retreating to her room, she crawled between the covers. It was early still. Lunch had been a long and leisurely one. It had lasted for more than two hours, plus the ride out there and back. And then there was the time Luke had spent with Cathy Tibbs, or Pine Branch, as she would always think of her.

But she couldn't imagine herself eating again and she wanted to look up some information to be ready for Luke the next day. Sara was always prepared. This project, foreign to her as it was, would be no different.

****

Sara drove into town and parked her car at the parking lot's edge so as not to draw attention to the fact she was there with Reverend Sterling. His SUV was sitting right in front of the office door. Tongues would wag if she left the rental beside it during non-scheduled church hours.

She ran across the lot and rapped against the wooden door. It sprang open instantly, as though he'd been watching for her. Luke Sterling was so handsome that the first few seconds she saw him made her heart flutter. *Or was it something besides his good looks?*

Gorgeous men practically littered the streets of New York. Many wound up across from her in the radio station's interview chamber. But rarely did they have this kind of effect on her.

Luke possessed an unnerving *knowledge* of her. He had a confident air surrounding him the way a scent halo surrounded the spritzing girls in department stores. She had never met anyone so sure of himself and his purpose, or one with such intensity. In her experience, the celebrities she'd met who were known for their intense presence were actually just focused on themselves.

Luke gave his attention to others, most notably to her. It sucked the oxygen from her lungs and left her speechless. His smile wasn't the only welcoming greeting. The aroma of cedar hit her instantly.

"Come in." He motioned inward, closing the door behind her after she entered. Reaching for her coat, he helped her remove it and hung it on a rack near the entry. For a moment she expected him to pull the side hem up to inspect for stains.

"I barely slept last night," she admitted. "I've got so many ideas."

He rubbed his palms together. "Fantastic. I love people with enthusiasm." Something clicked against his teeth when he spoke—*a hard candy maybe?*

Peppermint wafted beneath her nose. She looked around and saw the jar containing red-and-white cellophane-wrapped candies sitting on his desk. Following her line of sight, he held it out to her.

She took one, self-conscious about her breath. *I probably do still have the stale odor of coffee lingering on my tongue.* She had brushed her teeth before leaving home, but there was no reason to chance it. Sara removed the wrapper and popped it in her mouth.

"Here's what occurred to me..." She began to describe the various forums he could use to launch a radio show—everything from online presences including blog radio and podcasting, to pitching a local terrestrial radio program, to going straight to the subscriber station considering itself *family* programming.

He listened to her ideas, nodding and smiling. He then shared his. Surprisingly, they were vastly similar. "It appears we are on the same wavelength," he said.

He retrieved several outlines from his desk drawer. "I've been thinking about this for years. For you to turn up right now with experience in broadcasting feels like divine intervention."

"It feels like something to me, too," she admitted. Looking away, she knew she was blushing at the double entendre she had used.

They practiced interviewing each other. Sara loved his voice and told him so, declaring it perfect for radio. She recorded him on his laptop and played it back for him to hear. He was less impressed with it than she, but in her opinion, few people liked their own voices. In fact, aside from her father, she knew no one who did.

"It's different from my sermon voice, isn't it?" He replayed the frisky bickering between them soundtrack.

She shook her head. It was easy to forget he was a minister.

He misunderstood the gesture. "It isn't different?"

"Yes, it's different, it's just…"

He took her hands in his. "You can say whatever is on your mind. You don't have to tiptoe around me."

She caught his flickering eyes. They practically danced in a brilliant dervish, pulling her forward. "I like you very much," she whispered. She realized her thick, deep intonement resounded with her desire despite her resistance to let it surface. "But I don't think…I mean…"

She looked away; forcing the emotions he stirred into her mind's most hidden recess. Given way, she might stroke his arms, run fingertips up his side, press against him until there was no space left between them.

He reached forward, sliding butterfly touches along her chin. His face came close to hers, so close she could see the pores in his cheek. Her breathing quickened. Her chest rose and fell in quick bursts.

When he spoke his words sounded melodious. "You don't think you want to get involved with a preacher? Is that it?"

She was sure he could hear her heart pounding. Blood pulsed with urgency, filling her ears with the throbbing sound. She couldn't speak, only nod. Sara thought he was going to kiss her to prove her wrong.

"At least you are honest about it," he whispered. Releasing his touch from her face, he said, "You are safe here. This sanctuary belongs to the people of Bland. It isn't mine to use as I please."

Luke stroked the spine of a book, *The Last Supper*. His fingertip lingered over the chalice near the author's last name, a publisher's trademark. As though it had burnt his hand, he yanked it free. "Our business venture is purely professional, and I wouldn't jeopardize that either. But I like you as well. And after hours, if you are interested, I'd like to make my case as just a flesh and blood male."

She wasn't aware she was crying until he reached up and wiped the tears from the corners of her eyes.

"Why the tears?"

Fear, she wanted to say. She was afraid to get involved with someone, especially someone as dedicated to his job as Luke Sterling. And then there was Cathy Tibbs, the pine branch girl. Some part of Sara suspected he might have toyed with her. But if he held such a tight principle about what went on in the church office, he likely maintained it altogether. Besides, she remembered the girl had left crying. Maybe he had that effect on people. "I don't know," was all she said.

"Will you accept my offer then?" he asked.

"On one condition."

They had been dancing around each other, not discussing their first unofficial meeting. Time had arrived to ferret it out, time to bring twin brothers out from the closet.

His eyes widened. "Condition?"

"Yes. I believe we met before, though neither of us has had the nerve to talk about it."

"Oh?" His looking away was a guilty admission, a cue she'd learned to pick up on during interviews.

"You know what I'm saying. Before I can agree to a partnership with you, I'm interested to know what you were doing in New York last Friday. If it was innocent, why didn't you bring up our encounter when Cade introduced us?"

Chapter 12

Luke rubbed his chin. The white elephant they had been tiptoeing around had finally roared. "So it was you," he said.

Sara focused on him, zeroing in on his face as if her target's bull's-eye. "Yes. You know it was. Given your silence about the encounter, I have to wonder."

"Wonder?"

Narrowing her eyes to mere slashes, she squinted at him. "Is the kind reverend about to desert his flock? Were you interviewing for another church?"

Her accusation fell hard on him. He wouldn't dare consider leaving Bland now. There was so much work to be done, so many projects he had started but hadn't finished. He gasped. "Interviewing for another church?"

Sara used a professional tone, the one he assumed she pulled out for interviews. Her stare was close to being uncomfortable, as her eyes burned into his so intensely he couldn't retain the contact. She continued with a barrage of questions, each more intense than the one prior.

"I've heard nothing about you having any relatives in New York, nor about a sister church in the Manhattan area. Is there a wife there? A child? A Broadway show you just couldn't miss? What's the story, Preacher?"

There was also a mischievous undertone to her

cutting questions. She was toying with him. But what he had been doing there had always been a private thing, something just between him and God, the people he served there, and the one he always hoped to be serving…the one he sought each time he went.

He swiped at his face, one finger running along his bottom lip, a nervous habit akin to the knee rub. "Would you believe me if I said it isn't what you think?"

She peered back at him. "No. It's always what I think. I have a knack for ferreting out scandal."

Sara Jane Goode was tough and not likely to let him skirt the issue. *Should I tell her? Should I share my secret?* Something told him she would know if he was less than honest. And if he wanted her to open up with him, he'd have to give a little of himself. "I've never told anyone about this. It's been a secret."

Sara leaned forward. Her irises glittered in a blue-and-green mélange. "I'll take it to my grave."

"How can I be sure?" he asked, hesitating.

"Well, I didn't give away our previous encounter to Cade when he introduced us, or to my parents."

"Was that on my behalf or yours?" As soon as he asked the question he regretted it. Her face fell. Every twinkle and merry sparkle died out as if the light switch controlling her inner illumination had been turned off.

She swallowed so hard her Adam's apple bulged outward for a minute. "You mean—was I keeping it secret due to my behavior? Did I dread being discovered and outed as the"—her hands jutted outward to make air quotes around the next segment—"*bitch* from the plane?"

Luke wanted to backpedal, to retract the last

sentence. "I'm sorry, that came out wrong. What I meant…what I was trying to say…I…" He stopped the endless stuttering. If he wanted her to be truthful with him, he might as well confess it all.

"Go ahead," she coaxed. Her arms wrapped around her midsection in self-protection. "I'm a big girl. I can take the criticism."

Luke tugged on her arms, trying to free them from their imprisonment around her waist. Carefully stroking her forearms with the backs of his hands, he wanted to soothe her, to show how much he liked her and wished not to offend her.

"I don't want to criticize you." He moved closer, and pulled her forward slightly, pulling her arms free and by her sides. "I'm just trying to get to know you, to find out everything about you and to let you know there is no point in role-playing, and pretending to be people we aren't."

She pulled back a little. "What do you mean? I don't pretend to be anything."

"That's not true." He bit his lip again. *Why do I keep saying things I know I'll regret?* Retracing the track laid down by her tears, he stroked her face with one finger, trying to show tenderness, to uncover the softness she kept harbored behind a steely façade.

Sara took another step backward. He was losing her. She was erecting a wall he might never get around, over, or through. On impulse, he grabbed her and pulled her into his chest, hugging her tightly to him, stroking the back of her head with one hand while keeping the other firmly on her waist.

He could feel her breath coming in heavier pulls and drags. And then a giant gulp as she fought against the emotional wave he knew was coming. It broke then, against her iron will, it burst forward into sobs he suspected were long overdue.

Embracing her even more tightly, he held Sara to him. "It's okay. Let it out, let it all out. Tears cleanse the soul."

Slowly, her arms moved from their stiff positions—as sentinels at her side—to his elbows, and finally around his midsection. Her fingers twirled in his shirt.

Luke wanted to comfort her, to kiss away any pain she had ever had, especially any he had caused. Knowing that would be dangerous, he kept stroking her instead.

With her head against his shoulder, her face buried in his neck, he whispered in her ear, "See, it's all right. I'm still right here."

"Why?" she sputtered.

"Because I like you, Sara Jane. And I think you could like me, too, if you would give me a chance to prove I'm worthy of really knowing you."

She sniffled. The tears, having emptied their well, fell with less urgency. She lifted one hand from him to swipe at her face. "Then you have to be honest with me, even if it is something you don't think I'll understand."

Though he didn't really want to, he released his grip on her, turning the snug embrace into a slight hold. "You mean about New York."

"Yes. If you can't trust me with your reasons for concealing your trip to the city, then why should I trust you?"

He dropped his arms from around her and stepped back. His vocation mocked him. Its faith, love, trust, and understanding, seemed in direct opposition to what he was about to confess.

"You may be sorry you asked, because what I was doing there is an involved story. And it isn't going to be easy for me."

She pointed to her face, indicating her swollen eyes and tear-streaked cheeks. "Do you think this was easy for me?"

"But I'm supposed to be the counselor, the one with the answers. When I tell you what happened to me, you might not believe that ever again."

"Or it might restore my faith in people's ability to change and to grow. Who knows? It's a risk you'll have to take if you want me on board with your project."

He rubbed his face with both hands, knowing how hard the next few minutes would be. "Well, let's sit down again. I don't think I can do this standing up."

Chapter 13

Luke, agreeing to explain his foray, entranced Sara. Knowing she was about to hear something he had never told anyone before, made her feel special, though nervous. Bracing for the worst, she snagged the chair opposite the one he had just claimed.

For a moment he sat, silent, rubbing his cheeks and eyes with both hands. One fell to his right knee, massaging it, while the other knee bounced from the up and down movement his left foot incited.

This was familiar territory. She recognized the twitches, the nervous ticks, and the hard swallows causing his throat to bulge. Whatever his reasons for being in Manhattan, Sara could tell they were important, at least to him.

Clearing her mind, wiping away all thoughts of herself, she shelved her own issues and troubles in order to be fully in the moment.

No one has trusted me this much since Cade. Sara's pulse quickened. Panic swept into her stomach, churning its contents and causing nausea to swell. *What if I let him down? What if I fail to react in a way which upholds his pride and honors the trust he is giving me?* Sweat trickled beneath her hairline, beading her forehead.

Luke appeared oblivious. He looked to the right, then upward, and bit his lip, before releasing a loud exhale, continuing to rub his knee. "Okay, I told you yesterday about the career-ending college football injury."

She nodded. "Yes, I remember."

"Then I told you I found my calling." His chest rose and fell. In swift succinct movements, it expanded and contracted until she was mesmerized by it. "What I left out was the events between those two things."

Luke didn't speak for a while. Silence created a vacuum in the church office. Street noises failed to penetrate its insulated walls. The room cocooned them. Privacy was ensured for any parishioner during confession or prayer request.

This was the point where most people became uncomfortable and would be tempted to interject their own voice into the deafening hush. But having interviewed so many people in the past, Sara knew this was the sacred time when he was working out how to present his story. She didn't want to lead the conversation.

Her willingness to listen, to sit mute for as long as it might take, could possibly make a difference in how much he opened up to her. If he was being honest, and she had no reason to believe otherwise, it might take a few minutes to sort out the right words.

Luke inhaled deeply, picked up a pencil, and set it down. He looked up at her, then down, glancing back as if to check if her eyes were still trained on him. Finding them there, he spoke again, "Well, I think you first have to know I played football my entire life. My father, a high school football star, was sidelined with an injury before he made it to college. He not only taught me the importance of staying fit and healthy, but to play the game with my head as well as with my body."

He looked off into the distance and she kept her focus on him.

"He was so proud when I left to play for Columbia University. It was a really big deal for him. He was diagnosed with cancer in my first year, but I didn't go home to spend the time I should have with him. My football career was more important."

A cloud descended over Luke's face and Sara's heart broke for him. "If he played, too, I'm sure he understood," she said softly.

Nodding, his bottom lip caught in his teeth, he continued, "He did. But when he died, I flew in for the service and left immediately after, due to my career. I abandoned my mother when she needed me most." Shaking his head, he finally dropped it. His eyes were on something in his lap Sara knew wasn't really there.

Her heart was beating so loudly she thought he might hear it. The suspense from his story was building inside her. But she couldn't rush him.

He grabbed the pencil again, catching it between his palm and thumb, thumping the eraser end against the desk top. "I was a real jerk; full of myself, cutting out headlines in newspapers' sports sections, going through women as I had my pick—not caring if I hurt them."

His admission made a swift painful slice into her heart. It was why he had identified with her, understood without judging, what had happened with Cade. He hadn't always been the thoughtful man who sat before her today.

"After I was injured—when the hit ending my career sidelined me for good—I waited for my teammates to show up, my coach, the trainers and masseuses, the girls I'd been leading on, anyone. And do you know who came to my bedside?"

His eyelids peeled slowly upward and Sara ached with the disappointing news she was about to hear. "Your mother?" she asked.

"No." He paused and stared at her. "Nobody. My mother thought I'd be surrounded by the same people I imagined would be there. She didn't want to get in the way. She believed she was useless to me."

Sara was stunned by the abandonment he'd suffered at what was likely the toughest period in his life. "What happened? How did you get by?"

He grimaced. "I became angry and"—Luke glared up at her—"well…depressed."

"But of course. That was more than enough to cause depression. But where…?" She stopped talking. It wasn't time for her to question, but to listen.

"That's when I realized people had been hanging around me because I was the moment's star. As soon as my comet burned from the sky, they found someone else to idolize. I was old news."

He adjusted his position in the chair and swiped at his face a few more times. "Then a pastor stopped by my hospital room and invited me to spend Thanksgiving with his parish. They were serving at a homeless shelter. I thought it sounded like the most depressing place in the world. Although I told him I'd consider it, I didn't mean it."

Sara understood. How many times in the past had she accepted invitations for the sole purpose of making the issuer go away? With no intention of actually attending whatever she'd agreed to do, she had left a string of disappointments littering her pathway. *Maybe my mother was right to refer to me as USS Sara Goode.*

While she sorted out her own demons, Luke found his voice once again. "But then Thanksgiving arrived. I had just been released from the hospital, everyone else had their own plans, and the shelter wasn't far from my dorm. I hobbled down on crutches. I was surprised at how vibrant and alive the place was. And for the first time since the injury, I understood how blessed I really was. My depression began to dissipate."

With each slowly exhaled breath, a bit more light left his eyes. Sara imagined a lowering blind wouldn't have doused their shine any faster.

Although his words were indicative of the lifting darkness, going back to that time in his life had conjured memories that flashed across his face. The depth of his pain resonated in his voice. "It saved my life," he declared.

Though Sara understood his meaning, she sought clarification. "You think…you mean…the depression was that bad?" She tried to ask succinctly but the words wouldn't come out. *Had he meant he had considered suicide?*

The vacant expression in his face when Luke nodded made his meaning clear. She wanted to run to him, to embrace him, to apologize for making him recount the incident. *I am horrible.*

"Yes, Sara, the depression was such I considered ending my life. I've done a lot of research about this, especially during my theology studies. Sudden life changes, mood-altering drugs administered for pain, psychological restructuring of who we are in the world, abandonment by those we believe care for us—it all adds up to feelings of worthlessness." He frowned. "That's how I felt, useless."

Knowing it hadn't lasted, that he hadn't succumbed to his perceptions, emboldened her. "But obviously you found a way out of it."

"Yes, thankfully." Blinking a few times and taking some deep cleansing breaths, he shrugged. "I volunteered at the shelter that day and many others. It was through helping others I found meaning once again. So, to answer the original question you asked, what was I doing in New York?"

His lengthy pause compelled her to spur him. "Yes? New York?"

"I go back every year, on the Friday before Thanksgiving, and take some coats and food and money I've saved. It's my way to not only give back but to keep a toe in the space of reality. I never want to become so full of myself again I fail to see the suffering those around me are enduring."

"It humbles you," she said.

"Yes, I do find it very humbling, Sara." With his admission complete, he set the pencil aside and stilled its rolling along the desk.

"And so there is little patience for a self-absorbed woman in an expensive winter-white coat who is trying to maintain the seat she spent points to get?"

"Was I that obvious?"

"I guess I was," she admitted. "But why do you keep it a secret? People would admire you for it."

"Exactly. I don't do it for admiration. I don't want other people to know—plaudits for an unselfish act then become selfish. I don't want the action to become another prop for my career."

Is Luke Sterling for real? Does anyone still operate like this? Sara's heart dropped into her stomach. "You're joking, right?"

"No. I'm serious. I fully expect my admission remains as sacred as anything you might say to me. I have no intention of ever avowing to anyone else what I do at that time of year. It's that important to me."

"Luke, I don't know what to say. Your reason is so admirable."

"Okay, that's my little story." He leaned back, relaxed finally. "So why were you so cranky with that young couple?"

Sara groaned. *How can I follow his admission?* The truth behind her churlish behavior was terrible, but was all she had. "I was shattered by my show's cancelation. And I knew I was only going home because I'd exhausted all plausible excuses." She shrugged.

This time he had her caught in the cross hairs of his intense gaze. "So, you didn't come back to Bland because you were homesick and longing for your mother's pumpkin pie?"

"No. I haven't been home for Thanksgiving since I moved to New York. I've not even been coming for Christmas."

"But you show up when your life is falling apart and wonder why the red carpet hasn't been rolled all the way to the highway for you?" He winked at her and she understood he was partly serious while making his joke.

"It's that obvious?" She covered her face with her hands. They absorbed the heat coming off her flushed cheeks and she knew they were flaming red in embarrassment.

He adjusted his weight in the chair, leaning

forward conspiratorially. "Want some good news?"

She peeked through her fingertips. The grin she saw lit his face like a thousand kilowatt bulb being ignited behind his head. "Please."

"We've both just excavated some trauma. We've pulled back the covers on our souls and let the other peek beneath them. And we can still sit here, smiling and joking. Nobody ran away screaming."

"But I feel like that's what I should be doing," she protested.

He raised an eyebrow, giving his face an amused appearance. "Due to what I admitted?"

Sara's voice crackled. "No, because of my shame. I'm so embarrassed."

Chapter 14

Luke had wondered how much to tell her. Sara Goode was as slippery as Cade's initial warning about a greased pig. But he had no interest in playing games. He'd left that behind along with the football he'd taken to the field and placed on the five yard line after discovering he was no longer on the Lions' roster.

But he wasn't ready to talk about the night he'd met the gray-eyed man in the shelter, the man whose voice soothed every ache in his soul. Luke considered him a healer, and had never ceased looking for him again.

He spread his arms wide—indicating more than himself, the pastor's office, the church building, and even God's abundant wider community. "Don't be ashamed. There's no judgment here. You aren't judging me, nor I you. Things have happened to us. Try to remember things are happening to people every day."

Sara's face still blazed with her admission's flush. "Act with compassion. Is that what you're recommending?"

"It's a good place to start. Most of us are fighting some demon or battle and we can't know what the other is facing."

The color began to drain away, and she appeared to finally be getting his message. "Like my sister? My mother?"

"Yes, Sara. Exactly. I saw you catch a glimpse of compathy during the *Hanging of the Greens* dinner when you mentioned your sister and their mother-daughter pudding. You saw then, Beth had been feeling the same exclusion from your father's affections you have felt from your mother's, didn't you?"

She looked more surprised at that than at his confession. "You noticed?"

"I have been noticing everything about you since I bumped into you on the plane. We met under shaky circumstances but I think our determination to understand each other will make a good radio show. What do you say?"

She cut her eyes at him, narrowed them into slits as if tunneling her focus through binoculars. "There is energy to our give and take. It could work well over the air."

Luke grinned in spite of himself. She was giving in, seeing the possibility of a successful new venture. "We'd make a good team. I'll tell you anything else you need to know to help you decide."

"No, I don't need to know anything else. You've answered my questions in more detail than I expected. So I guess I can't hold out any longer."

His heart sped up, racing in his excitement over having just convinced Sara to come on board with his project. "Is that a yes? Are we going to be partners?" He held out his hand. After hers extended to meet his, he grasped it with eagerness between both palms.

"Partners," she agreed.

Luke resisted every urge to jump up and kiss her. He wanted it more than he had wanted anything since his football injury.

Watching her leave, he was amazed at his ability to reign in his emotions. The old Luke would likely have gotten her into bed by now and forgotten her by sunrise on the following morning. He was happy that was all relegated to his past.

Now he knew better. If she was worth his time and affection, she was worth waiting for, getting to know slowly and over many conversations' long courses. He wanted to hold her secrets safely in his heart before he held her body around his own.

Taking an oath to spread God's word hadn't stopped his ability to lust. However, it did change the way he acted about it.

****

Sara's invitation took Luke by surprise. Only a day had passed since she'd accepted his offer to launch a radio show together. "You've been invited to Thanksgiving at my parents' house. We didn't know if you've already planned to spend the day with your mother…or what…but…"

The mention of his mother caused a familiar tug at his heart. Luke missed her, and wished it would be possible to share the day with her. "My mother is in Iowa. Since I have the Wednesday night service, it isn't possible to get out there."

Sara's face brightened. "Shall I tell them to expect you then?"

It was on Luke's tongue to accept. He wanted to more than he could have imagined. "I'd love to come, Sara, really I would. But I've already told Cade I would have lunch with his family over at the Starnes' estate."

An eyebrow lifted. "Lunch?"

"Yes. And then Cade and I will probably toss the

117

ol' pigskin around to work off the calories."

The previously raised brow now inched for its twin on her forehead's opposite side. "Our dinner doesn't get cranked up until six or six-thirty, so if you're still interested…"

For some reason, Sara hadn't accepted his decline. She seemed to be searching for a way to include him. *What is going on with her sudden desire to share Thanksgiving with me?* His fingertip hooked along his bottom lip. "Dinner at six-thirty? Okay. Let's say I arrive about five-thirty."

The smile breaking across her face filled him with joy.

"Perfect," she said.

****

The Starnes' house vibrated with holiday energy. From the television in the great room the sound of bands playing Christmas music, during the annual Thanksgiving Day Parade, wafted throughout the house. Voices intersected the music in blurts, guffaws, and occasional whines—depending on their source— whether from the adults or the children.

Cade and Emily were immune to the kid noises, carrying on with whatever they were doing or saying even while adding a towel-swipe at a spill or refilling a sippy cup. Two bowl-passing rounds had circled the table. Those choosing to dine in other sections of the house had slipped in for second helpings.

Emily had risen from her seat and returned with a rolling cart laden with confections. Luke hadn't noticed her absence from the table until she appeared at his side with the offering of pies, cakes, and other sweet treats.

Glancing at every tempting morsel, he could

almost taste each one through sense memory. Luke held up a hand, warding off temptation. Engaging his willpower, he announced, "I'm skipping dessert."

Cade reached across from the table's opposite side and snagged a pie wedge, along with a trifle dollop, and a chocolate cake slice. His eyes grew into saucers as large as the dish he was using to scoop the various sweets into. "You're joking, right? No one skips dessert on Thanksgiving."

Emily glanced between them, unfazed by Luke's refusal. "Care for coffee?"

"Yes, thank you. I would love a coffee."

Handing him the cream pitcher, Emily reached for an extra take-out plate. "Here, you are—something for you to fix your dinner on."

He glanced at the disposable plate and then at Emily's confusion-laced face. "I appreciate the offer but I'm actually having dinner with the Goode family. That's the only reason I'm not tucking into the pumpkin cheesecake right now."

Cade set the cookie tray down with a thud and a raspberry thumbprint disk rolled facedown onto the tablecloth. As he peeled the sticky jam from the fabric, he issued a shocked look at Luke. "You're kidding. You're having dinner with Sara's family?"

Luke hadn't intended on keeping it secret. The congregation would learn shortly about his and Sara's conjoined efforts to get the radio program on the air, so he might as well be upfront about it. "Not kidding. Sara and I are working on a little venture together."

Mr. and Mrs. Starnes peered between the three of them as the name of their son-in-law's former fiancée was bantered about the table. Emily delicately placed a hand on Cade's arm. In spite of its tremble, she registered no emotion when she spoke. "So…Sara intends to stay for a while? That's nice."

Luke wondered what she was really thinking about Sara's return. He'd seen them talking amiably at church and had witnessed a shared hug. Things had appeared to be easy between them after the pre-Thanksgiving service last night also. Sara had been cooing over Cade and Emily's children.

"I hope so," he said. "Coffee's great, Emily. Finish your dessert, Cade, and we'll go throw a little pigskin."

Cade shoved the cookie into his mouth and set the desserts aside. "I'm finished for now, too. Some air would do me good."

Luke was carrying dishes to the sink when Emily stopped him. Dropping her head, she took the plates from Luke, and set them on the counter. "We're just surprised by Sara's sudden return. We both love her…still…in our own ways."

"Sara still loves you, too," Luke whispered.

Shaking her head, she fiddled with a drying cloth. "I don't know…but I hope you're right."

When she looked up, Luke could see the tears collecting.

Lifting his eyebrows in question, he hoped Emily didn't think Sara had returned to lay claim to Cade. "Hey, you aren't concerned about her presence here in Bland, are you?"

"No…I mean…it's not…but…" She couldn't finish the sentence. Fear emanated from her silence. Clearly, she was worried about the prior relationship between Sara and her husband.

Cade rushed up behind them. "Meet me outside.

I'll grab the football from the garage."

Luke nodded. "I'm going to carry over a few more bowls, and then I'll join you."

When the door closed behind him, Luke took Emily's hands, stopping them from their endless twisting and pulling on the dishcloth.

Her father returned for another dessert helping, and disappeared back into the living room where the broadcasted parade's finale was making its way along some street in America. With the meal finished, the sound had been cranked up. The parade announcers' voices bantered cheerily over one another as the horses' clomping echoed from the set. "Whoa, look at the stallions," someone said.

Emily found her voice, but the words sounded dull and flat. "Sara loves horses, as does Cade. I was never into them much. Horses, that is."

Luke gripped her arm, squeezed it to indicate his certainty. "Cade loves you, and the kids. You know this, Emily. Whatever happened between him and Sara is in the past."

"I hope you're right."

"You know I am," he said.

Cade's head popped back into the doorway. "Are you coming?"

"Yes, just finishing." He nodded toward Emily in a gesture he meant to be reassuring.

She yanked her head upward, indicating her agreement.

Outside, tossing the football in the crisp autumn air reminded Luke of his past. He missed it still in so many ways—not the game's politics, not the pressure he'd been under when playing for the college, not the intimidation, nor the constant attention to diet and workouts—just being outside, the ball's threads gripped by his fingertips, the white lines on the field, the sounds emanating from the band.

He also didn't miss the focus required in keeping stats for a career resume, or even the fans' attentiveness when he'd back up to throw a pass or nestle the ball into his stomach to run sideways and then forward into a hole between opposing players. The cheers, the stadium's blur, the scent of popcorn and hot dogs, the hard plastic mouthguard worn to protect his teeth, snug pants, shoulder pads, cleats biting into the earth— maybe he didn't miss it so much after all.

Every long toss with Cade returned him to the field, the place where he had shone as brightly as a star in the night sky, for a time. Then there was the shooting star crashing and burning from the heavens in a final glory blaze.

Cade's return passes got harder and more forceful.

Luke had to leap into the air to snatch one high and to the right, his long fingers hitting the edge and twirling the ball downward into his cradling arms. "Getting out some aggressions?" Luke teased.

Cade played innocent. "Why would you think that?"

Luke rubbed his knee. "You've forgotten my knee. If you keep up this abuse, I'm not sure I'll be able to stand in the pulpit Sunday morning."

"Maybe you should forego dinner and go home and ice that thing down. You've been on it a lot lately."

Something was not being said. Silent fury underlined Cade's words.

Wincing, Luke realized Cade might be bothered by

his acceptance of the Goodes' dinner invitation. "Maybe. But I've already said I'd go. So…"

He pulled his arm back and let the ball go with more force than he'd meant to put behind it, a reflex from his younger days with the spring-loaded notch still etched in his nerve endings. The football shot straight at Cade, like a rocket from a missile-launching pad.

"Did Sara's mother issue the invitation?" he asked, scooping his arms to the side to make a pocket for the airborne ball.

"No, but she confirmed my expected attendance last night after the service."

Cade glanced up at Luke. The ball, although initially landing in his bent grasp, flipped upward, smacking him on the nose. Blood squirted forward, continuing to ooze through Cade's fingers as he shoved both hands against his face.

"Oh, no!" Luke ran forward to check on him. "Lie down, get your head back. I'll get ice." He helped Cade to the ground, tilting his head back, before bolting for the kitchen, ignoring his grumbling knee as he rushed full speed ahead.

Emily returned with Luke, paper towel roll beneath her arm. Luke had opted for frozen peas in place of an ice pack. "Let's get this on quickly," he suggested, breaking the individual peas apart and placing the entire package onto Cade's swelling face.

Emily knelt beside her husband, her voice an octave higher than normal. "Do you think it's broken? Should we get him in the car and drive to the hospital?"

Cade squeezed her hand. "No, it's not broken, just bloodied. I've had it broken before, and I know the difference."

"I'm sorry," Luke said. "I must have thrown it with more force than usual."

Cade's voice was nasally, the swelling membranes making it sound as if it came from a barrel. "No, it was my fault. I was distracted."

Emily stroked his head. "What distracted you? You're normally so focused."

"Just talking to Luke and looked up too soon. Thought I had it."

Throwing a glance at Luke, as forcefully as the ball had been tossed to Cade, Emily seemed to be sizing up the situation. Turning her attention back to Cade she said, "How are you now? Shall we try to get you up?"

"Yeah," he said, elevating himself to his elbows. "The bleeding has stopped. I'll be fine."

The soft tissue surrounding his eyes had already started puffing upward and outward by the time they got Cade into his house. Luke feared his friend's whole face would be black and blue by Sunday's service.

A story concerning the local minister and ex-fiancé of the woman he was now seeing would likely set the gossip mills on fire. Her return to town via being dismissed from a prominent Manhattan radio station would just be added fuel. When Cade showed up with a battered face, chatter would worsen.

He'd just have to deal with it when the time came. Right now Luke had to go home and change clothes before attending the holiday dinner with the Goode family.

Chapter 15

It was the first Thanksgiving Sara had spent at home in so many years she feared she wouldn't recognize the holiday. In countless ways, it was just as it had been every other year in memory. The menu was the same, the aromas wafting throughout the house were all familiarly Thanksgiving-scented—pumpkin, apples, roasting turkey, sage, rosemary, cloves, and cinnamon.

The brown-and-white transferware dishes—from her grandmother's china hutch, now perched in the dining room's corner—were the ones they had set out every November. Removed with great care to prevent chipping an edge, they were washed by hand, nestled onto bronze chargers on the golden tablecloth, and framed by the recently-polished heirloom silver. A gleaming tea glass sat high and to the right at each place setting. The centerpiece cornucopia brimming with gourds, apples, pears, and oranges, also sported cat's tail spikes, colored cob corn, and cinnamon stick bundles tied together with raffia.

Whenever the back porch door slapped open—as it frequently did to allow desserts to rest and cool on its chilly back table—evergreen's piney fragrance, from the still-in-progress roping assembly, punctuated the entire house with a festive scent. Although Sara's parents didn't drink much wine, they had purchased a few Sauvignon Blanc bottles to have on hand for Thomas' parents and whoever else might desire a glass.

Sara washed pots and pans as quickly as her mother emptied them, keeping fresh utensils at the ready for her. It was nice. She couldn't remember helping her mother in the kitchen before. As a child she would have accompanied her dad to the cattle barn, assisting him with the feedings, brushing down the horses, whatever needed to be done outside.

Beth would have been inside with their mother. But now, with Beth on the hill, *her hill*, tending her own children and preparing the dishes she'd been assigned—sweet potato casserole, green beans, and pecan pies—gave Sara a new perspective. She was seeing the inner workings of the meal for the first time. "How did you used to manage all this by yourself?"

"It's what I do, what I know how to do," Sadie answered. "I'm glad to see *you're* starting to appreciate it."

The words stung. "I've always appreciated it. I just didn't understand how much work was involved."

Her mother's voice and demeanor matched, both brusque. "Well, now you do."

Sara wasn't sure if her remarks were meant to be cutting or simply made offhand. She decided to let it go. "Yes. And I'm happy to be here, to be helping in whatever small way I can."

Sadie nodded toward the potato sack resting in the bin by the door. "You can wash those if you'd like. I'll need to peel them and get them into some water soon."

Putting away the remainder of the clean utensils, Sara dumped the contents from the potato sack into the sink. "That I can do."

As she rinsed each tuber, watching the earthen bits clinging to them release and disappear down the drain, Sara was reminded of the little slights and wounds she'd likewise love to wash away. She'd been carrying them around as if they were glued to her side. Willing them to take the same liquid baptism, she imagined all the hurts being cleansed from her heart.

It was healing. Humming subconsciously, she was unaware of the emanating sound until her mother started giggling. "What are you laughing about?"

"You," she said, good-naturedly. "Who would have thought my all-business daughter, the one with absolutely no domestic proclivity whatsoever, would be humming a tune while peeling potatoes?" She shook her head, but continued to grin.

Sara laughed too. "You know, I'd hate to have Mr. Higgins walk in right now. He wouldn't recognize me."

"Who is Mr. Higgins?"

A sharp pain pulsed behind her eyes as she recalled her last day on the air. *Surely I mentioned him at least once before*. But on closer examination she realized she rarely mixed her family and work lives. *I doubt he would know who Sadie Goode was either.* "My boss—well—ex-boss, anyway, you know, the one who gave me my dismissal."

"Then Mr. Higgins is a fool. He should have realized what a dedicated employee you were." The little nod Sadie gave to accentuate her declaration shook a curl onto her brow. She swiped at it with the back of one hand, the other buried in her apron.

Is Mother taking my side? Is that possible? Dumbfounded, Sara stared, agape. "He was only doing as he was ordered. I don't think he had much say in it."

"Still…" Her mother yanked the oven door open and the turkey's aroma permeated the room. "Help me get this behemoth out onto the counter one more time."

Sara quickly dried her hands and grabbed the extra oven mitts. Dragging the roasting pan to the rack's edge, they lifted it and set it out onto the counter for its last basting. Then it was back into the oven and the timer reset.

"Better get this extra dressing in the bottom oven," Sadie said. Removing the roasting carrots, she tossed in the casserole stirred together from corn bread, turkey stock, butter, celery, pine nuts, onions, parsley, and sage. "By the time we get the potatoes cooked and mashed, the turkey will be ready to come out, and we'll drain its juices for the gravy. Then the rolls will replace it in the upper oven, and the dressing will be finished and hot."

"I'm amazed. You have this down to a science."

"Probably not unlike you and your shows. It just takes a little pre-planning and forethought."

So she did listen to my radio broadcasts! Sara smiled. This was turning into the best Thanksgiving in memory. Luke was coming and she'd have someone to sit with her at her end of the table, knocking knees with the handsome preacher.

Oh lord, she thought, *did I just think about the preacher in an unholy way? Yikes!* Peeling away a thin layer from the potatoes' outer flesh, she rinsed each before dousing them in a cold water-filled pot. *Calm down. You're just amusing yourself.*

****

The day passed into evening with unprecedented speed. The house at 1550 White Pine Drive filled with the sounds and scents of holiday merriment. Benjamin and Darla squealed with laughter as they chased each other through the living room delighted to have both sets of their grandparents present to dote on them.

Sara felt as though she'd slipped through a time warp. Thanksgiving was the same and simultaneously totally unrecognizable. Although there were numerous resemblances to her childhood's holiday up to this point, there were also noticeable additions. Thomas' parents, the children, and now Luke, made for an interesting mix in conversation she hadn't anticipated.

When all the food had been carried to the table, Sadie laid a hand on Luke's shoulder. "It isn't every Thanksgiving we are treated to a minister in our midst. Reverend Sterling, would you like to ask the blessing?"

Luke beamed at Sara's mother. His megawatt smile radiated not only from his widely spread lips and gleaming white teeth, but sparkled from his cornflower eyes, instantly besotting everyone's attention.

Grasping Sadie's other hand in his, Sara saw him give her mother a wink—charming her even more than she already had been by his manners and grace. "Thank you for your request, but I'm not here tonight as your pastor, just as a friend. Ben should return thanks tonight." Luke nodded toward Sara's father, who broke into a smile.

Ben shuffled his feet, but his chest swelled with an inhalation and a nod. He was clearly pleased with the deferral. "Well, if you insist."

Sara couldn't keep a grin from breaking across her face as well. Nothing was more meaningful to her than hearing her father's deep voice, conjoined with bowed head in supplication, asking God to use the food for nourishment in their bodies and their bodies in the Lord's service. It was the touchstone she carried inside her, even when racing across the line between Godliness and materialism, with the latter most often winning.

Thank you, she mouthed silently to Luke, who winked at her in response. But she noticed his preoccupation as the evening wore on. At first she thought he was merely being observant, listening to the way she communicated with her sister and mother. It was becoming obvious he was barely listening at all.

Normally talkative, especially in a group, he was quiet and withdrawn. More than once he had asked someone to repeat a question. Picking at his food, he appeared to be pushing it around on his plate more than consuming it. Although he continued to genuinely beam when looking directly at someone around the table, she noticed small changes the others likely missed.

The smile faded quickly, not lingering across his cheeks as it usually did. He frequently looked down at his hands, staring at his palms. As his lips puckered inward, the bright light in his eyes dulled to a lusterless film.

As soon as they rose to clear the table for dessert and coffee, she leaned over him to remove his plate and whispered, "May I speak to you on the porch? Privately?"

Nodding, he scraped his chair back and met her there a few moments later.

Knowing time was limited because someone could burst out onto the porch with them at any minute, Sara cut straight to the point. "Is something bothering you tonight?"

His expression remained flat, unemotional. He swiped at his face, resting a forefinger against his bottom lip, the telltale sign he was contemplating something. In his usual manner he answered with a question. "Why do you ask?"

Shivering, she wrapped her arms around her midsection. It had been warm, nearly hot, in the kitchen with the ovens going and the stove blazing. The air outside was surprisingly cold, but not damp. There would be no rain or snow, just a frigid late autumn chill. Snatching an afghan from the swing, she draped it around her shoulders. As she pulled it snugly across her body, she spoke with unarguable certainty. "You're a little distant tonight."

His face distorted at her words. "I'm sorry. I'm worried about Cade."

She was taken aback at hearing Cade's name, certain the shock of it played against her face. Luke would likely see it there, with his vision adjusted to the darkness. "Cade? Why on earth would you be worried about him?"

Dropping a hand to the porch railing, he rocked backward on his heels. "I had lunch with his family, as you might recall my mentioning."

"Yes. But why would…what would…?" She didn't know how to ask the question. *Was Cade ill? What had happened?*

Turning from her, Luke leaned fully across the railing, his elbows propping him up, a foot hooked over its bottom rung. His head was cocked to one side, but his ever-vigilant eyes scanned the fields beyond. "We were playing football after the meal. A pass I made to him popped off his arms and hit him in the nose. I'm afraid he'll be sporting a black-and-blue face by Sunday morning."

Sara recalled the Friday night game against a rival team on home turf in which Cade had suffered a broken nose. She remembered his vivid description of hearing the bone and cartilage crack, feeling the warm wet bleeding trickle turn into a torrent, filling his sinus cavities and nasal passages. He would know how serious the damage was from personal experience. "Is he all right? He didn't break his nose again, did he?"

Luke shook his head. "I don't think so, but there'll be talk. Imagine it—lunch with him, dinner with you, and in the interim, I black both his eyes and bloody his nose."

Sara couldn't understand Luke's concerns. He was Bland Chapel's pastor, not a hooligan. "But not on purpose. It was an accident—a game risk—right?"

Luke's foot slid from its perch. His elbows relinquished their roost, and his head snapped toward hers. In that instant she was glad for the dim light. He wouldn't be able to see her concern and the old memories flashing across her face.

And she was prevented from watching disgust reflecting off his features, although she could hear it in his voice. "It's a small town, Sara. It won't play out that way. Besides, I sensed some uneasiness in Cade about you and I seeing each other. Are there unresolved feelings between you two that need ironing out before you get involved with someone else?"

Out on the familiar porch, Sara felt seventeen again. Luke could have been Talmadge Brooks, the guy she had met during college tours. He'd followed her to Bland, tried to convince her to go out with him.

Talmadge's gull-wing Ferrari had sat in the tall grass like an eagle waiting to fly away, and she'd longed to perch in its passenger seat and accompany the bird on whatever flight it was poised to make.

But she'd felt bound to Cade. Now she could see it more clearly, could read the silent messages she'd communicated to the man in the sports car. She had wanted out of the relationship with Cade even then, and yet was still attached to its comfort. Knowing she couldn't have it both ways, she'd turned Talmadge down and watched with a heavy heart as his car roared away.

Cade had been a security blanket, her first experiment with love, with hand-holding, whispered longings, deep kissing. He might still remind her of those young, carefree, infatuation-filled days, but it was nothing more, especially now that he had not only a wife, but two beautiful children depending on him.

"There is nothing between Cade and me besides some nice memories," she assured Luke. "Puppy love, a shared past. He hasn't said anything to you to indicate otherwise, has he?"

Luke shot her a cautionary look searing from stormy eyes. She knew what that meant. Losing patience, she poked his chest with her forefinger. "Don't give me the pastor-parishioner confidentiality bull. You brought it up. Remember?"

"But…but…" His face registered a desire to open up, but his refusal to do so left Sara seething. It was a window into what life would be like as a partner to a minister. He would always bring home the fallout from whatever he'd absorbed from flock members while never being able to disclose what it was ripping him apart.

"Fine. Have it your way. Punish me for something someone else said, while—"

The door yanked open, its hinge screeching. Heavy-heeled footsteps thumped against the porch floorboards. Thomas was hauling a giggling Benjamin in his arms. "There you two are," he said. "They're waiting on you inside."

Trailing a faint smile, Sara turned toward the interruption.

"We'll be right in," Luke said.

She met Thomas' stare, reaching out to tickle Benjamin on the stomach. "Do you still have room in there for dessert? Some cookies? Maybe a little ice cream?"

He howled in laughter. "Ice kweem," he enunciated.

"Ice kweem, it is." Sara chuckled. "Come on little man. Let me see what I can dish up for you in the kitchen."

"Awl wight!" he shouted.

Taking Benjamin from Thomas, she saw him join Luke at the porch railing. They watched her disappear from view. He would probably talk of her to Luke; maybe even say something about Cade, something Beth would most likely have shared in confidence.

Here it is. This sinking feeling in my gut is more like what I recall from previous Thanksgivings. This is like the holidays I remember—being talked about and belittled.

Thomas and Luke returned, enjoying a laugh about something the rest weren't privy to. It rankled. It angered her too much to pretend otherwise. While she kept her voice and demeanor playful and soft with the children, she shot dirty looks at Beth. They were pointless as her sister was oblivious to them.

Choking down dessert, playing hostess, clearing dishes, refilling coffee cups, Sara busied herself and avoided Luke.

He tried to meet her eyes. He attempted to get her attention and made inclusive comments. But this wasn't the place to iron out the reasons they could never work as a couple.

He was as married as Cade, only Cade had a fat, gold band occupying his left hand's third finger announcing his commitment to the world. Luke's devotedness was much trickier to wrap the mind around. His obligations hid in the church office behind the raiments in the cedar wardrobe. One couldn't decipher exactly what they were.

Feigning interest in Thomas' long-winded, mind-numbing chatter about his business endeavors, Sara managed to stay away from Luke for a while. When she couldn't take her brother-in-law's prattle any longer, ran out of dishes to wash, and the children became too tired to play or engage with her, she initiated conversation with Thomas' parents.

They were nicer and more interesting than she'd remembered—a true gift for the evening. For the first time since Beth had married into their family, Sara saw them with a curious mind and an open heart.

But soon the Moores left, followed by Thomas and Beth and their children. It was time to say goodnight to Luke, who'd finally gotten her message. Realizing she was too angry to talk with him, he was now picking her father's brain about the cattle industry.

Sara laid a hand on her father's shoulder, extending a cold stare at Luke. "Dad, will you show the preacher out when he's ready to leave? I'm going on to bed."

Jumping up, Luke asked, "Can I speak with you before I go?"

She shook her head. "I'm tired and talked out. I suppose you'll want to take tomorrow off from our work plans."

Luke turned drooping eyelids up at her. He looked wounded, his lips turned down, a forefinger resting on the bottom one. "No. No, I'd love to see you in the morning. Same time okay?"

She shrugged, unsure as to whether to stay at a nice distance for a few days. "I don't know. Maybe…"

"Please, Sara." He reached out and touched her hand.

Beneath the long fingers and strong tendons, Sara felt the slight tremor. Meeting his eyes, he communicated wordlessly. He had offended her and knew it. He wanted to make amends and didn't know how if she wouldn't talk with him.

For several long minutes they each stood frozen to the floor, his hand against hers, his eyes pleading silently. Sara wanted to stay tough, stick to her plan to avoid him. But in spite of herself, or perhaps due to the late hour and the long day's work, she acquiesced.

"Okay, I suppose I could meet you for an hour or two anyway."

Keeping contact with her hand, he drew her forward, bringing her ear to his mouth. "Would you see me out? I'm ready to go."

Turning back to her dad he finally released her from his grip and offered a handshake to Ben. "Thank you for a lovely evening."

Her father stood, nodded. "Anytime. Come back and we'll finish our discussion about Charolaise cattle."

"I'd like that," Luke said.

Quietly, she and Luke proceeded to the porch. In the darkness, the cattle's soft lowing became the night's music. As she listened to the familiar childhood sounds, Sara's toughness slackened.

"I'm sorry," he blurted out suddenly. "If you'll forgive me, I won't let it happen again. This is so new to me. And I've not been this attracted to someone in a long time, maybe ever. It's…disconcerting…especially since I don't know if you intend to leave…or stay…"

She imagined the soulful expression in his blue eyes, the way his hair fell across his brow. Weariness washed through her body, draining its resistance and strength. Dropping her guard, she opened the door to her heart—just a crack really, but an opening all the same.

Through that crack the truth tumbled forth. "I can't compete with the entire congregation, Luke. I can't change how they think about me for leaving home to work in the city, or for leaving Cade, or for what they perceive as my fast-and-racy lifestyle. It's who I am, Luke, and I can't change that either."

"I don't want you to change. That's part of the reason I'm attracted to you, or at least…I think it is." He shuffled toward her. "And there is no competition. I'm here with you because I made the choice to be here. Do you understand what I'm trying to say?"

It made Sara angry to be vulnerable. Softening toward Luke was clearly a risky position. Ire gathered. "No, I don't."

He slid closer. "You don't?"

"You talk around things. You bring things up you won't finish. You start to tell me something, drop little innuendos, then clam up. I don't know how to deal with that. I'm direct, maybe too forward, but it's how I got where…well…where I was. I'll make it back to the top. You'll see."

"I don't doubt that, Sara." He took another step closer, then another, until he was by her side.

She could feel his presence radiating electricity. Her breath quickened, matching her pulse in speed. Gasping as strong arms tugged at her, he pulled her into him as easily as he might have snagged a football from the air.

His breath, hot on her cheek, ruffled her hair when he exhaled. Speechless, she simply draped her arms loosely around his waist as he nudged a swath of hair from her ear, whispering into it. "I just want to be with you when you do," he said.

"But—" she protested.

Luke didn't give her a chance to finish. "Allow me a few mistakes you absolve me of just because I ask to be forgiven. Please. And I'll do the same for you."

This was something nobody had ever solicited from her before. Nearly always the one to render apologies, she'd rarely had anything resembling a forgiveness request from anyone other than her father. It broke past Sara's wall, knocking through it, rendering it into a debris-strewn heap.

"Ah…Luke." She sighed. Shaking her head, Sara surrendered, feeling her whole body go limp with its acceptance of him. She couldn't believe how much she desired him, especially given his profession and the fact he wouldn't likely desire a sexual relationship outside marriage. It wasn't going to be like any other courtship Sara had known as an adult. He wanted to know her and fall in love with her if it was meant to be, not just fall into bed and see what happened as a result.

His fingers wound 'round her curls. "Is that a yes?"

"Yes, it's a yes." She caressed his cheek with hers, knowing his lips were close, so close, yet not hers to take and manipulate and taste.

"Perfect," he said. "Until tomorrow then." Releasing her, Luke turned and walked across the porch, the vibrations of his steps resounding through each long pine board into her body.

The sensations ceased as he stopped. Spinning around, he made the trek back to the spot where she stood and gripped her face with his huge hands, bringing his lips toward hers. Pausing for a moment—a long torturous moment when she couldn't decide whether to fall into him, or pull away—she could barely breathe. *What is he going to do? How should I react?*

The swiftness of his emotional display left her defenseless as his lips traced her cheek's outline, and continued along her nose. His thumbs were beneath her chin, holding her, gripping her steadfastly.

Soon, those thumbs began to move and caress and slide along her neck's backside, up along the ridge of her jawline, behind her ears. His fingers trailed paths in her hair, reaching around her head, inching slowly.

The entire universe swallowed Sara. She became light. A need and a passion greater than any she had felt before engulfed her, threaded through her like oozing lava before the eruption. Panting, trilling, cooing, she longed to taste Luke, to bond with him.

Finally yielding to need's pull, attaching his mouth to hers, searching with his tongue the promise of returned lust, he moaned with desire. "Oh, Sara."

She was swept away. The longing overpowered her rationality. She lingered on his taste; his kisses' honeyed sweetness assuaged any and all previous angst and anger.

Finally, her mind returned long enough to send cautionary warning alerts. The small inner voice whispered; *he's a preacher*. Pulling back, she gasped in horror at her behavior.

"I'm sorry," she blurted. "That shouldn't…I…it…" The words failed her as she panted to recapture her breath.

Luke struggled to maintain contact with her. "What's wrong? Why are you sorry?"

Every step she took backward, he met by walking forward, seeming unwilling to allow her to put space and distance between them. "You…you're the pastor…at the church…and I…we…the kissing…" Her hand flew upward to her lips, still burning from the connection with his. They felt like traitorous things, wanton objects betraying her guilty desires. Surrounded by darkness, at least he couldn't see the embarrassment she knew was flushing her cheeks.

For a moment he dropped the connection with her, letting his arms fall from her body. He took two steps away. Then, with determination, he lunged forward. "I'm not here as your pastor. I'm just a guy, a flawed one at that. I don't always say the right thing nor have the best answer. Sara, my profession may color your perception of me, but I'm asking you, once again, to give me a chance as you would any other person."

His words landed hard on Sara. It was easier to think about dating him as *just a guy* than it was to contemplate dating a preacher. His job did bear weight on her opinion of him. He represented God's word, holiness, moral conduct, and strict religious behavior. How could that possibly mesh with physical longing and white-hot desire?

She could feel his fingers prying hers apart from their locked position. Then, gently, softly, he threaded his through hers, palms touching, and heat from their proximity once again coursing through her body.

His facial outline and broad shoulders formed a silhouette. "What do you say? I know I've asked you this before, but I can see you're having trouble with it. Can you do this Sara? Can you ever see me as an ordinary man?"

Can I? Her lips moved, but no words came out.

Luke wasn't the kind of person who gave up easily. He slid his feet closer to hers, his chest now mere inches away. Slowly and softly, even that gap was sacrificed and he was holding her to him again, their hearts thumping wildly in unison.

One large hand cupped the back of her head as if it had been carved in the shape of his palm. Gently, he lowered it into the crevice between his shoulder and neck. The other scooped around her, claiming her spine as its territory to trace with abandon.

Chills pulsed through her, fanning out from every spot he touched.

"Will you? Hmm?"

"I…" How could she find words when his touch radiated electrical currents through her body? She had a sharp, sudden inhalation as he lowered his chin, pushed hers upward with his, and landed feathery kisses on her throat.

"Say yes," he pleaded. His hot breath fanned the growing flames once again.

"I…"

"Say it," he pleaded. "Say you'll give me a chance, please." Before she could answer his lips were once again working their magic along her face, her mouth. He nibbled her bottom lip and she caved, diving into his mouth's hot promise driven by wild, prehistoric need.

His face was so close to hers she could make out details even in the dark November night. With their bodies pressed together, there was no denying the enormous arousal both were experiencing.

Steamy breath escaped from them, blending into one superheated yearning space. "We could be good together," he whispered.

"In bed, you mean?" she moaned.

He held her gaze captive and she wished for light, for sudden illumination so she could see the expressions playing across his face. "Yes, of course. But that isn't what I was petitioning."

"What then? What are you asking? What do you want from me?" There. She'd said it. She'd put the question to him, even though she might not like the answer.

"It's simple. I'm asking to date you, to see if this wild attraction is more than a physical longing."

"What if it isn't?

"A better question would be—what if it is?" With that, he backed away a few inches, leaving space to allow her mind to process his query.

A cool, swift breeze blew between them, chilling

her. She snatched the afghan once again, draping it around her shivering body as tightly as possible to shield her laid-open heart and vulnerable emotions from their sudden exposure. The wrap wasn't enough to keep the raspy, thick-tongued desire from her voice when she finally spoke. "You certainly know how to frame a question."

His voice, too, was deeper and more emotional than normal. "Not if it doesn't get the desired response."

"I suppose it couldn't hurt to try, but I don't know what the rules are. I've never dated a preacher."

"You're not dating a preacher, Sara. Respect my job, but—"

His failure to understand her position was too expansive. Agitated from unfulfilled longing, she felt her nerve endings pulsing with anxiety. "You keep saying that," she snapped. "You keep advising me you are 'just a man,' but you're not. You are a minister of God's message. I find the former enormously attractive, but the other…" She dropped the sentence and her eyes. Her sharpness didn't appear to bother him.

He grinned, his teeth flashing blue-white in the sliver of moonlight popping suddenly from behind the hill's crest. Trailing a finger across his bottom lip, he said with amusement, "Enormously attractive, huh? I'll take that as a 'yes,' and leave before you change your mind."

True to his word, he escaped the porch with a deftness she doubted she could have managed as swiftly without running into a chair or a post in this darkness.

Feeling the afghan against her ankles, she lifted it back around her and watched his taillights disappear, wondering what she had just agreed to. How in the world would it be possible to ever see Luke Sterling as an ordinary man?

Chapter 16

Luke was overjoyed that Sara had agreed to dating, to giving him a chance. He was also eager to get the radio show up and going. Once again he remembered Cade referring to her as a greased pig. Slippery, apt to run, hard to catch—she would be difficult to hold onto.

He had to remember not to put too much pressure on her, or she would go back to New York in a flash. Her family already pushed every figural sensitive button she had. Luke knew she needed a compelling reason to stay in Bland, and he intended to see to it she had one.

Working on the radio show proposal consumed what little spare time he had. From Thanksgiving through Epiphany—January sixth—he had a full roster. But he made sure to carve out time for Sara. The next few days flew by.

Sara spent most mornings with him working on radio show strategies, helping to develop a programming schedule and a possible sponsors' list. During these hours, sitting in his church office, he was careful to keep it all business. There could be no impropriety, no cause for scandal.

They were occasionally interrupted by visitors— Cathy Tibbs at least once every other day, the mailman, the florist looking to place a floral holiday spray on a particular grave or to deliver an order for a service. And then there were church employees and volunteers—the cleaning crew, the pianist stopping by to practice a piece for the cantata, even Beverly the choir director popped in and out for various reasons.

He kept a respectful distance from Sara, knowing if he as much as bumped into her, an onslaught of desire would course through his body. She affected him more than anyone had in so long he couldn't remember such an urgency.

To her credit, she was equally careful with him. Obviously used to professionalism, she made no effort to be nearer to him than was required to look over an outline or approve a possible interview roster.

In the afternoons he visited the sick and shut-ins, starting with the hospital before going door-to-door to the infirmed and elderly, both in his parish and those who weren't Bland Chapel attendees. He was sure God didn't care about denomination.

Occasionally one would ask a favor. Could he pick up a package for them? Would he mind carrying in some firewood, repairing a broken step, or changing a light bulb? It never bothered him to do the small things he was able to, though other people sometimes chastised him for it.

Luke knew mountain folk were proud and dignified. Most had earned a hard living until they physically couldn't anymore. The two elderly Jones sisters, living in a house with a wood stove for heat, ran low on firewood from time to time. He and Cade kept an eye on the bundles by the back door, replenishing as they dwindled to thin sticks and the heaviest logs too difficult for the ladies to carry inside.

Cade always managed to find a deal on a cord of

wood, or knew about someone with fallen trees they wanted removed from the yard or some forested acreage about to be cut for timber where the smaller trees would just get skidded over and left in a heap. Luke had spent many Saturdays running a chain saw or a wood splitter, stacking the splits on Cade's truck bed, and hauling the wood off to somebody in need.

Cade Norton was a fine man and a good friend. One thing was certain—Luke would have to find a way to keep their friendship intact while pursuing a relationship with the woman who had broken Cade's heart. That was going to be tricky.

Mountain men, even modern ones, didn't like to talk about their feelings. But Luke could tell by Cade's behavior, whenever Sara's name came up, it bothered him. It wasn't sulking, but the mood was altered. The ease with which they conducted themselves diminished.

This was new territory for Luke. Everything was new and often confusing—the immense attraction to Sara, the strained relationship with Cade, the extra demands as he made time for dating, and the thrill of seeing a dream taking form as he and Sara developed the business plan for the radio show.

In the evenings he picked Sara up at her parents' house. Occasionally they stayed in and watched a movie or played a board game. She preferred remaining in to going out. "Out" meant they came upon others in the community, and she had made it clear she didn't care to be gossip fodder.

The football incident with Cade had faded pretty quickly, mostly because he had laughed about it and said he should have known better than to try to play football with the former star quarterback for

Columbia's Lions. Cade's cheerfulness and determination at showing up for church with a bruised face, while slapping Luke on the back like old times, belied any hostility that might lead to chatter.

Emily and Sara occasionally sat with heads together, laughing over something. All was going well.

Soon Luke had convinced Sara he could be trusted, a deep friendship was forged, and she confided her issues with her family. And there were issues. Though some had mended, others—especially with Beth—worsened the longer she stayed.

He dropped in one evening to find the entire house in an uproar. Ben stormed out the front door, his face red, while women's voices raised in anger wafted in varying loud waves from within.

Ben jumped backwards upon finding Luke just stepping up onto the porch. Startled, squinting at him, he managed a cursory, "Hello."

There was no denying a full-fledged argument was going on. Luke tried to joke with Ben about it. "Are you under attack?"

He grimaced. "Sounds like it, doesn't it?"

Another outburst met his ears. He could hear two women yelling at each other simultaneously.

"What on earth is happening?"

Ben glanced at his feet, head bowed as it rotated side to side. "I made an egregious error. I strongly encouraged Sara to loan Beth her fancy designer coat. Beth brought it back with a huge stain...well...more than a stain. I actually think it's paint."

Luke grimaced this time. He knew what the coat meant to Sara, had witnessed its specialness to her. "Paint?"

"You'll see." Ben jerked his head toward the house. "Sara's carrying it around like a wounded fawn. I'm sure she'll shove it under your nose in a minute."

"Ah, the white coat," Luke muttered.

Just then the door burst open and a very angry Sara appeared on the porch. "Yes, the infamous winter-white coat…which cost me a fortune," she snapped.

Trying for a sympathetic tone, Luke spoke softly. "I heard."

Her face was flushed and her eyes, pulsing behind the widened lids and blood-shot whites, were wild with anger. "Beth ruined it!"

Surely there had been an apology. Perhaps he could remind her of it. "So, what did she say?"

"That's just it. What she said was worse than what she did."

Sara held the coat out to him. A huge black spot made it look as if it was a partially-completed art project meant to make it look like a pony print.

"It's ruined!" Sara snatched the coat to her chest.

Her sister wafted by, dark head in the air, in a blaze of superiority. "It was an accident," she insisted. She flipped her wrist as if tossing a minor offense away. "Get over it."

Watching Sara's face as it reddened even further, Luke saw her chin jut forward looking a bit like a chicken prepared to peck a worm to death. When she spoke, her words were enunciated with unusual properness, anger tingeing each one. "Get over it? You bring my coat back with a most likely non-removable dried paint spot on the back, and all you have to say is 'get over it'?"

"Yeah, that and get a life, Sara. It's just a coat!"

The vitriol in Beth's voice was clear and obvious.

And there was something else. Was it glee? Luke snapped his head in her direction, trying to detect the emotion most clearly matching her tone.

Sara was livid. "You're not even going to explain how paint got on the back?" She stopped yelling at her sister only long enough to slap a hand across the coat's ruined back.

The noise frightened Darla who had trailed her mother outside and now ran back inside the house yelling for her maw-maw.

The door snapped opened, jerking quickly backward with a slam. Sadie's slight figure appeared on the scene, hands on her hips, both elbows jutting outward as if to broaden her girth. Glancing at her daughters, circling the coat the way buzzards did rotting flesh, she shouted, "What on earth is going on out here?"

Ben and Luke huddled in a corner, waiting for a response.

Beth was the first to answer, pointing at Sara. "She's all crazy because her precious coat has a little stain on it."

"Stop the fussing, Sara, and take the thing to the cleaners. You should have known better than to buy a white coat anyway," her mother chastised her.

Sara didn't appear surprised to hear her mother taking sides with her sister, but she looked wounded just the same. "What I should have known better than was to let her borrow it. If Dad hadn't insisted, I wouldn't have. And by the way, it isn't 'a little stain.'"

She held it out to her mother who took the coat and inspected the dark spot, scratching at it with a fingernail. "What is it?" Sadie asked.

"Paint!" Sara yelled. "Who gets paint on the back of a coat, unless it is on purpose?"

"I told you it was an accident. I had to pick up my car and I accidentally backed into a recently-painted part they had hanging from the ceiling. If you're going to be such a baby about it, I'll send Thomas out to pick you up a replacement. I saw The Daily Dollar carting in a new shipment on hangers today," she said to her mother.

"The Daily Dollar?" A maniacal laugh escaped Sara in a sudden sarcastic rush. "Do you think you can get a garment like this at The Daily Dollar?"

Luke could tell Sara thought her sister had damaged the coat on purpose. With Beth's remorse lacking, he was beginning to think so as well. Even the suggestion of replacing it with something ripped off a rack at the discount store sounded horrifying.

Beth's chin remained in the air, bitterness oozing from her voice. "A coat is a coat."

"To you, maybe, but this isn't ready-to-wear. It's couture!"

Sadie stepped between them, dangling the coat from outstretched arms. "I'm growing weary of this, and you are frightening the children, Sara. How much would it take to replace this thing and get you two to stop arguing?"

Luke saw Sara's lips start to move and then freeze. He understood something Sadie might not. Depending on the designer, the coat's price tag could be more than Ben's entire corn crop had cost to put in. It might be unbelievable to the mother that Sara would spend so much on a coat designed for style and not function.

Such expenses should have to come with a warranty, he thought. But those who couldn't afford the loss usually didn't make the investment.

Sara had been a fool with her money and her sister had known it. Beth had ruined the coat to keep her from having an extravagance she, herself, couldn't afford. And Sara wouldn't be able to again anytime soon.

"You can't afford to replace it," Sara said, her voice softening. "I would never ask you to do that, anyway."

Beth seized the moment to make the dig work in a little deeper. "Yeah, do you hear her? Miss *I'm so special and important I wear garments from couture* is telling us we are just a bunch of hicks who don't know anything about fashion," her sister accused.

"Well then,"—her mother tossed the coat at Sara— "get yourself another one. Your father and I can't be responsible for such silliness."

She turned around and took Beth by the arm. "Come on, darling."

Beth looked back over her shoulder and sneered as she accompanied their mother back into the house.

Luke squeezed Sara's shoulders. "Why don't we take it to the cleaners? I know one in Wytheville whose specialty is getting difficult stains to give up the ghost."

Ben, whose face had grown even longer and more heavily clouded, nodded. "That's a fine idea."

Agreeing, they left for White's Cleaners, an appropriate name given the object being taken in for stain removal. But even the proprietors held little hope for getting out the paint stain.

Luke was certain the relationship between the siblings would never be mended unless the coat could be restored. "Do whatever you can—anything—everything," he insisted.

Chapter 17

Beth's behavior over the coat made Sara nuts. Vengeful ideas occurred to her—sneaking up the hill in the dark and painting crude messages on the side of Beth's car with permanent spray paint, tossing a rock through the picture window overlooking the fabulous view, and pouring hair remover into Beth's shampoo bottle. The difference between now and when they were children and teenagers, was Sara could think about doing these things without feeling compelled to actually do them. Ten years prior, she might have done at least one of them.

The brooding interfered with her work. Preoccupation with her family caused Sara to be less attentive to Luke during their usual morning routine. *I'll apologize when I see him later tonight*, she decided. *It would be so much easier if I had enough funds to rent a hotel room and only see my parents when they could meet me at a restaurant, sans Beth.*

When she walked into the house, her father's voice startled her. "When are you and Beth gonna outgrow these dust-ups?"

He was sitting alone in the living room, on the couch, reading over a newspaper, or at least pretending to. Sara tiptoed toward him, hoping her mother wouldn't approach, having heard the squeaky screen door opening. Slumping onto the sofa, Sara stated what she was certain could not be disputed. "She ruined my coat on purpose, Dad."

Her father snapped the paper together, ruffling it to get the edges aligned and the creases folded in the exact locations they had originally been. When he had finished with the noisy fluttering, he laid it in his lap and turned his attention to her. "That's a mighty big accusation. Couldn't it have been an accident?"

Sara shook her head. "If it had been any other person who had done it, then yes, it could have been. But with Beth, no way."

He sighed. "Maybe that's the answer."

She felt her face twisting into a scowl. "The answer to what?"

He shrugged. "I'm thinking you expect the worst from Beth, and get it every time."

How can he place responsibility back on me? Is he taking Beth's side? He's never questioned my right to be offended before. Reeling, Sara used her best warning voice and even had the audacity to point an unpolished fingertip in his direction. "I don't want to talk about Beth."

"Yeah, but if I hadn't suggested you loan her the coat…" Lifting his shoulders, he held them up only a moment before allowing them to drop in surrender. "Somehow this feels like my fault."

His regret and sadness deflated her anger. It was difficult to remain upset when her father was taking the brunt of their quarreling. "Dad, you are certainly sweet to think it's your fault. But it isn't. The truth is simple though. She has never liked me or any of my achievements."

"No, Sara. That isn't true," he protested.

Unwilling to be swayed, she held her hands out to him, offering up memories as sacrifices. "Don't you remember the army of dolls you replaced because she ripped their arms, legs, or heads off? Then she'd just do something to the new ones, too. And the trophies I received had to be put onto overhead shelves to keep her from destroying them the same way she had the first two I won for softball."

His eyebrows inched inward as if on a race for the bridge of his nose. "But you aren't children anymore."

"No, we're not. However, the feelings and the animosity are still there. Who doesn't know not to walk into a greasy garage wearing someone else's white coat unless your intent to cause some damage to it exists? Am I right?"

He refolded the paper lying in his lap into thirds and tossed it onto the hearth. "I understand your point, but—"

Here it is. The fault is circling back to me, as it always has. Even when she had been innocent in the initial tiffs between them, Sara had been the one expected to forgive and forget. It wasn't happening anymore. She was tired of being Beth's insecurities punching bag. "But what?" she snapped.

"You're not being rational, not seeing the entire picture."

Sara inhaled briskly. The hostility forbearance toward her father was forgotten. Her face blazed hot with rage; her temper flared beyond any controllable level.

Every emotion she had buried—anger at the station, disgruntled feelings about Cade's surprise marriage to her best friend, the eyesore house on her hilltop that acted like a knife in her gut whenever she thought about it, the way her mother had shunned her upon arrival, and now her father defending her sister's crime against her and her coat—rushed out like the spout from a sperm whale's blowhole.

Everything poured out in vitriolic discourse. "Oh, I see, suck it up, Sara! *She* wanted your spot on the hilltop so we gave it to *her*—suck it up, Sara. *She* destroyed your priceless, irreplaceable coat on purpose—suck it up, Sara. How about some sucking it up for Beth? Where's the *suck it up, Beth* advice?"

"That's quite enough, Sara," her mother said from the doorway.

Both Ben and Sara jerked their heads toward Sadie's voice. Her arms were crossed over her chest in a defensive position. In spite of her diminutive stature, the stance exuded a powerful front. "I won't have you disrespecting either of us in our home."

"It's because it's about Beth, isn't it? You weren't so upset about Beth's venom yesterday."

"Beth has never been rude to either of her parents. She's like us, solid, reasonable, not…" Sadie stopped, falling short of completing the sentence.

Sara was pretty sure she knew what the words on the tip of her mother's tongue were. She felt the sting as strongly as if they'd been uttered. "Not what mom? Not a dreamer? Why can't you ever frame me in a positive way? I'm a thinker, a doer, a traveler. Why must you always think of me as a loser?"

"Stop it," her father shouted. In one smooth action, he leapt up from his seat. His voice boomed—low and thunderous—like the rumble before a mighty storm. "This is my fault. I should never have allowed Beth to build up there."

Both Sara and her mother quieted before his rancor. Sara could count on one hand the times she had heard him bellow out so.

Normally Dad was content to let them work things out between them, privately making it up to Sara if he'd felt she had been slighted or unfairly treated. Going for ice cream, hot dogs, four-wheeling along mountain trails, or meandering through the Native American Museum housing artifacts found on nearby farms had been his normal means of restoring peace.

He pointed up the hill. "I knew it had been promised to you but you were so happy in the city, rarely even coming home."

He hung his head. "Stupidly, the other day I thought if I could get you two sharing clothes, then maybe you girls could get to sharing ideas. I was wrong. Now look at what's happened." His shoulders slumped in defeat.

Sadie jerked a thumb toward Sara. "Don't blame yourself, Ben, because this one is a hot head."

A fresh wind coursed through Ben's body, his spine yanked to attention, taking his head and shoulders upward. Pointing to Sadie, he said, "That's quite enough from you."

Sara inhaled deeply, unused to her father standing up to his wife.

Sadie gasped. Her arms fell from their entanglement to land stiffly by her sides, hands fisted. "Well!" she snorted.

Ben's voice rattled the rafters, though he had ceased yelling after the first attention-grabbing outburst. His tenor defied questioning. "No, I mean it.

I've watched you shun this girl since she walked in the door last week, and I've had about enough. Maybe if we'd put our foot down with Beth a long time ago she would have learned a little more respect for her sister. Instead, you encouraged their rivalry. And so have I, by abdicating my responsibility. It ends today."

Neither Sara nor her mother spoke as they focused their eyes on him.

He pointed once again to Sadie. "You're going to sit down and the four of us are going to have a chat."

Although she huffed, Sadie did as he directed. Both women watched Ben punch a number into the phone. He settled back into his chair and spoke with authority. "Your mother and I need to see you…alone. Yeah…good…Thomas can watch the kids. We're in the living room."

****

Sara couldn't remember the old clock ticking as loudly as it was right then. She felt a bit cleansed, but still anxious. *Who knows what the next few minutes are going to reveal?*

Finally, the door opened and Beth's footsteps echoed across the wood floor. "Dad?" she called out.

Ben stood. "Have a seat, Beth. We're having a family meeting."

She looked around the room. Upon seeing Sara she groaned. Her arms dropped lifelessly to her sides. She tilted her head backward as though staring at the ceiling. "Oh God. Are we going to talk about her coat again? Geez!"

Ben pointed a finger at his older daughter, his eyes narrowing in caution. "Not one more word from you, until I say you can speak."

Sara watched what little color was there drain from her sister's pale face. Neither had been spoken to in such a chastising voice since they were small children. It was discomfiting.

"We've got a few things to iron out, as a family, and nobody is going to walk out the door until we are all squared away. So be warned."

The three women glanced at the floor and each other, but no one dared challenge the gauntlet he had thrown. "Beth, I want to know the real reason you wanted to borrow Sara's coat."

She rolled her eyes. "I thought it would look nice with my outfit," she replied off-handedly.

"Lie!" Though he kept Beth in his glare, he pointed his finger at Sadie. He knew his wife's penchant for defending Beth. His action communicated a silent warning. She bristled, but didn't interrupt. "I'm too old, and time's too precious, to beat around the bush. Try again. We all know it was more than that."

Beth adjusted her posture, shrugging her shoulders. "I wanted to see how I liked a white coat."

"Lie," he said again. His nostrils started to flare, presumably along with his temper. "Try again."

Beth stiffened. She crossed her arms over her chest and tilted her chin upward. "Well if you aren't going to believe me, what's the point of my speaking?"

Ben Goode narrowed his eyes into slitted, focused, laser-like beams onto Beth.

For a moment, the grimace on his face frightened Sara. She had no idea what he was about say or do, but could tell it would be a game changer.

"Ray Bulger wants a hilltop plot right up there beside yours, Beth. He wants to build apartments between your picture window and your view of the lovely scenery you currently enjoy. The only view you'd be enjoying then would be heat pumps, water tanks, and garage doors. Though that would probably tickle Sara right now, the only thing keeping me from selling that land is my respect for you. So try again. I want you to act and speak like an adult now, and make me believe it."

Beth squirmed in the seat. She looked at her mother, clearly communicating an SOS signal through her panic-stricken eyes. It wasn't forthcoming.

She perched on the chair's edge, pointing at Sara. "I…she has things…things I'll never be able to have with the children. I wanted to see how such a top-notch coat would feel draped on my shoulders. I…wanted to impress the ladies at the school." She bowed her head in apparent shame.

"And you wore it into the garage for what purpose? There's no way you didn't think there would be something filthy waiting there to brush up against it."

She shook her head.

Ben took two steps toward her. "So what your silence is saying is that you meant to ruin it. Am I right?"

Sara might never have finagled an admission from her sister, and Sadie would likely never have attempted one. But the threat of a ruined view gouged the truth from Beth.

With eyes bulging from her flushed face, she let the words pour forth. "It felt powerful to know I could ruin something of hers. She has always ruined everything for me."

Sara gasped, but didn't speak. She had suspected

her sister despised her, but had held hope it wasn't true. Even Sadie winced.

Ben closed the gap between him and Beth. He knelt beside her, draping an arm around her shoulder. She was crying now, the admission's guilt shaking her shoulders.

With a much softer voice, he asked, "What has Sara ruined for you, Beth?"

"The day I got to join the quilting bee, she made the basketball team. Woohoo for Sara, nothing for Beth. She made friends effortlessly, while I struggled—still struggle. She traipsed off around the world and every single time we ran up with someone we hadn't seen in a while, all you could say was something wonderful about Sara, telling them all about her travels. Don't mention Beth. Pretend you don't see her. Pretend she is nothing and nobody."

She paused for a second. "Even now, when she comes home for longer than a short breath, all the oxygen is sucked from the room for Sara's use."

Though Sara was hurt by her sister's outburst, she knew it needed the release. Resisting the impulse to defend herself, she diverted her eyes, and listened.

Inhaling deeply, Beth continued on her rampage. "And it isn't just you two, or the people we knew from childhood. Look at the preacher—the man every single woman in town wants to date—he takes one glance at Sara and is over the moon."

The tears continued. "And you both love having Luke Sterling around. You don't particularly care for my husband. You all make fun of Thomas, don't you? He's too loud, he's too short… But let Sara bring home a man…" Her voice faltered.

Sara was shocked. This whole event was draining. The room was quiet except for the sound of Beth's sobbing, punctuated by the clock's adamant ticking.

Between Beth's sniffles, Sara heard footsteps crossing the porch. "Luke's here," she warned. The words sounded like loud gongs echoing in the painful inner chamber. "Should I send him up to see Thomas for a few minutes?"

"Yeah, I think that would be perfect," her father agreed.

She slipped quietly from the house and motioned for Luke to follow her to the car. "Dad's holding a little family meeting and Thomas is alone with both kids. Do you think…I mean…would you mind going up to sit with him for a few minutes? I'll see if I can hurry this along."

"Sure." Luke grinned and leaned in to plant a kiss on her forehead. He was getting braver about the places he kissed her.

Sara felt the energy from his kiss enter into her head, rush through her veins, and spill into her abdomen where it throbbed and ached. She wanted to race after Luke's SUV, tackle him to the ground, and explore his body. She took a deep breath. All the animosity toward her sister dissipated as she exhaled.

She didn't even want to go back into the house. But since this was about her—and she had started it—she returned. Her family, in their original seats now and all eyes turning toward her, waited as she crept back into the inner sanctum.

"What did you tell him?" Beth asked. She was snorting into a tissue someone had given her while Sara was away.

"I told him we were having a family meeting and Thomas could probably use his help with the kids. He's on his way up the hill right now."

Beth rolled her eyes again. "The last thing I need is for the preacher to think I'm a psycho."

Sara resisted the urge to tell her to stop acting like one then. Instead she asked one simple question. "Why do you do things to hurt me, knowing I'm your only sister and your ally?"

Beth lifted her head and met Sara's cool gaze with stony eyes. "It feels like retribution. It feels like I'm getting a little piece of me returned. It feels good. I like it." She glanced around the room. "So, Daddy...I guess I'll be having a welcoming party for the new neighbors, right?"

Sara sat down next to her father. "I don't know how to fix this, Beth. Sadie, do you have any ideas?"

His wife was sitting with one hand over her mouth as if to stifle the usual automatic responses that typically flew out on their own. Her hand starting to nervously tap her lips, she looked from one to the other of her daughters. "Sara, why don't you apologize to your sister, and we can put this whole nasty scene behind us."

Ben squeezed Sara's shoulder, giving her the signal to stay quiet. "Why would Sara apologize to Beth? You misspoke Sadie. You meant to ask Beth to apologize."

Punctuating with quick hand motions slicing through the air, she indicated it was all over. "No. I said it correctly. Beth isn't good at apologizing. It's much easier to get Sara to say she's sorry and then it's over."

Ben wasn't having it. "Sadie, that isn't going to work. Sara hasn't done anything to be sorry for. The damage has been done—intentionally by her admission—by Beth."

"Yes, but…"

"No buts. Listen, Beth, you need to apologize to Sara and replace her coat."

"I'm sorry." She sniffed.

"Tell her how much the coat cost," their father encouraged.

Sara didn't want to admit the actual price she'd paid for the coat. It was too much, too expensive. "Really Dad, it's…"

He punched her lightly on the arm. "No, she made the choice to ruin it. She should have to pay for it. Go on, tell her."

Sara knew she would never get him to cease badgering about the cost. She'd have to tell them, especially as she had been the one to make such a drama over the garment. "It was $5,875.00."

He laughed. "This is not a time for joking, Sara. Now tell her the real price."

"*That* was the real price."

He stopped laughing. His voice elevated to a tone reserved for shock and surprise. "You paid nearly $6,000.00 for a coat?"

Sara gestured toward Beth. "Yes. That's why I went a little more than ballistic when she ruined it on purpose."

Beth jumped up from her seat, her face frozen in a horror-stricken expression. "I can't pay thousands. Why would someone waste money like that? That's ridiculous. With two kids…Dad…there's no way…"

"Then you shouldn't have ruined it, should you?" Ben barked at her.

"Listen," Sara started to explain. "I took the coat to a cleaner in Wytheville. They haven't made any promises but are going to try to fix it. Maybe they will. I'll forfeit the coat if Beth will forfeit her jealousy. I don't want to argue anymore. I'm tired of it. Beth, I've never done anything intentionally to hurt you. I never would, not even now."

"So this stops right here? No more acting out between you two?" Ben swept his hand out to include their mother. "Three?"

"Agreed," Sara said. Beth and Sadie repeated it, although half-heartedly.

"My three girls…er, women,"—Ben exhaled—"you all mean the world to me." He grabbed them all in a bear-hug.

"Can I go home now?" Beth asked. A lifetime of being the lesser daughter resounded from her dull question.

"Yes, and send the preacher back down this way," Sadie said, finally getting to extend authority.

Ben settled back onto the sofa again, picked up the newspaper he had been reading, and opened it. He flipped, turned, and rattled the pages, filling the atmosphere with much-needed normalcy.

Sadie followed Beth out to the porch. Sara leaned against her father's shoulder. "We are hard on you sometimes, aren't we?"

He patted her on the head. "But worth every minute." He flipped the page again. "I love ya, honey. I swore the day the doctor put you into my arms I'd protect ya. I just didn't know it would be from the other people I already loved and had sworn to protect as well."

Sara heard the weariness in his tired, listless voice. She regretted her earlier angry words. "I'm sorry," she whispered. "I love you, Dad. I shouldn't have said anything. It wasn't worth upsetting you this way."

He peeped over the top edge of the newspaper. "If it was upsetting you, it was already upsetting me."

"Did you mean what you said about Ray Bulger and the mountaintop? Didn't you give the whole hill to Beth?"

"Actually, I only deeded Beth the acre on the side next to the wood line. She chose to build on the point furthest west. That leaves plenty of room up there for you, if you ever want to live up there. Then the view will belong to you."

Sara grinned as she realized she had been harboring an unnecessary hurt. And maybe she felt a smidgen of satisfaction that Beth now lived with an uncertain view. "You are a real rascal, Daddy," she said with laughter in her voice.

The door slammed and Sadie returned to the living room. "Beth is a mess. I hope she makes it home safely."

"Well if she can't make it to the top of the hill, she's in more trouble than we knew about," Ben added calmly.

"Sara, don't you need to freshen up before Reverend Sterling gets here?"

"You know, that's not a bad idea."

She left for her room.

****

Dripping eye drops into her reddened eyes, Sara doused her face with some powder and swiped lipstick across her wind-chapped lips. Not sure if her parents were having some private discussion she wasn't privy to, she didn't leave her room until she heard Luke's car outside. She came out to meet him as if nothing had happened, rushed him from the house, and into the car.

After they reached the main road, he asked, "What's going on?"

"Family drama," she said simply, hoping to avoid explaining the whole ordeal.

"I've certainly seen plenty of that before," he said. "Is everything okay with Thomas and Beth?"

His assumption startled her. "You think something might be wrong between them?"

"Isn't that what the meeting was about?"

"No. It was about me, if the truth be told. They're fine, as far as I know."

"Okay, but you know you can talk to me. I can keep a secret." He paused for a second. "Is there something I should know about you?"

She burst into laughter. "There's probably a lot you should know about me, but you're going to have to find it out the hard way. I'm not going to make it easy on you by just blurting out my deep, dark secrets."

Luke slipped the car into the pizzeria's darkened parking lot, cutting the engine. "Oh yeah?" He leaned over and cupped her face in his hands. "You positively stimulate me...in every way. Another challenge only makes you more interesting, if that's possible."

Her throat constricted. As much as he asked her to think about him as any other man, she couldn't get his vocation out of her mind. *He shouldn't be this sexy. I shouldn't desire him so feverishly.*

The words tumbled out over tightened vocal chords, sounding as if she meant something sexual.

"You stimulate me, too."

His eyes glimmered. One lid lifted at his eyebrow's arch.

She started to correct herself, but thought better of it.

He leaned toward her face, turning away at the last second. His lips brushed her ear lobe as he said, "I'm glad to know it."

Her cheek brushed his, and the palm resting on her chin slipped downward across her stomach. Igniting an involuntary gasp as her whole body tingled, she realized some inner core portion wanted more. It had her in its grip, dangling her over an anticipatory cliff's edge.

Sara's internal voice began its bantering barrage. *What does he see in me? Does he feel this temptation as strongly as I do? Does he just think I'll be easy because I've lived a faster, freer existence than the locals?*

As though hearing her thoughts—*Were they just thoughts, or did I speak them aloud?*—he pulled back, leaving a cold space around her.

"Come on, before I lose my self-control." His voice indicated his self-discipline might already be off on holiday.

Sitting in a quiet booth a few minutes later, he managed to snare the truth from her concerning the family meeting. At first he simply nodded, absorbing the sparse details, and then he did the last thing she expected. Luke sympathized with Beth. His casual tone suggested he assumed Sara's agreement with him. "It can't be easy to have a younger sister who outshines you."

She was still dabbing at her pizza slice with a

napkin, trying to soak up the extra oil bubbling on the surface. "I'm jobless…and maybe homeless in a few days. What is there about my current status that would perpetuate jealousy?"

Setting his pizza aside, he started to lick his fingertips. Probably due to her grin as she watched, he snatched a napkin. "But you've done things she will never do. You've met politicians and authors and entertainment superstars."

This was a mistake people often made about her. They assumed the people she met did so because they desired to meet with her, that a relationship ensued where casual conversations would occur over the phone. It was only business. They likely forgot her face and name within three seconds of leaving the studio.

Grabbing the parmesan shaker, Sara sprinkled her wedge. "Only for the meeting's sake," she explained. "They don't want to get to know me. Nobody asks about my life—"

"Yet—"

Fearing what he was about to say, she held the cheese shaker out to him. "Care for some?"

"No, thank you."

He started to speak again, but Sara wasn't finished with her rant. "I'm just doing my job, and they are getting publicity."

She shook more parmesan on her pizza, realized her mistake, and knocked it off with her fork. "Why would my career bother Beth? She doesn't even want to work, for heaven's sake."

Luke leaned back against the tall booth, his hands gripping the table's edge. "Do you hear the judgment in your voice when you say things like that?"

Sara furrowed her brow, feeling the frown distorting her face. *Why isn't he defending me instead*? "What do you mean?" Even in the dim lighting she could tell he was assessing her flippant attitude.

He lowered his chin and locked eyes with her. "Did it occur to you that your sister wants to be accepted for whom she is, and not the person you think she isn't?"

She sipped her soda and thought about it for a while. *Is he right? Have I been judging Beth in the same way she has been judging me?*

He let her digest his words along with the meal, eating the pizza slice he'd doubled over on itself as if a sandwich.

Does my sister value other things and wonder what is wrong with me for not seeking them? "I guess I have thought Beth was lacking because she didn't want what I wanted, because she didn't have ambition. Do you think she intuits this and judges me because I haven't wanted to settle down and start my own family?"

Luke smiled. "Just sit with that thought for a few days, and see how it turns out."

"I can't believe this. You've been around my family for a scant few days—well, me for a few days, the rest you've known for a while—and you've managed to analyze what we haven't been able to see in three decades."

"I told you." He laid his hands open in front of her. "I'm a good listener."

****

Things improved around the family house. Beth was less snarky. Their mother noticed the improvement and was more receptive to Sara. It was a better environment all the way around.

The more time Sara spent with Luke, the more she realized he was indeed a good listener. After seeing him every day, holding hands, looking into his eyes, she wanted him fully. She was becoming insanely attached to him.

He kept leaning in, as though thinking about it, and then pulling away. Just seeing his heated gaze was enough to set her blood to boiling. It was frustrating, although she knew it wasn't a failing in him, but strength.

Compared to Bland, everything in New York had been in fast forward. Kissing happened on the first date. If there was no chemistry behind the lips, there wouldn't be a second date. Chemistry with Luke was obvious. Electricity crackled off his skin and through his bright eyes. It seared into her with such burning force Sara thought she might combust at times.

He would hug her, hold her hand, caress her cheek, look into her eyes with torturous longing, but he avoided kissing her again on the mouth. The memory of their Thanksgiving kiss on the porch steamed inside her. Though she had experienced the weight from his lips along her cheek or atop her forehead, she craved them once more smashed against her own hungry ones.

Longing for his touch endeared Luke Sterling to her more than any man ever. The realization ignited something else, a pulsating panic.

With nothing pressing calling her back to New York, she lingered at home. Luke's question reverberated in her head, thumped in her heart. *What if?*

Chapter 18

Snow started falling in early December. White powdery dustings produced the perfect backdrop for simple beribboned evergreen wreaths appearing on gates and front doors around Bland. Christmas trees sparkled in picture windows—their curtains pulled into frames for the holiday symbol.

Thick, dense cloud cover assaulted the sky until its natural blue was as leaden as the frosted dormant grass. The air had a bite, a real damp coldness causing Luke's knee to throb. He was in a good mood in spite of the heavy winter storm the weatherman predicted. *More snow's coming*, he thought. *My knee's as good a predictor as the barometer, maybe better*. Stepping outside, he slid on the walkway and realized a faint sleet had already begun.

Carefully picking his way back to the door to phone and warn Sara, he heard the engine's clatter before he saw the vehicle it rattled in. Turning, he watched Sara pull into the parking lot in her father's old truck. Avoiding the slippery sidewalk, Luke rushed to meet her.

"Go back home," he called out. "There's a big storm coming. They're predicting at least a foot of snow."

Sara shivered. Looking skyward at the ominous snow cloud layers, the prediction seemed to sink in. She yelled back, "Okay." The old truck screeched and groaned at her rough and unsteady gear-shifting. Turning around, she slid from the parking lot onto the forest-shaded icy pavement. Fishtailing onto the road, the skid continued.

Luke ran for the truck, reaching it just as the sliding ceased. Her right wheels ended up in the road's dirt shoulder. Sara gunned the engine and her wheels spun in the frozen mud.

"Hold on," Luke called out. "It's too lightweight in the back. I'll get my truck and pull you out."

Maneuvering his SUV in front of her dad's truck, he tied a rope to the bumper, then carefully pulled her out of the ditch. After disconnecting the two vehicles, concern for her well-being consumed him. "I'll follow you home to make sure you get there safely," he said.

Her breath frosting in the air, Sara argued, "That's not necessary. I'll be fine."

Her assurances meant nothing to Luke. Sticking with her as she made the trip back to her parents' house, his heart fluttered with every skid, every slip. Luke knew she rarely drove in New York and had likely lost the innate ability and the nerve she had once had about trekking along treacherous roads.

The storm had turned into near-blizzard conditions before they reached White Pine Drive. Sara's dad, his shape barely visible in the heavy snow flurries, was pacing the porch when the two vehicles pulled to a stop at the farmhouse.

Luke exited first, half-stomping, half-sliding to the truck in an effort to help Sara from it and to the door.

"Thank goodness you found her and talked some sense into her," Ben said. He reached out to grasp his daughter's arm to support her climb up the steps.

Luke, hands on her back, helped hold her upright. Her fashionable shoes—not designed for such weather—failed to grip onto much. The steps were icier than the road.

Ben insisted he come inside to get warm and dry. Sadie made coffee and fussed over them while Luke's coat was positioned in front of the fireplace to dry out.

With the tacit crisis over, Ben leaned forward. Merriment sprinkled his hazel eyes with a twinkle Luke had seen normally reserved for the grandchildren. "I cut the tree this morning." Ben's announcement was clearly expected to please his youngest daughter.

Sara grinned. "The Christmas tree?"

"Yep. The kids and their mama picked theirs out. You might be interested to know our tree this year is one you helped plant back during high school."

Surprise etched Sara's voice. "One of the firs we covered the hillside in as a future investment? One of our special trees?"

Ben nodded; his face aglow. "What's more special than having my baby daughter home for Christmas?"

Sara ran to him girlishly, locking him in an embrace. "Thank you, Daddy."

Holding onto her father for a moment, Luke knew she was consciously reliving a memory of her youth, taking her back to a time in her past she held precious and dear. He hoped it would act as glue to stick and keep her in Bland. He wanted to express his own gratitude for her father's gesture.

The aroma of brewing coffee mingled with the scent of baking sugar cookies wafted outward from the kitchen, mixing with the evergreen tree's piney fragrance as it waited to be decorated. Logs burned in the fireplace, undoubtedly sending smoky tendrils up the chimney and across the snow-covered hillside. Ben's outdoorsy mix of tangy leather and hay aromas completed the perfume Luke knew he would hold in his own heart as *Christmas with the Goodes.*

Though he hated leaving the cozy atmosphere, he knew he needed to. "Guess I'd better be going if I'm going to stand even a remote chance of making it back."

Sara's head snapped toward him. Her brilliant eyes pleaded with him. "No. Stay and help us decorate the tree. Please?"

He wanted to play it cool, but the desire to be near her overwhelmed the one to be coy. "I'd love to," he said. "Ben, do you need some help getting it in the stand?"

"I sure do!" He slapped Luke on the back and they traipsed off to the back porch together.

The snow didn't let up during the tree-trimming party, but continued to assault the valley. By the time they realized how deep it was, even four-wheel drive vehicles couldn't get far. Emergency systems were warning people to stay off the roads. Trees were downed by the icy snow's weight, taking power lines with them. By dark, the power at the Goode residence flickered and failed.

Luke was stuck there, though he didn't mind. They had plenty of food; roast chicken, sourdough bread, cheese, broccoli salad, and sugar cookies. Eating the meal cold, sitting before the fireplace, they drank beverages heated over the flames to help warm them from the inside out.

Ben was in his element. He began to tell a story of Wyoming during such a snowfall. The sheriff in a small town near Cody let him and his friend come into the jail just to have a place to sleep for the night.

Luke listened with rapt attention as his mind conjured the western white-out.

Sadie readied the spare room and showed him where he would be sleeping. He *oohed* and *aahed* over her hospitality. Her harshness with Sara had softened. Was it just for the sake of appearances?

Armed with gas lanterns, flashlights, and candles, the Goode house glowed, even in the power outage. After Ben and Sadie went off to bed, Luke and Sara stayed up, talking. It was easier in the golden glimmer than in the harsh daylight. And it was seductive.

Words whispered by flickering firelight danced through Luke's auditory senses, fanning the flames beneath his flesh. Instinctively, he reached for her, pulling her into his shoulder's crook.

Leaning into him, she peered into his eyes. As his hand lifted to stroke her face, hers feathered his neck with uncertainty. Every touch left a trail of desire in its wake. It was torturous to want her so desperately.

He wasn't likely to breach the mores he had chosen to live by, and he would definitely not advise her—as a parishioner—to do so. Yet, he had asked her to think about him as only a man. But was he able to do the same?

Her long curls tickled his nose. "You are so dear to me already, Sara. I haven't felt this way in a very long time."

Her cheek grazed his, and whatever oath or promise he had made, disappeared into the valley where sharp longing and desire resided. Nature took him.

Sighing—was it coming from him or from her? She turned her head just enough to smash her lips against his. His fingers wound into her hair and his palms cradled her head as his lips left her mouth and sought every other surface of her face—her eyes, her nose, her forehead.

"Sara," he whispered over and over. He wasn't sure how much more he could take before his lizard brain, the part science dictated had evolved to survive as a species, snuffed out all reason. "Sara, I want you so badly. I've got to stop, or I'll lose myself to this passion."

Her breath had become labored, close to panting. "I know what you mean. I want you, too."

It was there. The fire wasn't just being reflected in her eyes, it was blazing inside them. If he continued to stare into the flames, he knew he would be consumed. Pulling her against his chest, he tried to calm his thundering pulse.

"Stay in Bland, please. It would break my heart to see you leave now."

With one arm wrapped around his midsection, the other running through his hair, she cuddled into him. "Where else would I go?"

Luke reached for her hand, slid it toward his lips, and laying it open, kissed her palm, He nervously fingered the ring around her third digit, spinning it around to get a better look. The band sported two hands, one on either side of a heart engraved with the letter *G*. "That's interesting," he said.

She peered down at it. "It's a Claddagh."

Glad for the sudden distraction, he lifted her hand

upward to see the ring better in the dimness. "What's a Claddagh?" he asked. It was nice to have something to talk about, think about, besides how much he wanted to devour her.

"A Claddagh is an Irish family ring," she explained. Love swept through her quiet voice. "Many people wear it as a wedding band. I wear it because it reminds me of my Irish roots and the strong line of women I come from, the ones who wore it before me."

He stared at the *G* again. It was weather-worn, not as sharp as it must have been when initially engraved, but still pronounced enough to make out. "But isn't Goode an English name?"

She grinned. "It's not for my last name, but for my dad's mother's family—Grady—probably O'Grady at some point in time. He gave it to me after she died, and I've worn it proudly ever since."

Luke stroked her memory-softened face. "You have a sentimental soul, Sara Jane."

"Well, don't tell anybody," she teased.

He held up two fingers in oath. "Scouts honor," he assured her.

She settled into him and he held her until both starting nodding off. Giving up their positions by the fireplace, they reluctantly ambled off to their rooms and into cold beds.

The sheets' chill instantly awakened Luke. Sara's voice replayed in his mind. *Where else would I go? Why do those words bother me? Shouldn't the statement have been assuring? Comforting?*

In the darkness, with the complete absence of noise, his thoughts raced wildly through unchartered territory meeting snags and bogs and demons. *I wish she'd said—There is no place else I'd rather be. Or, Bland is my home and always will be.*

But he couldn't change what she'd said, or how she might have been feeling when she'd said it. All he could do was accept the fact she was here now, and worry about some future departure when, and if, it occurred.

Chapter 19

While waiting for roads to be cleared, Luke and Sara resurrected the board games she remembered playing as a child; *chess, Monopoly, Scrabble, Battleship*, and even her mother's *Pollyanna*—circa 1967—in better shape than the newer ones due to the pristine care Sadie relished on her belongings.

Interestingly, Sara's memories of playing the games produced a fondness of her childhood with Beth. During those rare times, perhaps because there weren't other children around to have fun with, they had behaved—well, mostly.

Looking over the bedraggled *Monopoly* money brought a few squabbles to mind. Many bills were dog-eared or torn, some browning where the glue on the tape had leached into the paper. Three deeds—Baltic, Reading Railroad, Park Place—were recreations Ben had cut from old box lids and scribbled across.

Luke and the Goodes ate their meals cold or warmed over the fire—an advantage of having a wood-burning fireplace. Food spoilage wasn't a concern. The snow served as ice packs around the large coolers Ben stored the refrigerated items in, while the freezer on the back porch remained closed and protected by the frigid air.

The leftover chicken, with a few canned vegetables and extra broth, became a stew. Sara's father dropped biscuit dough strips into the simmering pot and covered it with the lid, producing a fine version of chicken and dumplings.

Sadie seared bacon in a blackened cast iron skillet. Eggs, scrambled in the same pan once the resulting bacon fat had mostly been dipped away, sent appetite-inducing, smoke-scented aromas throughout the house.

Wet clothing from snow-sledding escapades and animal tending was draped over racks Sadie had snapped into place along the fireplace wall. Drying overnight, they were ready to don once again the following morning, even though as wood smoke-scented as the bacon. It was a small price to pay for sustaining warmth and food preparation.

Sara watched her parents manage with ease. They'd done this before, knew the drill, and had all the right implements. If the electricity continued to fail, they'd be fine.

Blackouts scared Manhattan residents, especially Sara. She had no idea what she would have done there without power for several days. Her apartment building had emergency generators with enough back-up propane for only a day or two, but nothing sustainable for long periods.

She had no ingenuity where her tiny apartment was concerned, although, she probably would have had the sense to store her perishable food on the small fourth-floor balcony. This at least was a vantage point as opposed to the units on the lowest level where the area's homeless population could snag the items.

Homeless. Did New York get this wintry blast? What is happening to Marge? Is she warm enough? How can I find out?

Panic wound itself around her heart as she worried for the woman whose bed was an outdoor bench and whose ceiling was the winter sky's canopy. Warmth came from the subway station if—and only if—she had a ticket. Sara remembered the measly few dollars and spare coins she'd left for her. It was all she'd had on her at the time, but wouldn't be enough to sustain Marge for very long.

I should have gone back. I should have left her with more.

Luke returned from helping her father with the animals, his arms laden with firewood he carefully stacked in the box near the hearth. "What's on your mind," he asked. "You look worried."

"I was just thinking about…" Curiosity bubbled. "How can you tell I'm worried?"

"Are you kidding?"

She shook her head. *How can he understand me so well? How can he recognize my emotions when I often don't?*

Slipping his bark-covered gloves off, he rubbed his hands together over the languishing flames. He stirred the wood and added another log to keep the fire blazing. "It's pretty clear by the expression on your face."

Sara ran a hand across her face as if wiping a blackboard with a fresh eraser over her furrowed brows' chalky outline. "What expression? I'm positive there is no emotional outward countenance written here."

Luke placed his coat on the rack, to warm, and shivered. Touching her forehead with a nearly-frozen fingertip, he traced a line between her eyes. "Right here," he said. Caressing her cheek, he said, "And here."

Sara shivered as well, though not from the cold. His touch scorched her face, heated her veins with urgency. *How does he do this to me? Is it knowing he won't touch me inappropriately? That he respects me? Is it the sheer want of him, knowing that won't happen any time soon?*

As if reading her mind further, Luke leaned forward, cupping her chin in his palm. His thumb traced a line across her lower lip's bottom edge, and his gaze locked on her mouth. Luke appeared to taste her with just his eyes, drinking her with only his mind.

The sensations birthed by his tender touch melted Sara. The forest scent, smoky and piney, wafted beneath her nose as he leaned in and buried his nose in her hair, now inhaling her as well. It was the sexiest, most tantalizing moment in Sara's existence.

Slithering away, afraid she'd breach an invisible barrier and do inappropriate things, Sara put distance between them by exiting the room, Returning with a pan for popping corn, she extended it by its long handle into the flames. The noise made her think of herself, bursting into some soft, supple condition in place of the stony hardness she had developed in the city.

It worked to keep them apart for the afternoon as they nibbled the salty popcorn and drank half-frozen, slushy-from-being-submerged-in-the-snow sodas. But by nightfall they were curled up together on the weathered old sofa, absorbed in each other once again and confiding secrets.

Sara learned about Luke's first love—and first heartbreak—and more about his quarterbacking years in college. She shared her adventures taking the train from town to town through Italy, Switzerland, and France. Luke teased her about being a Ben-clone.

But sharing those intimacies, and seeing herself from a different perspective, wasn't as alluring and provocative as the sensations his fingers stirred by simply touching her face. Luke was telling her that he knew her in every stroke, every tender caress.

Her shield was down and he had made it past the fence she had kept firmly between herself and any other potential man in her life. Not even Cade had been able to penetrate this deeply into her soul.

Sitting beside her, he trailed fingertips along her arm and brought her hands together, both now grasped in one of his large ones. "You can tell me. Whatever was bothering you earlier, I'd love to know about it. I'll listen."

She shook her head. *Why worry him about a homeless woman he had never met?* "It's nothing, really."

The grip tightened as he flinched. "Is it Cade? Do you want to tell me about Cade? It's all right if you do. You know by now you can tell me anything."

There it is. She knew sooner or later the subject of his friend—her old love—would surface. Thinking up a dodge, she used his position against him. "He's one of your parishioners. Would it be right?"

Laughing as she poked him in the ribs, he lightened the moment's heaviness. "Your family members are in the congregation and that hasn't held you back."

"Do you really want to know?" She hoped he would say he didn't.

"Yes. It might help me understand you, and him,

better."

Sighing, Sara pushed herself up off the sofa. "It's not pretty," she warned. She turned away from him.

"If you don't want to…" He apparently mistook her reticence as a lack of trust or continued emotion, both untrue.

She glanced over her shoulder at him, trying to burn the image of him into her memory. It might change as he listened to her foul deeds. He might leap off the couch and make a run for it after he heard what she had done. "No, I just want you to understand what you're in for."

"I'm ready," he assured her.

She gathered her thoughts. Standing with her back to him, she stared into the fire. The hearth glowed orange as the flames danced across the large logs. *How much does he know already? What has Cade told him?* "Surely Cade has talked about this. Do you really want a rehashing?"

"I'm not asking for Cade's viewpoint. I want to hear it from *your* perspective. How do you see what happened?"

I see it as your and my relationship's demise, she wanted to say. Luke wouldn't want to continue seeing her when he knew. Who would?

Chapter 20

Luke braced. He could tell by Sara's hesitance to talk about Cade and the relationship they had shared, that she was either still in love with him or had something to hide. *Will she be honest about it? Can she?*

He heard her long, deep inhalation. She released it slowly; the only sound besides the fire's crackling. "We went to school together. We had known each other...have known each other...always. I played every sport a girl could at our school at the time, and so did he. We were a pair of jocks, really."

The flames kicked higher, the fresh log catching ablaze. Images of Cade, Emily, and Sara as they might have been in high school etched into the burning wood of Luke's imagination. It couldn't have been more vivid had an artist seared them into the actual logs before they were thrown onto the grate.

"I was also on the dance squad, so we were always on the field alongside the football players. Cade and I became a regular couple. We dated all through high school." Sara paused. "Then changes happened."

Luke conjured the field he had played on, the drums' cadence as the band struck out across the turf was a soundtrack in his mind. He didn't speak.

"We graduated. Cade was picked up at one college and I was offered a scholarship at another. I spent two summers abroad, the one in Europe I told you about, and another in Asia. And through it all, we remained a couple."

Sara turned from the fire, as if the happy images she saw there had suddenly turned to ash, dismal gray remains replacing the once-colorful scene. She stared at his face, squinting and frowning as if reading his mind.

Luke tried to wipe all visible emotional signs from his mien, leaving behind a clean slate, a nonjudgmental front to encourage her honesty.

Placing one hand on the mantel, the other resting on her hip, she continued, "We graduated college. The next logical step, we both agreed, was to get married. He was…is…a wonderful person. We planned a big wedding. Emily was going to be my maid of honor."

Luke's outburst was involuntary. "What? What about your sister?"

"We weren't close then either. She was pregnant and sick all the time. Anyway…" Sara shook her hand back and forth to indicate that wasn't the story's important part.

"Sorry. Please continue." He settled back again.

"Yeah, so, we planned this huge wedding. It started out small and just grew and grew. One day, he and I were talking about it and he said, 'This is the biggest adventure of my life. I want it to be so wonderful and huge I will always remember it.'"

Luke didn't have to guess the amount of pain still attached to whatever came next. It was draining the light from Sara's eyes.

Before he could speak she blurted out an incidental memory. "Cade was wearing the same kind of clothing he wears now; denims, checked shirt rolled up at the cuffs, white-wool-lined sheepskin jacket, and Robin Hood-like pull-on boots."

Luke tried to assure her with a nod there was nothing to be ashamed about, nothing he couldn't handle. "I can imagine that."

"It happened so suddenly." She snapped her fingers. "My chest opened and swallowed some dark and hopeless entity. I was sane one minute, and without hope the next. I could see our future all laid out. My entire life was planned ahead like one of those trips to Europe where you see thirteen countries in nine days—not a single minute for myself. Not one adventure that wasn't on the menu. I felt as if my life had just come to an end."

"What did Cade say when you told him about your fears?" Luke asked.

"Say?" Sara gave him an odd stare. "Oh, I…didn't tell him."

Luke felt his eyelids widening, knew he was wearing shock on his face that was as visible to her as his shoes or shirt. But he couldn't suppress it. "Why wouldn't you? Surely you were close enough, after being a couple all those years, to share your fears."

"I thought I was just too stressed, had eaten too many sausage and cheese pizzas, or maybe just experiencing the settling-down fears people commonly described. I expected it to pass. But it just got worse. His words kept replaying, over and over, 'the biggest adventure of my life…so wonderful and huge I will always remember it.' And I realized not only was it going to be our biggest adventure, but it was going to be the last."

Sara rubbed her face with both palms. Admitting

her failing wasn't easy for her. Turning from Luke, she continued. "I could see my life's map on the last page of the whole book ending with the marriage to Cade. Not one more adventure to be had. I realized I didn't want to marry someone who needed pomp and circumstance to remember the day. I wanted my wedding to be memorable, not because of the event itself, but simply due to the person I was marrying." She coughed and her shoulders shook.

Slipping from the sofa to assure her with his presence, Luke stood behind her. "So what did you do? Clearly, you didn't go ahead with the wedding."

"I did the worst thing possible. I left a couple of days before the wedding. Just packed up and left. I didn't talk to Cade, didn't explain it. I just disappeared from town and didn't look back." With the last statement her head fell forward, chin to chest.

Luke waited for a moment before speaking. He had heard rumors, hushed whispers. Innuendo was dropped whenever her name and Cade's were simultaneously mentioned.

When it became clear she had nothing else to say about that time in her life, he placed a hand on her back. Her muscles twitched beneath his palm. "How did Cade handle it? What did he say when he found you?"

Whirling toward him, the motion knocked his hand free. "Found me?"

"Yes. When you saw him next, what did he say?" He tried to bite back the questions, but they poured from him. "Did he try to convince you to return? Did he offer to move to the city? What was his reaction?"

Sara shook her head and made a gurgling noise. "What do you mean? I…I…didn't see him again until a couple of weeks ago when I got back into town."

Stunned, Luke couldn't hide his shock. "He didn't follow you? He didn't track you down?"

"I left no bread crumbs. I made two short phone calls to my parents so they would know I wasn't dead or anything. By the time I had settled myself in New York, knew I was going to stay there, it was six months later. He was obviously being consoled by my best friend at that point."

Luke couldn't prevent surprise and near-disbelief from oozing through his voice when he spoke. "Even Emily didn't know where you were?"

Sara kept shaking her head. "No. I didn't call her. I knew she would tell."

"But, if she was more important to you than your own sister, if…?" When the right words didn't come, Luke's hands circled empty air, trying to produce them from the ether.

Snatching his fingertips and grasping them in her shaky grip, Sara broke his concentration. "I was running for my life. I was drowning, choking, being dragged down by this two-horse-town's weight. I needed adventure. I wanted to see plays, and hear concerts, and have some sort of stimulating career. My talk show was perfect for me—talking to famous people, being at the forefront of things."

Her face brightened when she mentioned her job, but only until she cited its loss. "I have been devastated by its loss. You can't imagine how much it meant to me." Wearing the pain like a mantle, her shoulders sagged.

"You talk about your former job with more emotion than you do your ex-fiancé. Maybe he wasn't the right person for you."

"Clearly you must think I'm awful. It's okay." Sara held up her hands. "I even think I'm awful. What kind of person does such a thing to someone else?"

Luke wrapped his arms around her, resting his chin on her shoulder. "I think you are a wonderful person. One who got caught up in an overwhelming situation that took on its own life. Maybe you didn't handle that part spectacularly well, but I've seen worse methods. Let's be clear, going through with a marriage you know is wrong for you isn't smart. But I see some mistakes Cade made along the way too, and one was in letting you run."

"Letting me? He couldn't have known," she protested.

"He should have seen the panic in your eyes and stopped the craziness that was making you so stressed. I can assure you, if you and I were engaged and our wedding loomed, I would go after you if you ran away." He grasped her tightly to his chest.

She turned in his arms, searching his eyes as if for some animosity his voice camouflaged. "You don't despise me for doing such a thing?"

"No. I love you for being so honest." As he calmly spoke, tears burst from her. They streamed down her cheeks, and he longed to comfort her. Luke's hands caressed her back, while his lips kissed the tears from her eyes.

Sara reached inside his sweater, her fingertips brushing against his stomach before they swept around to stroke his back.

He sighed and devoured her mouth, his tongue searching for fullness, pouring his soul into her.

She matched his desire, pressing her body tightly against his. There was no denying how much they desired each other.

"I've got to stop," he said. "But I don't want to." He pulled her to the sofa, his fingers brushing her throat's soft fleshy hollow.

"Oh, Luke," she moaned. "I want you too much. I feel like I'm drowning in desire. It keeps plunging me down, down, down."

Hearing her say the words that expressed how her ardor matched his own, swelled his longing into such passionate desire he was nearly powerless to abate it. Using every ounce of reserve in his body, he stepped away, walked off, and returned with boots and coats. "Come on. A nice long walk in the snow ought to cool us off."

Chapter 21

Sara stood on the porch and watched Luke's SUV follow her dad's big tractor as it cleared a path to the road. Thoughts from the previous night's admissions and burning desires that had been somewhat squelched in the snow raced back to her, pushing all else from her mind.

Luke clearly had feelings for her. He had said he loved her. *He didn't just say he loved me. What exactly had he said? It was more like he loved my honesty, possibly that he loved me for being honest.*

She laughed at herself for splitting hairs. She had been so surprised he hadn't raced from the house in a flurry, calling her names including *shrew* and *hag* that she feared she might not have heard correctly.

Glancing about at the surrounding mountains, she wondered if she could live in Bland. *Could I be a preacher's wife? What would life with Luke Sterling be like?* She played scenarios in her mind until both tractor and SUV were lost to her sight.

She walked back in the house to resounding pings. Her phone had buzzed back to life. It had gone dead in the electricity outage that had been restored only an hour ago. A message backlog filled the screen. Several were from the radio station.

Texts started appearing. She read them, one after the other. It took a minute for the news to sink in. She read them again, enlarging the font size to make sure she had understood correctly.

Sara squealed with delight. "I've been given a reprieve," she yelled. "The network wants me back. Yes!" She danced around her mother who had just come into the room.

"Sara, what on earth is wrong with you?"

Joy spilled over as she shared the news. "I've been called back to my show. Listener complaints flooded the station. *Sara's Surprises* is back!"

Her mother didn't look quite as thrilled. "So?" Before Sara could interject, Sadie's voice became accusatory, sharp, and angry. "What about that young man you've been leading on? What happens to Luke?"

Sara hastily ran her thumbs across the phone's screen, typing out excited messages before hitting *send*. Energy coursed through her body, competing with the sudden surge of electricity traversing the power lines. "We can still see each other. I'm not leaving Planet Earth, just going back to the city."

Her mother pointed to the tree. Disdain coated her words. "And your father? He thinks you're here for Christmas. He cut that tree down just to make you happy."

"But this opportunity is—" She didn't get to finish. Her mother turned her back and fled the house, letting the door slam behind her.

Sara sent a message back to the office.

—Will get back with you. Snowed in.—

What am I going to do? Luke is coming back tonight. We'd been seeing each other every night before the blizzard hit. I'll talk it out with him. He'll have some insights. That's it. I'll wait for him, and we'll discuss it together.

****

Luke telephoned, saying he had too much catching up to do, after being snowed in at their house, to drive over that evening.

Sara stewed about her choices and wished he were there to bounce ideas from. Luke was such a good listener. *And his kisses...* Sara couldn't get them from her mind.

Her desire for him was fierce, electrical, soul searching. It was as if she had gone somewhere else entirely, floated outside herself. That had never happened before. *Is Luke the right man for me? Could I be the right woman for him?* These thoughts consumed her.

She sent another text message to the office.

—*Phone service iffy. Anticipate a better signal tomorrow. Hope you get this.*—

Buying time, she didn't want to accept the offer until she could discuss it with Luke. And she didn't want to talk about it with him over the telephone. She needed to see and be able to judge his reaction by his facial expressions.

Sara tossed and turned, unable to sleep. The moon, as if a torch extended from the heavens, lit up the snow. She watched the patterns its shading made against the drifts and the vibrant brown dashes of deer rushing in to feed on the hay bits left by the cattle. They huddled together near the barn where the wind could be blocked from their cold bodies.

She padded off to the kitchen for warm milk and then sat watching the living room hearth's dying fire. Before its complete demise, she tossed on another log and picked up the book Luke had been reading. Setting it aside, Sara realized she couldn't reason sharply enough to digest anything deeper than a comic strip.

The decision weighed anvil-heavy on her. What would Luke think about her going back to New York? *Will he make me choose between him and my career? If he does, which will I choose?*

Her throat thickened with the same uncertainty she had felt right before her and Cade's planned wedding. Her pulse strummed unevenly beneath her flesh, bottoming out, and fluttering to come back to life—like a stalling engine. She struggled for breath.

Anxiety consumed her. Every trick she knew wasn't good enough to stop the panic attack. When the sun began to rise, turning the snow to peach-colored grandeur, she went to bed. Sleep was not to follow. She listened with rapt attention as the household snapped back to life. But whenever someone neared her doorway, she turned on her side and pretended to be out cold.

"Don't bother her," she heard her mother say as she puttered in the kitchen. "She was rambling about the house late last night. Must've had trouble sleeping." The oven buzzed, sending the message it was either warmed up to the desired temperature or whatever was baking had reached its time limit.

Sara nearly laughed at her father's feeble attempts at tiptoeing through the house. His efforts to be quiet resulted in louder-than-normal steps. The tractor roared by the window, his previous reasons for stealth having been forgotten as he delivered more hay to the cattle. The cows began to bellow and moo, vocally expressing their happiness at getting more food.

These were the same sounds she had heard in this room as a child, the soundtrack of life on a farm in rural Virginia. Newer additions joined the chorus—quick, short footfalls running across the floor. Benjamin and Darla had arrived. The slower tapping sounds from a longer stride followed. *That would be Beth*, she thought.

She hadn't seen Beth since the coat incident. The snow had left a huge drift across the drive leading up the hill and it was a steep climb on foot.

"Where's Sara?" Beth asked. Her mother's answer was given too quietly to hear. A rash of *shushes* met her ears. Beth was reminding the children to keep their voices down and they were telling each other the same thing.

"Shh," one said. The other repeated it and erupted into childish giggles.

Sara finally pulled herself from beneath the covers and crept to the kitchen in desperate need of coffee. The pot was empty, so she set about making some fresh.

"Sorry for the noise," Beth said from the doorway. "We were trying to be quiet."

"It's all right. I wasn't really sleeping anyway." Sara brushed it off before turning wide-eyed toward Beth. *Did she really just apologize for something of her own free will?*

"Auntie Sara," Benjamin called out. He raced across the floor.

"Hey there, buddy," she answered.

As she swooped him up in her arms, he giggled louder. "Daddy said we could build a snowman today. Do you want to help us?"

His sincerely happy face was joyful with

anticipation of a day spent playing in the snow that had previously been too deep and hazardous to be out in. Wiggling in her arms, his pent-up energy demanding an outlet, she settled him back onto the floor.

Darla bounded up beside him. "Yeah, Auntie Sara, help us."

Sara patted her on the head. "Okay. Just let me drink some coffee first."

"Yay," they chorused. Clasping their little hands together, they spun in a circle on the floor. "She's helping, she's helping!"

Sara gulped down her coffee. When she had enough caffeine in her to make her feel alert, she threw on some thick clothing and met the children in the yard for snow games. A little play might be good for her, too, and it would help the day pass.

Outdoors Sara wouldn't be looking at her watch, consulting the clock, or fixating on her phone too many times to count. The hour and minutes was displayed on nearly every object nowadays—the television listed the time, the microwave and the oven had built-in clocks—everything held a reminder of the passing time.

The children went home for dinner. Sara showered and changed into fresh clothes, letting her hair dry by the fire, accepting the curly spirals it turned into when left to its own devices. Now she was thankful to watch the minutes click by. It meant she was nearer to seeing Luke and getting his opinion about the radio show.

Her father came in for the evening, and she set the table for four. Luke was having dinner with them tonight. Six-thirty came and went. Seven came and went. His cell phone went straight to voice mail.

The need to discuss the job offer grated on her,

made her anxious and nervous. Sounds caused her to jump. She ran to the door and watched the driveway for his car. Sara dialed his number again, left a message, and chewed her nails—an uncommon thing for her.

Over the next couple of hours her mother's friends telephoned, a neighbor rang up looking for a lost dog, and Beth called twice. Sara's heart thumped with wild abandon and sent her pulse into a rampage with each phone jingle. *Where is he?* Worry for his safety overtook that of her needs. *Is Luke okay? Has there been an accident?*

She had almost surrendered her phone-answering duties when his voice sent relief through her veins. "Luke, where are you? Where have you been? I've been so worried."

"Sara, I'm so sorry. One of the parishioners fell in the snow and has broken a leg so badly it needs surgery. Another collapsed with a heart attack shoveling the snow from his sidewalk. I'm at the hospital with them and their families."

"You aren't going to make it over tonight either?" It was a selfish question, one she wanted to take back, but simultaneously needing the answer.

"I wish I could, Sara, but…my flock…the parishioners…" His voice faded, despair underlining his tone.

"Right," she said. "Of course." Although she meant the words, the loss to herself—the long day she'd spent waiting for him—disappointed her.

"I'll call you tomorrow," he assured her.

"Yes, of course," she repeated.

Despite understanding his obligation to be with his parishioners, she felt a little let down. She had wanted to talk to him so badly. But now he was with others. That was how it would always be. A pastor had to tend his flock. He couldn't put her first.

"So where is Luke tonight?" her father asked.

She explained and he nodded. "At least you are the right one to understand his situation."

"What does that mean?"

He squinted at her in confusion. "You've been putting your job before family for years. Please tell me you don't hold Luke to a lesser standard."

She nodded and knew instantly what she had to do. "You're right, Dad. And I've got to resume that position. I'll never be the kind of woman who can sit at home and wait on a man. I've got to get back to New York. My life depends on *me*."

Sara hurriedly stuffed her belongings into her bag and raced for the door, stopping only long enough to send a text to the station.

Though she heard her father's voice as she sped back through the house—"But Sara…"—she didn't listen.

It was nearly midnight when she tossed her bags into the car and fishtailed down the slippery driveway, sliding to the road with heart-pounding fear. Thankfully, the main arteries were cleared, salted, and sanded. She sped away from Bland before she could change her mind, hitting I-81 in Wytheville bound for Roanoke.

****

It was two a.m. before Sara arrived at the airport. Fortunately, a space was available on the five-thirty a.m. flight, but the two-hundred dollar rebooking fee put another ding in her budget. Had it not been for her network-issued press credentials, she wasn't certain she could have obtained the seat. It was just one more perk of the lifestyle she enjoyed.

Once Sara had garnered her ticket, she turned off her phone. She couldn't bear to see Luke's name pop up as he called again and again from the hospital. The desire-filled kisses they had shared haunted her, leaving her with longing she hadn't known existed.

In addition to being physically attractive and inspiring desire, Luke was a good man. He deserved a partner who would be there for him totally, not one who had to do things her own way. She swallowed the knot threatening to choke her. It squeezed her chest, making breathing difficult.

Her flight number was finally called. She boarded the plane with swollen red eyes, deflecting the surrounding people's stares.

I'm doing the right thing. So why does it feel so wrong, she wondered forcing the memory of Luke's face and his echoing voice from her mind. His smile was harder to eradicate. It looped through her like a movie trailer the entire stretch of the flight. *Stop it*, she warned herself, grabbing her luggage from the carousel and hailing a cab into the city.

The slush from the taxi tires didn't cause her a great amount of concern. There was no longer a white coat to be ruined. She'd left it, along with her heart, in Virginia.

Having not slept for two nights, Sara was more tired than she could ever remember being. All she could think about was returning to her apartment, falling into bed, and letting the city's sounds lull her to sleep.

Her apartment looked stark and had a funny odor to it after her Bland expedition. Perhaps it always had and she just hadn't noticed it. She called her office and arranged an interview schedule for the following day. Then she crawled into her stale bed and slept.

****

Sara slept for the rest of the day and night, awaking early and racing into work an hour ahead of schedule. It felt comforting to once again experience the city's pulse, to breathe the smoky, polluted air, and drink the chemical-laced, metallic-tasting water.

She made the same single phone call to her parents she had made when she ran from Cade, assuring them she had arrived safely, and hanging up before they could voice opposition. She silenced her phone so as not to hear their return calls. Burying herself in her work, she was ignoring all calls from Virginia.

*I'll feel full again—whole, renewed—*she assured herself. *I just need to get back in the saddle, get a full day of radio programming accomplished. That's all.* But the end of the day, and the next, brought no relief. The sad fact was she had never felt emptier in her life.

Leaving Cade hadn't been this gut-wrenching. She relived Luke's kisses over and over, the way his hands caressed her face, his breath ruffled her hair. She missed him with her whole heart, it now protesting its newfound emptiness.

When she could take her staid apartment's loneliness no more, she wound her way through the festive streets, trying to build up the Christmas spirit she had felt in Bland. Leaning against a store front with her eyes closed, she mentally conjured the image—snow-covered mountain peaks, columns draped in evergreen roping, wreath-festooned front doors, Christmas trees with sparkling colored lights, the tree her father had sacrificed for this Christmas.

Fleeing the memory as surely as she'd run from Bland, she continued along the avenue until the scent of butter and sugar stopped her in her tracks. Blythe's Bakery announced its delicacies each time the door was jerked ajar, tantalizing the passersby. She glanced at the trays being hauled from the display case. Instead of seeing the round lady in the white coat, she was transported to the farmhouse in Virginia.

Her mother would be in the kitchen, from which wafted the aromas of sugar cookies and coffee. Her father, in the living room, sat between the fireplace and its neighboring evergreen tree. And Luke…

Oh, Luke. She could hear his soft laughter, feel his fingertips entwining with hers. The memory, teasing her with delight, flickered for a minute before disappearing as sirens split the air. Beeping car horns, squealing tires as brakes engaged too quickly, drowned out the tinkling bell of a Salvation Army Santa Claus leaning over a change-filled kettle. Her footsteps quickened.

Restaurant doors burst open, revealing fierce activity for a split second, before closing just as quickly. Inside Sara knew people laughed and sipped beverages with holiday names—the Silver Belt, San-ta-gria, Peppermint Daiquiri.

Peppermint. She laid her hand against the

chalkboard sign announcing the menu. Luke smelled like peppermint and cedar. *How I miss his laughter.*

The restaurant's maître d' opened the door and pointed to her. "Care to come in from the cold? You can wait for your party inside if you'd like."

"No thank you. Just checking the menu."

The door shut, and Sara shuffled down the street searching for the elusive Christmas feeling. It defied her, shunning her attempts. Somehow she wound up at Rockefeller Center. The wet streets and skating rink glittered with the tree lights. Glancing upward she saw the Herald Angels silently beckoning. She picked her way through the crowd and back to the quiet area at the wire sculptures' bases.

After a few minutes she heard laughter. Looking around, she saw two feet behind the park bench. With merriment in her voice at the joy of seeing her homeless friend, she said, "I see you, Marge McKay."

Pulling herself out from her hiding place, she said, "I thought you went home."

Sara rolled her eyes. "I did."

Marge squinted, sizing her up. "So what are you doing back here?"

Sara shrugged and picked at a lint speck on her pants. "I missed the city and my old life, I guess."

"Liar!" She giggled.

Shocked at her outburst, Sara snapped. "What?"

Marge turned her impish face toward Sara. "If you are so happy in your life here, what are you doing moping about now?"

"I can come here if I want to," she replied. "It's a public place."

"Well, if you got family back home, and you're

here instead of there, they must not want you very much."

Marge's innuendo hit hard, causing her to wince from its emotional wound. "They want me a lot, as a matter of fact."

"Then you just don't want them," she argued.

How can someone with no real knowledge of me know me so very well? "What's it to you?"

Marge shrugged her bent shoulders and began coughing. It rattled in her chest and she had trouble getting it to stop. The toboggan hat she wore, obviously meant for someone much younger, danced with its long tasseled tail.

"You need to see a doctor about your cough," Sara warned.

"Ain't no doctor interested in giving free care to the homeless," she replied between coughing fits. "It'll pass."

Sara tugged on Marge's sleeve. "Come on. I'm taking you to the hospital."

"No, you're not." She jerked free and coughed a while longer. "I'm just like you. I want to be left alone."

Sara bristled. "Who said I wanted to be left alone?"

"Make up your mind. You say your family wants you home for Christmas, yet you are out here plodding about by yourself...alone. I was once like you."

"In what way?"

"I couldn't accept the tide had changed for me. I kept pushing and pushing, rowing against the current until it took me under." She had a faraway look in her eyes, as though she could see not only past Sara, but beyond the city's skyscrapers. Her hands fluttered in the air as her voice softened. "If I had my time to do over, I'd turn around and release the oars." The rattle returned as she breathed.

It alarmed Sara. Rattles indicated fluid buildup. She needed medical care immediately. "I really think you need to see a doctor, Marge. I'll pay for your care. We just need to get you some medical attention."

The old woman shook her head, the tassel from the toboggan's tail now bouncing both up and down and side to side. "Doctors can't fix what's wrong with me."

"How do you know?"

"I know. Just like I know about you." She jerked her head at the Herald Angels. "They're never wrong."

Confused, Sara thought it likely Marge's oxygen was getting low. "What are they saying now?"

"They're saying I'm finally going home. And that you'd better do the same or you'll be right here, all alone…with no Marge to—" She broke into a coughing fit. "Not everyone can hear them, like me. I listen to them. So you listen to Marge." She pointed a mittened thumb at herself.

"Marge, you're talking nonsense. At least let me get you a room for the night, out of this damp, cold air."

"I've only waited 'cause I knew you'd—" She coughed. "I knew you'd come back. You just can't let go." Pursing her lips, she shook her head.

Sara insisted again on taking Marge to the hospital.

The woman got angry. "If you want to do me any favors, get off my bed. And go back home…before they forget about you."

Sara rose, left all her loose bills and change on the bench, and promised to check on Marge the following day.

The morning papers relieved her of fulfilling the promise.

Homeless Woman Found Dead on Bench
in Rockefeller Center

Sara knew instinctively it was Marge. She had finally *gone home*, just as she'd foretold.

Chapter 22

Luke was beside himself. He drove out to the farmhouse on the Goode's property every day, hoping for word, praying Sara would come home. All he'd received for his efforts up until now were blank stares from her crushed parents.

Ben grabbed his shoulder in a gloved hand, giving it a squeeze. "She's afraid of attachment, Luke. If it's any consolation, the fact she's hiding from you likely means she is experiencing feelings that she has a problem dealing with."

"What should I do?" He recalled the conversation he'd had with Sara when she'd confessed what had transpired between her and Cade. Hadn't he promised he would come after her if she did the same to him? But it was the holiday season. He not only had services to oversee, but sick and injured parishioners in the hospital needing his visitation. What *could* he do?

Ben stared off into the distance. "Well, I guess…" He paused. "Look, I don't know what promises you two made between you, and it's none of my business. But I s'pose…I mean…if you have to ask…well…" He shrugged.

Luke knew he was hinting at something. "Go ahead. I can take it."

Sucking in air, as if the words needed a fresh oxygen supply to make them congeal, he faced Luke.

"You're lucky she was only here for a month. Any longer and you might have been so attached you'd just walk away from the pulpit and go right up there after her."

Ben's words shot through him. Luke tried to reason, to see how it could even be made possible. "If I decided to do that, to go after her, where would I find her? Is there an address to her apartment building lying around somewhere? And even if I knew where to go, who would look after the church and the flock that depends on me?"

Reaching inside his coat, Ben pulled an old envelope from its inner pocket, slapping it down on the table by the chair. He shrugged. "I can't stop you from observing things, like a return address, on your own."

Luke snatched the envelope, snapping a picture of the address with his telephone. "That answers a part of my question, but—"

Grinning, Ben gently retrieved the greeting card from the table and placed it back inside his inner pocket. "You young people have to be told everything these days."

"Such as?"

He held up a hand. "I appreciate your dedication to the church, son, but don't you have some pretty dependable deacons? If you had to oversee an emergency, who would you call?"

"I'd call Cade Norton. But, in this situation..." Luke couldn't imagine asking Cade to stand in for him while he did the thing Cade should have done so many years ago.

Ben shrugged again. "If you know what to do, where to go, and who to call, and you don't..."

For a moment he looked down his nose at Luke before tucking his chin and glancing upward. "Well, it's a choice then, isn't it? You're choosing to let her go. And that's okay too. As long as you realize you are making a decision."

The words flattened Luke. It was a choice. No matter how he justified it, he was choosing to stay in Bland instead of boarding a flight to New York.

The front door yanked open, banging against the jamb as two sets of small feet clattered through the house. "Maw-maw," Benjamin and Darla squealed, "Paw-paw."

Luke heard the shuffle of Sadie's slippers as she scooted to the children, probably issuing hugs the instant they saw each other.

"Excuse me," Ben said. "The little ones are calling for their grandpa." He crossed the room and disappeared.

The children's shrieks echoed back to Luke. *Family.* He missed them.

Lost in his thoughts, he failed to hear the more subtle steps Beth's shoes made against the rug-lined hardwood. Her voice startled him as she called his name. "Luke…Luke Sterling…hello?"

Glancing up, he saw a brown paper package tied with jute roping. A white tissue paper lining corner jutted outward from the edging. "Oh, Beth…"

"How are you holding up?" she asked.

There was no point in hiding the truth. He was in love with Sara, warts and all. And he wasn't holding up well. In fact, he felt as if he was coming apart, his bones threatening to shatter from the extra stress weighing down on his heart. "How do you think?"

She sat down beside him. "That bad, huh?"

"Yeah. That bad."

Beth set the package aside. Her sharp features were more obvious when she frowned, as she did now. "You know, there are a few things I've never told Sara, but wish now I had. One is that we all love Cade and always did. But he was a fool for letting her go without a fight. And she was right not to settle for a man who didn't think her pursuit-worthy."

Luke winced. "You're telling me I should go after her."

She gave a sarcastic chuckle. "I'm the last person to give advice. But I do wonder what's stopping you?"

Luke's heart was palpitating. He hated to admit the real road block. But if he couldn't tell Beth, he would never be able to tell her sister. Taking deep breaths, he stilled himself for the challenge of admitting his failing. One word. A single four-letter word packing more punch than a symphony. "Fear."

It glanced off her. "I recall a preachment you delivered about the phrase 'do not fear' appearing at least twenty-nine times in the Bible."

Grimacing, Luke bowed his head. "You know, there's nothing that hits a minister harder than having his own sermons delivered to him."

A hand landed on his right knee—the damaged one—but it wasn't his, it was Beth's.

He thought he detected a slight tremble as she muttered words as surprising as the gesture. "I've been whispering the phrase, 'do not fear,' beneath my breath for the last hour. I'm fearful of facing my husband and admitting an expenditure we can't afford. I'm going to have to get a job and put the kids in daycare, or get

Mom and Dad to look after them. That's hardly fair since they do so much already."

Suddenly Luke was outside his own thoughts and thinking about someone else, concern for Beth filled his lungs where oxygen had barely been allowed. "You seem pretty level-headed, Beth. I doubt you would have spent money frivolously."

"Frivolous? No. Unaffordable? Yes." She shook her head. "What's your fear? What's keeping your butt in that chair instead of going after the woman I believe you're in love with?"

Another single word answer, but the one taking him back to the locker room on the day he was released—the one when his coach had turned his back, slapped another player on the shoulder, and fled from him as if he might be some noxious disease carrier. It had nearly killed him. "Rejection." *I can't face that again. What if I don't recover this time?*

Beth snagged her lower lip between her teeth. Merriment flashed across her face for a brief instant. "What if you had an excuse to go to New York? What if you needed to make a delivery? A special Christmas delivery?"

Pointing at her, Luke found his voice. "You're up to something. Spill."

Snagging the package by its twine, she tossed it into his lap. "I need this delivered to Sara. Before Christmas."

The package was soft, but thick. He dangled it by the knotted string. "Why? What's in here?"

"Her coat. I got it back for her, stain-free."

"No way. They got the paint…? But it had dried. Beth…?" He gasped. Suddenly it made sense. "This isn't her old, stained coat, is it?"

Her mouth dropped open. She started to nod a yes, and then slowly began to shake her head sideways. "The paint residue turned loose, but a big gray circle"— she raised her hands in a dinner-plate-sized shape— "like a target, remained."

"And you purchased a new one for her, with money you couldn't afford to spend, in order to make amends?" Luke hoped it was true. And then he hoped it wasn't. He wanted it both ways—the coat returned whole to Sara, but without the added financial burden to Beth and Thomas.

With quivering lips, she admitted, "Yes."

Luke was floored. He toyed with the twine, pressed on the paper covering. He just kept fiddling with the paper, wondering what had gotten to Beth, to make her do such a thing.

Her hand reached up to swipe away tears collecting against her cheeks. As if reading his mind, she answered his unspoken question. "She was right. I did it on purpose."

He remained quiet as she sucked in a giant inhalation before continuing, "I had gotten used to Sara's absence. I liked it—liked having the attention from *both* my parents. Mom's always preferred me, Sara's right about that, too. But Dad? No, he was all Sara's, and we knew it from the time she was born. Ruining the coat was a dig at her. I had no idea it was so expensive."

Ben appeared. He'd apparently overheard at least part of the conversation. "That's not true. I love my girls the same. But your mom made it so hard on Sara—well, I guess I overcompensated." He sat beside

Beth and pulled her against his shoulder.

She sobbed openly, unable to stop.

Ben rubbed her head with his big, giant workman's hand. "I'm so sorry. This is my fault, too. I'll chip in on the debt."

Her chest heaving, sobs breaking the words, Beth shook her head. "I can't…ask you…to do that. You've already…given me so much."

Luke watched the father-daughter healing taking place in front of him. He ached to run from the house, jump on a plane, and be in Manhattan before nightfall. But he was needed right then to facilitate the bonding of Sara's family, so they would be ready to receive her fully when she came home once again.

It dawned on him suddenly. "I have an idea," he said. "Why don't you two earn the money together? We can all go to New York!"

Beth and Ben looked from one to the other, shrugging. Ben was the first to speak. "What are you going on about?"

Luke rubbed his hands together, and raised an eyebrow. "A little business venture."

Beth had ceased crying, the tears having left streaks down her face. Looking stunned and confused, she asked, "What do you mean?"

Luke pointed at Ben. "Meet me outside in an hour. I've got a proposition to present. If it's accepted, we'll need some equipment and a truck." With that he sped from the Goode house straight to the Norton house.

****

Cade Norton stared at him for a few minutes. "You've lost your mind. It isn't possible."

Luke slapped him on the shoulder. "Oh, ye of little

faith. Why are you standing here, stalling, when there's work to be done?"

"But it's two weeks until Christmas. Who's—?"

Luke grabbed Cade's jacket from the hook by the door and tossed it to him. "Are you going to argue, or get busy?"

He chuckled, pointing a finger at Luke. "She's under your skin, isn't she? You're doing this to get Sara to come back."

Bracing for his reaction, Luke squared his shoulders, faced him, and prepared to confess his love for the woman who had once broken Cade's heart. "And if I am, would it matter to you? Would you still help me?"

Cade turned away and then back to face him. "You can't mean it."

"I do. I am in love with Sara Goode. But there are some issues in her family that must be addressed before she'll be willing to come back. I have to help them. And I need my best friend to help me help them."

Cade looked wounded, his face bore the shattered expression of someone simultaneously shocked and repulsed. "Why would you even ask me if I would? Surely you know the answer."

"You aren't still in love with her, are you? I didn't even know you guys then. What happened wasn't my—"

"Criminy, Luke, I'm in love with Emily. I realized a long time ago Sara was oil and I was water. Yes, I went through a terrible period of rejection and self-doubt, but I didn't know real love until Emily."

Cade grabbed him by the shoulders and pulled him into a hug. "As my best friend, how could you doubt my feelings toward my wife? Toward you? Toward the girl I shared my childhood with?" His eyes spoke the volumes remaining unsaid.

Luke recalled the scenes of Sara running from the church upon seeing Cade and Emily together, Emily nervously pulling at her skirt during the dessert reception after the *Hanging of the Greens* service, and the attitude he'd perceived from Cade when they'd played football after Thanksgiving lunch. "But you two…the sparks…the uncomfortable moments…"

"Pride. Wounded pride, guilt, and ego. Also a bit of protectiveness toward you, knowing first-hand how difficult she is and how flighty she can be when cornered."

Luke's mouth dropped open. He couldn't believe what he was hearing. "So, you're sure you don't mind? You're not still in love with her, still aching from the breakup?"

Cade winced. "Of course not! Did you just hear anything I said? Aren't you the one who's supposed to have the answers to these things? Why on earth do I have to explain human behavior, as despicable as it can be at times, to the counselor?"

Relieved beyond words, Luke embraced his friend again. "I love you man. I've never been happier to be chastised in my life."

"Well then, come on. We've got work to do."

Chapter 23

Local talent filled Sara's calendar for interviews—dancers, actors, singers, the producer for a special Christmas production on Broadway. She recorded several shows each day to stockpile enough new ones so that no reruns or *best of* shows would have to be aired during the days immediately following Christmas. New voices were too difficult to acquire during that sacred time.

She had been given a reprieve, and wanted to make full use of it. If her fans had caused her good fortune by advocating for her return, then she owed it to them to give them fresh programming. She now felt compelled to add at every interview's conclusion—"Good night, Marge McKay, wherever you are."

From her return show's first farewell, people began to talk about it. The radio entertainment release featured a headline asking:

Who is Marge McKay?

Sara didn't need headlines to think about Marge. The woman's voice rattled in her head just as the cough had rattled in Marge's chest the night before she died. *"I'm just like you. I want to be left alone."* And, *"I kept pushing and pushing, rowing against the current until it took me under. If I had my time to do over, I'd turn around and release the oars. Go home."*

Marge was haunting her in a continuous loop. Sara

attributed it to exhaustion, although she'd only been back a week. Christmas was just a few days away. At least there would be a break then, and she could rest. She dragged herself back to her apartment after the final interview of that day.

Tomorrow would be the twenty-first and she'd do the last few interviews for the year. She had downloaded a video of the ballet whose prima ballerina was on the schedule. There was another featuring the lined-up child star performing in the latest successful Broadway remake. With CliffsNotes on the novel she hadn't read, and the town's most famous Santa Claus—one who grew his own beard and had cheeks so plump he could have been the character for whom the book jacket of a holiday favorite was painted—she had all the information she would need to breeze through the next set of guests.

What will I do then? She toyed with the idea of going back home. She wanted to, but—she had left in such a hurry she was sure she'd made everyone angry, or hurt them in some way—it was best if she didn't.

Thinking about Luke, she recalled his conversation about the homeless shelter here in New York. Maybe she should find one and serve up plate lunches in Marge's memory.

Find one? Why do I need to hunt them out? How is it I have been in Manhattan for years and have no idea where the shelters and emergency housing are located?

The berating lifted as her mind swirled with possibilities. She only had to choose one of the many opportunities, or ditch them all for a few days in a tropical paradise detailed in the brochure that had shown up in her mailbox the day before.

Sara stood in the entryway of her apartment's building, facing the front façade. It was lined with compartments, each having its own little door stamped with the corresponding apartment number. She didn't have to search out 24-J. Its location was as familiar to her as a gunslinger's holster to his shooting hand. Every day she stopped briefly to retrieve her mail before heading upstairs.

She expected she might receive a few Christmas cards. There had been several sent to her at the station, mostly as thank-yous for interviews. None were personal. There wasn't a single card from a friend or relative.

Her mind quickly shot another chewing-out round at her. *My relatives expected me to be in Bland. My friends? What friends? I had Luke…but…*

Luke… Thinking about him ripped into her heart, shredding it. Her palm rested against the mailbox front, she bowed her head, swallowing hard. *Don't do this,* she warned herself. *Don't think about him, don't dwell. If he loved me he would have come after me. Even he said as much.*

Lifting her head, shaking it as one might a child's erasable drawing toy, Sara forced all thoughts of Luke from her mind. She unlocked the miniature door. As she pulled it open, a mail avalanche pushed outward from the small receptacle, spewing in a heap at her feet. Stooping to gather the various letters, credit card offerings, and bills, she snatched up an advertising brochure for the restaurants and cafes in the city operating during Christmas.

"Just what I needed," she said aloud.

"Are you referring to me?"

The voice reverberated in the empty vestibule. *It sounded like…no…of course it couldn't be.* She turned, saw no one, only a dark shadow spilling from the corner.

She was hearing things. She shook her head again, stood with the mail pieces fanning this way and that from her shaking hand. To her amazement, the shadow began to grow, spreading toward her. Soon it became more than a silhouette.

It couldn't be. Surely she was talking to herself and no sound would return to her from inside the small chamber. "Is it really you?"

The voice quivered, but the words were clear. "Yes, Sara. It is."

Closing her eyes, she assumed she was now seeing things as well as hearing them. But it felt good. *What harm is there in letting my imagination conjure Luke's lifelike image.*

"What are you doing here?" she asked. She was too shocked by the illusion to say something more welcoming.

Luke's image offered his hand. "You forgot something when you left Bland in such a hurry."

Her heart pumped wildly, thundering as it thickened her throat, forcing blood through her veins at breakneck speed, and making her flesh tingle. Luke Sterling continued to walk slowly toward her. He stopped about a foot from her.

His palm was still outstretched. She wanted to take it. She wanted it more than she could articulate. Yet she felt like stone and couldn't move. Her feet, frozen to the floor like great icebergs, weighed her in place.

His fingertips lifted, landing gently against her

cheek. The touch sent chills from her chin along her spine. They circled to her stomach and raced upward to her heart. She wasn't seeing things, imagining things. He was real. Luke was standing in her apartment building's vestibule, touching her.

"What did I forget?" she asked.

"You forgot to tell me goodbye," he said.

His face was dangerously close to hers, though dimness and teary eyes darkened his features. "I couldn't," she protested. "I couldn't tell you goodbye."

"Why not?" he whispered.

Something wet rolled down her cheek and he brushed it away. The tears were spilling over, free-falling. She could see now he hadn't shaven and his eyes were bloodshot. *Or are my own eyes reflecting back at me?*

He took another step toward her and she went limp, dropping everything; the mail she'd just collected from the floor, the briefcase she'd gripped in one hand, her handbag from beneath her elbow. None of it mattered. Nothing mattered aside from the man standing impossibly before her. Sara's arms reached for him involuntarily, as though they weren't connected to her brain. She grabbed fleece into her fingers as they fisted inside his jacket.

The distance was closed. His fingers curled around her head as they tugged tangled spirals of hair toward him.

There wasn't thinking, only reacting. The stubble on his face scraped her cheek. She didn't care if it sanded her flesh away. The bristling was evidence he was truly there with her.

His lips gently brushed and then pressed against

hers as if he couldn't hold back the urgency with which he searched her mouth.

Have I ever needed anyone as much as Luke?

Cold air blasted through the yanked-open door. A couple, as mashed up against each other as she and Luke were, strolled merrily along without stopping for their mail. It broke the spell long enough for Sara to realize she had dropped all her belongings in the path other people needed to walk through.

She bent to the floor. Luke followed, helping her gather scattered envelopes and advertisements.

A flash occurred in her mind, a screening of all the times Luke had helped her put things in order, including herself. In what felt like an hour, but couldn't have lasted for more than a few seconds, she saw glimpses of Luke catching her running from the church, upset at seeing Emily and Cade with their beautiful family...Luke listening to her problems, giving her a new focus...Luke at Thanksgiving dinner with her family...Luke pulling her dad's truck from the ditch she'd slid into...Luke helping her father with the cattle and the firewood during the winter storm...Luke caring more about seeing her than worrying about gossip in the small town...Luke...

Suddenly everything was clear. The gulf she had thought existed was only within herself. Luke had always bridged the gap. And here he was again, during the holidays, sitting in her apartment building's entrance waiting on her to arrive.

Taking him by the hand, she pressed the code into the interior door leading to the steps up to her unit. "Come with me," she said.

He didn't protest. He followed her, carrying part of

her load in addition to a large bag of his own.

Once inside her apartment, she shed her coat and took his from his shoulders without asking. She hung both on hooks by the door.

The tears had dried, leaving behind salty residue. "How did you find me?"

"Your family. Most notably your sister."

He raised an eyebrow at her surprise. "She asked me to deliver a message."

Sara turned sheepish eyes toward him, feeling more than ever like a heel for skipping out on everyone. "Do I want to hear it?"

"I don't know." He shrugged. "But I think you should."

She braced, her hips hinged against the small table. "Lay it on me."

"Beth said your parents, and her children, deserved a Christmas with *all* their family, including you. *And* she's sincerely sorry if something she did or said was keeping you from your home."

Her sister's apologetic words being delivered by a man who had treated her so kindly made Sara feel worse, not better.

He held out the parcel he had been carrying. "And she sent this."

Taking it from his outstretched hands, she caressed the rough twine, the smooth brown paper. "Beth sent this to me?"

"Yes. Go ahead. See what's inside."

She could tell by his oncoming grin and the finger resting against his bottom lip that he knew what waited for her beneath the wrappings. She opened it slowly. Inside was her winter-white designer coat. She yanked it from the tissue paper and turned it around. The stain was gone.

Sara ran her hand over the coat's back, feeling for some difference in the material's texture. It appeared to be the same coat, only spot-free once again. But there was a new-fabric sheen and slickness her coat had lost with the washing from the baby spit-up. "This isn't my coat," she said.

He locked eyes with her. "It is now."

"You bought this? But…"

"No, Sara. I didn't buy it. Beth did." He ceased talking and just allowed her to absorb the words.

Running her fingers across the label, it was obviously an original. Confused, she protested, "But Beth and Thomas can't afford such extravagances as this."

Luke continued to meet her eyes. He shook his head. When he spoke, his words were soft, though their meaning hit her with force. "No, Sara, they can't. Although the paint was removed from the coat, it left behind an ugly gray circle. Beth bought this as a peace offering, as a goodwill gesture, even though it meant financial strain, a temporary lifestyle change, and possibly putting the children in day care for a while."

Sara gasped. "No. I won't accept it. I'll send it back…I can't…"

Luke pulled her to him, gently, softly stroking her back. "You can't do that. She needs to make this atonement and you need to bury the past by accepting her gift with a thankful heart. Let this be the olive branch that restores your family."

Crying again, Sara felt her heart breaking for different reasons than it had ached before. Perhaps her family did love her, did want a relationship with her. Maybe Luke and her dad had both been right when they'd told her she looked for the bad in Beth and so got it every time.

But there was another reason her heart ached now. Hoping Luke had come this far to reunite with her, she now realized it had been for another reason altogether. He'd come as the pastor, the community church counselor—not as a man wishing to be her lover.

Releasing him, she peeled herself from his chest. "I see. Why didn't you just mail it? You really shouldn't have put yourself to so much trouble."

As she turned away, Luke snagged her arm, tugging her backward. "Sara. Don't turn away, please."

"I'm sure you have a flock to attend. I don't want to keep you from it." She hated wanting him. The desire to hold him to her, to confess her love, nearly overwhelmed her, but she put her back up instead, stubborn in the wake of discovering his arrival had a reason besides her.

He appeared shocked, stricken. "What? You're asking me to leave?"

Swallowing everything she ached to say, forcing her feet not to run toward him, she visualized the strength she would need. She turned what she hoped were cold eyes toward him. "You have done what you came to do. Thank you."

"I did what I came to do? What are you saying? I came to do much more than deliver a package."

Glancing at her watch, trying to give the impression she had somewhere pressing to go, she spoke hurriedly. "Then you'd better get to it."

Luke's hand covered his mouth, a slight quiver

detectable. "I sense I'm keeping you from something, so I'll just get out of your way."

His long legs needed only seconds to cross the room of her small apartment. Looking back at her, he said, "I hope you and your coat will be very happy together. Goodbye Sara."

Gripping the coat to her chest, tears threatening an avalanche, she heard the door shut before she snapped to her senses. *What's wrong with me?*

Dropping the coat, she ran for him, throwing open the door, looking up and down the hall. "Luke!" But he had already disappeared.

Chapter 24

Luke was devastated. Every fear he had harbored, every reminder of what it felt like to be rejected, manifested itself once again. *Why did I do this to myself?*

This was worse than Columbia. At least what happened to him there hadn't been his choice. He hadn't chosen to be injured, hadn't issued the call on the field resulting in his guards leaving him open to a sack.

The moment came back to him in an agonizing flash. He'd leaned back, his weight on his right leg, arm poised behind him for the long toss. His receiver wasn't there yet, but he saw him tearing across the field slightly in front of Princeton's defensive back—the man assigned to keep the receiver away from what would undoubtedly be the game-winning touchdown, if the pass was good and cleanly caught.

His career had been based on trusting his guards to keep him safe from tackles while his eagle-like focus remained on his target, the player turning…turning. This was only the ten millionth time he'd replayed the event in his mind. He could see his target's hands cupped and ready to catch the football.

Luke had smiled to himself in supreme knowledge's instantaneous split second. The opening had arrived. His man was in place. Pushing his weight into the ground, forming the fulcrum through which his arm would sling the ball forward so hard and fast it wouldn't be intercepted, he cocked and… He wanted the scene to change, to be altered by some tear in the continuum between time sleeves.

Never had his wish materialized. Today was no different.

His hands swiped his face as the pain jabbed at him like a phantom limb. It wasn't physically possible to still feel the ripping and tearing, yet he did. Every time he'd thought about it, relived it, had flashes of it, it was the same.

Panic rose, bile gathered in his gut. He collapsed on a bench and rubbed his knee while his inner voice jeered at him. *This isn't like Columbia University. You didn't deserve their exclusion, but this… You asked for it this time. She rejected you, you fool. What made you think Sara would want you? Didn't Cade try to warn you?*

The other end of the bench registered weight. Someone had joined him there. He glanced up and saw Beth, her hands rubbing together in the cold. "So?"

For a minute he was too shaken to respond. *What is Beth doing in the Lions' locker room? Oh wait, that's not where I am.*

Gasping, Luke reeled back into the present. "Beth, hi."

Her expectant face betrayed her nervous curiosity. "So…"

Collecting himself—pushing all emotion, wounded pride, and hurt feelings deep into the part of him he used as a container for things he couldn't show—he thought up a response. "She loved the coat and your gesture. I think you have your sister back."

Tears careened down her face, relief from the anxiety bursting the dam open. "I was so afraid…I thought she might…I don't know…send it back or something." Half-laughing and half-crying, she continued to alternately sob and chuckle. Then she suddenly ceased both, glaring at him.

"And you? What is happening with you two?"

Luke wondered what to say. How could he tell her the awful truth? Yet, he could see no way to keep it from her. Eventually she would know. They would all know. Maybe he could get another church in another town, start over fresh. But no, he'd put so much work into…

Beth shook him gently. "Luke, what is it?" Her eyes sought his as it dawned on her face that her sister had rejected him. "She didn't!"

He tried to smile, to give her his best *I'm okay* face. "I guess I'm not the right speed for someone like Sara. I'm just a dusty old pickup truck and she's a Ferrari."

The witticism didn't work. He felt the tears pecking at his eyelids and just let them fall. It had been too much to process—the trip to New York, the football injury memory, the painful rejections, his loss of Sara.

Beth pulled him into her shoulder. Evergreen scents—pine, cedar, fir—wafted beneath his nose.

"Hey, hey," a voice called out. Deep and resonate, Luke knew its owner. "Are you going to be my son-in-law?" Ben asked.

Luke pulled away from Beth's comforting embrace and shook his head. "I'm afraid not. It's not what I thought. She's…"

Ben's gloves were stained with sap and resin. He

tore one off and laid a stern hand on Luke's shoulder. "Where is she? Where is Sara?"

Beth jerked her head and rolled her eyes.

Ben twisted halfway around, then back. "I'm going to talk some sense into her. I love Sara, but sometimes she's too much like her dad…stubborn and unyielding."

Beth grinned at him. "That's not what you've been telling us all these years."

"Well, I am now. It's a red-letter day." He made writing motions in the air with his hand. "Take notes."

Beth jumped up. "Let me. I want to talk to her first. If what I have to say doesn't work, then I'll call in your big guns. Okay?"

Luke had been listening to the father-daughter chat, using the time to center his emotions. He rose from the bench in defiance. "No. Nobody goes after Sara. She doesn't even know you're here. Let's finish what we came to do and leave."

Ben grimaced, looking bewildered. "You can't mean it, son? You aren't going to give up this easily, are you?"

"There's nothing to relinquish. I was obviously mistaken about our relationship. Now let's go sell some trees while there are still some interested buyers."

Ben and Beth looked at each other, but they did as he asked. The trio walked back to the tree lot and continued the brisk selling of the special trees Ben and Sara had once planted for just such an occasion.

Chapter 25

Luke was devastated. His plans to pursue a relationship with Sara hadn't panned out as expected. Perhaps Cade had been right to warn him, to try to stop his downward spiral. Shattered and rejected in the same city in much the same way he had been once before left him reeling.

A wormhole of emptiness began to eat its way through his belly, clawing at his gut, hollowing out his head. Concentration dulled. Luke wasn't the same person he'd been in college, but he was responding in much the same way as he had when he'd been replaced on the football team. *Depression.*

If he were counseling himself, his advice would be to find something to fill his time, take his mind off himself and Sara, and work toward the betterment of others. There was only one solution—the same one he'd unintentionally gravitated to after the injury. And he knew who could help him.

Finding his friend and fellow pastor, Jacob Hennings, he suggested a trip to the Mission for the Homeless. *Maybe he'll be there*, Luke thought, *the healer with the gray eyes.*

"Sure," Jacob agreed. "I have a few things to deliver there anyway." They gathered the donations and picked up some coffee, cups, creamer, and sugar at the store.

"Just one more stop," Luke said, "Blythe's Bakery."

Jacob grimaced and scratched at his chin. "Are you hungry already?"

"No, it isn't for me. Betty Blythe used to save the day-old breads and baked goods for me to donate to the mission. I called her yesterday and she's got something special for us to take along to the shelter."

"Will there be enough for the entire place? There normally isn't much left on her bakery shelves at day's end."

When they reached Blythe's, Betty rushed forward, looking the same as she always had, maybe a little rounder and possibly a little grayer. Warm, sweet, and spicy hits mixed with the yeasty fragrance of freshly-baked dough in the boxes she had stacked on the front glass case.

Peeking beneath the lid, Luke realized it wasn't old pastry she couldn't sell being offered up, but warm, freshly-baked cinnamon rolls. The heat from the contents was reducing the icing to little more than a glaze as it slid down the edges of the rounds. Lifting another lid, he saw molten cheese oozing from the edges of ham-filled savory croissants.

"Betty," he gasped. "You could sell these out in a matter of minutes."

Betty lifted her chin, winking. "Hush now, Luke. You take those on to those people a little down on their luck. I won't have my name attached to stale pastries during Christmas."

"You're a doll," he said.

The aroma of Betty's treats preceded Jacob and Luke into the shelter. Shelling them out with napkins and cups of coffee, Luke searched every face, looking for the one with the gray eyes.

Though it had been years, he knew he would recognize the man. *How could I ever forget the one who'd saved my life?* The pastries were disappearing quickly. Hungry men tucking into the warm delicious treats kept the noise level low. They were too busy chewing to talk.

Jacob walked up behind him, gesturing toward a cinnamon roll. "Hey, save one of those for Mark."

Luke lifted the last one from the box and laid it on a paper plate with the napkin he'd used to snag it. "Which one is Mark?"

Motioning to the back, Jacob singled out a man in a long-sleeved, black knit sweater and wool pants. "That's him. He hasn't made it over here yet. Mark's our head volunteer. He runs the place."

Luke pushed the roll-laden plate toward Jacob. "Want to take this over to him?"

"No need. He'll be by in a minute. I'm going to start another pot of coffee."

Luke busied himself tidying up the area. Stashing the wrappings into the boxes, then stacking them into a tower to make removal easier, he was about to head out to the garbage bins when a shadow descended from behind.

Dropping the boxes back onto the tabletop, Luke turned. The man Jacob had indicated as being in charge, now stood before him in tailored-to-fit garments. His head was bent over a coffee cup. Luke wondered if someone had donated the clothes or if he'd had a round of good fortune.

"Oh hello," Luke said. "You must be Mark." One

hand lifted the plate from the table's surface; the other began a half-extended proffering for a shake. That was as far as Luke got.

As soon as the man lifted his chin, Luke's world spun backward into the past as he absorbed Mark's features. He had a short, trimmed beard and his eyes were all-knowing—those of a seer or a prophet, steely cold, but simultaneously calming. The granite orbs Luke had thought about and sought for years.

"It's you!" Luke nearly dropped the plate he was holding out to the man.

He didn't appear to be as shocked and surprised to see Luke as he was to *find* him once again. "I wondered if I'd ever see you again. My name's Mark, by the way."

Luke found his fortitude and fully extended his hand. The man grasped it in a firm shake. "Luke. Luke Sterling."

Mark's captivating stare locked onto Luke's. "What brings you back down here?"

Perhaps it was the effect of his oddly-colored eyes, or the impression he'd once made on him, but Luke felt suddenly nervous and emotional. "I'm a preacher now. I turned my life around, partly thanks to you. Well, mostly thanks to you."

Mark lifted the roll, bit a chunk off, and lowered the rest back onto the plate. "To me? In what way?"

"I was at the lowest point in my life when I first met you. I was clinically depressed, actually. You gave me a fresh insight, a new and unexpected view on the world. If it hadn't been for you, I might not even be here today." Saying this gave Luke new purpose, easing the pain from the recent rejection. Perhaps this was what he was here to find—even if things never worked out between him and Sara.

"Well then, I'm glad we crossed paths again."

Luke remembered Mark's previous dishevelment, though he had the calm, innate serenity the rest of the diners, including himself, had seemed to lack. It was what Luke had wanted more than anything—the inner peace radiating from that homeless man in a shelter. "All is well with you?"

When Mark answered, his words were weighted things. "I managed to get straightened out, too. Clean and sober, I reunited with my family." He nodded then, a few too many times in a row.

Luke sensed there was more in his story but wouldn't press. "Jacob says you run the shelter now."

"Yes, I feel as though I belong here. I tried to follow in my dad's footsteps, join his firm, but just found no joy in the world outside this. I returned as a volunteer. I live onsite, full-time, though I take most Thanksgivings off to visit family."

Luke snapped his fingers. "So that's why I haven't seen you in all these years? You're not here at Thanksgiving."

He smiled an almost other-worldly smile. "It's the best time to get away. We have the most volunteers then. Something about the parade and the ensuing holidays has people aching to ladle soup and carve turkeys."

Luke hungered to question him, wondering about the man who had made such an impact on his life. But something in his demeanor stopped him. Mark didn't appear to want to be identified beyond the mission's walls. Separated from his ego, he seemed content to be the overseer, administering aid, hot coffee, and warm blankets.

On the walk back to the parsonage, Luke waited for Jacob to bring some subject up, anything he could use as a springboard to dive into Mark's curious past. As they neared Jacob's home, it became clear he was no longer thinking about the shelter's overseer.

They were walking by a string of small markets, little more than stands that sold a few basic needs. Tilted wooden bins brimming with fresh fruits and vegetables lined the street-side outer walls. In the meager December offerings, root vegetables—potatoes, turnips, yams, celery, onions, carrots—and citrus— oranges, grapefruits, tangerines—accompanied a few mixed greens, bell peppers, apples, chestnuts, and some brown, papery-skinned ginger knobs.

Picking at the ginger, Jacob chose one resembling a giant's thumb with ridges around its girth and motioned he was stepping inside. While he made his purchase, Luke glanced around the shop's interior. A rack behind the register housed cigarettes, looking like tiny books lying on their edges. Snack bags were gripped by clips on a carousel, bottles of wine lined a far wall. He didn't have time to survey the offerings on the center aisles, as Jacob had completed his purchase and was ready to go.

Luke's curiosity rumbled and rolled around his mind. "So you trust this Mark guy?" He asked in his best nonchalant voice.

"Mark…and his family," Jacob replied.

"You know his family, too?"

Jacob sneezed. He held out the bag holding the ginger, a lemon, and two oranges. "Feeling a cold coming on, I might need a toddy tonight."

"Oh…yes…a toddy. Right."

Jacob pointed to a side street. "Shortcut."

Luke hadn't been watching where they were going. "Right," he repeated.

They had only taken a few more steps when Jacob stopped. "What's on your mind?"

"Is it that obvious?"

"Yes. Remember, Luke, I've known you more than a little while."

Luke chuckled. "It's Mark. There's something about him…I…"

"You probably already know more about him than you think."

His words settled over Luke. *How can I know anything about the man? What is Jacob hinting at?* "Are you sure?"

"Well, most Americans know the Duchamp family. His silver-spoon upbringing didn't keep him from getting hooked on drugs and alcohol. He's come a long way. Miraculous really."

"So he didn't fish today's clothing from the donations bin?"

"He might have, actually. He's cool that way. Come on. Let's not linger in this night air."

Chapter 26

Buzz. Buzz. Buzz.

Sara pulled the covers over her head. Who'd be buzzing the door at this late hour? Her efforts to ignore the jangle were useless. It continued after a brief pause.

Buzz. Buzz. Buzz.

It was obviously going to continue until she gave the sleep intruder a piece of her mind. Stumbling from her bed, she made for the door, stumping her toe on the small coffee table.

Dancing around with the just-injured foot grasped in both hands, she blurted out, "Ouch, darn it, what the…?"

Buzz. Buzz. Buzz.

"Wait a minute!" she screamed, knowing they wouldn't hear her until she activated the intercom. Hopping to the door, she hit the intercom button. "Who is this and what do you want? Do you have any idea what time it is?"

"Actually, it's barely ten p.m.," a familiar voice answered. Sara couldn't quite put her finger on whose it was. "I thought you kept later hours up here in the city. Now you're acting like Grandma."

Ah. Now she recognized it. But why would Beth be in New York? I must be dreaming. Yes, that was it—a nightmare. But this couldn't be a dream or Beth's familiarly sarcastic tone would have been nicer, with a sweeter vocabulary.

"So are you going to buzz me in, or what? I'll just keep hitting this call button until you do."

Punching the release on the inner chamber door, Sara heard a swift, "Thanks. I'll be right up."

"Oh, God," Sara groaned. Removing the chain locks and twisting open deadbolts, by the time she jerked the door open, Beth was standing before her. Her disheveled sister had brown bits of something stuck to her cheeks and forehead.

"Hi, sis," she called in greeting. Before she could respond, Beth gave her a swift hug.

Sara felt the sticky goo from her sister's cheek tug at her hair. She had to pull the strand away from Beth's face. "What happened to you? Did you get into a fight with a Christmas tree?"

Swiping at the resin, Beth merely spread it instead of wiping it off. "Several actually. I've been selling them down on the corner."

"Selling trees? Down on the corner? That's why you're here?"

"Among other reasons."

Pointing at the grinning Beth, who watched the realization settle over her, Sara squealed in surprise. "You're in New York? Selling Christmas trees? Like on a real lot? You?"

Beth laughed. "They pay you to interview people? Really? Like on a real talk show? You?"

Sara turned away and then back again. *Has some future-Christmas ghost just landed in my apartment?* "Who are you? And what have you done with my sister?"

Beth pointed to the brown paper package wrapping

still wadded on the floor. "Opening presents early? Bet I can guess what was in that one."

Crossing her arms, Sara stood at attention, finally feeling awake. "Go ahead, apparition. Guess."

"A very expensive winter-white designer coat. It was from your sister, who had been a fool and wanted to make an atonement gesture."

Sara grabbed her to her chest. "It is you. I don't believe it." She ran to the door and looked out into the hallway. "You're not here by yourself, are you? Who did you come with?"

Crossing her arms over her chest, mimicking Sara's previous stance, Beth grinned. "Dad. He and I have a little project going so I won't have to throw the kids into daycare and get a menial job because I ruined something I can't afford to replace."

Another shock wave reverberated through Sara. This wasn't possible, couldn't be. "You and Dad? You two did this together? You came here together?"

Beth's eyes squinted into slits, her forehead furrowing downward with her eyebrows. "I thought Luke told you."

"Oh. Luke is in on this?"

"It was *his* idea." She smiled and rocked back and forth. "He wanted to see you, wanted to make sure you wouldn't have any reason to refuse him if he offered— well, it's not my business…" Beth began to survey her damaged fingernails.

Sara grabbed her again, yanking her hands downward. "What exactly do you mean? What did Luke do?"

Beth motioned to the coat, the sticky resin on her face, and then just past Sara's apartment landing.

"Everything, Sara. This is all Luke's doing."

Sara's brows raced toward each other, grimacing. She could feel them meeting in the space above her nose, having gone as far inland as possible. "I don't understand."

Taking her by the arm, Beth led her to the small sofa that would barely be called a loveseat at home. They settled side-by-side on the tight space. "Then let me enlighten you...before you make the biggest mistake of your life."

Sara started to protest.

Beth shook her head. "No, you don't. You listen first. Then, if you wish, you can order me out of your life again. But I have something to say and you're going to listen."

Surveying her sister's broken nails, gruff appearance, stained clothes and face, Sara figured she owed her that much. "Okay, just this once."

"Good." Beth paused a second, as if searching for the right words. When she found them, they poured forth incessantly. "I never really blamed you for leaving Cade. Though others did, and I didn't correct them. Secretly, I thought he was a fool for letting you go. I knew any worthy man wouldn't be tossed away so easily. But Luke...my God, Sara!"

Hearing his name sent chills along Sara's arms and legs. She pulled her pajama sleeves downward, shivering, but remained silent.

"Do you have any idea what he had to do to get here? Have you given any thought to a pastor's responsibilities, during Christmas, and to his parish suffering illness and injury following a crippling snow storm? Have you considered the lengths he'd have to employ to put people in place to cover those things?"

Beth watched her, waiting for a reply she didn't have. Shaking her head, Sara signaled she hadn't.

Beth's voice trailed judgment. "I didn't think so."

Sara knew she deserved it. She should have thanked Luke before dismissing him—really thanked him—and not let her hurt feelings get in the way.

"Sara, how well do you know Luke?"

She hadn't been expecting such a personal question. "What?"

"I mean, do you have any idea how emotionally hard it was on him, in particular, to face your possible rejection? To come here and ask you to…"

It dawned on her what Beth was trying to say. "He didn't come here for me, Beth. He came to reunite the two of us and our family. It's just part of his counseling work as a preacher."

"You really are a fool, Sara. He came here for you. This"—her hand motioned between them—"was just to remove obstacles for you, to make it easier for you to accept him."

"How can you know this?"

Beth laughed. "How can you not? For someone who's supposed to be smart, you sure have a lot to learn." She shook her head. "He's been moping around for days, wanting to hear from you, hoping you'd come home."

"Moping? Wanting?" Sara began to see the light. She hadn't let herself admit how much she wanted him to love her. "Is he still here?"

"I think so. Dad will know."

"Where is Dad? Why didn't he come to see me?"

"He wanted to surprise you after you and Luke

reunited. But that didn't quite go as planned, did it? And now he's waiting for you and me to mend our fences. You do know that Dad's sacrificed a lot for his family, don't you?"

Sara collapsed into sobs. "I've been awful to everybody. Do you think they'll ever forgive me?"

"Hey, if I can, anybody can."

"I thought I was the one forgiving you," Sara protested.

"Whatever..." Beth joked. She hugged Sara to her in sisterly affection for the first time in a really long time...maybe ever.

Chapter 27

It was early, in New York, for tree lot activity. Eight in the morning didn't find too many people wandering around looking for a tree. To save money, Ben and Beth were staying in the camper at the lot's rear near the park. Luke was staying with Jacob Hennings.

Jacob had proven to be a real friend, lining up this corner space for them through his Manhattan contacts. Without his help, Luke knew they could never have found a spot as ideal. Yet, it still had issues.

Thievery being what it was, they had gathered the remainder of the unsold trees, propped them up against the camper, and locked a chain around the whole grouping. It was tedious work, requiring them to be carried once again each morning to the street corner where they could be noticed by passersby.

Luke had just righted several firs when Ben tapped him on the shoulder. "Can you handle the lot while I go warm up for a few minutes?"

"Sure," Luke said. Sipping coffee from a paper cup, his mind wandered back to the previous day. A bleak emptiness assaulted his gut—one that would take more than a hot beverage to fill. *What possessed me to think Sara would ever want me?*

"Nice trees you got there," he heard a voice say. *No, that's ridiculous, just wishful thinking.*

"Yeah?" He set the cup aside and looked around. Nobody. Shaking his head, he picked the drink back up.

"A little dry, but nice."

"Dry? These are the freshest trees in New York. They were still in the ground last week at this time."

The muffled voice came from the lot's far corner. "So you say."

He walked toward the sound and spied a pair of boots among the tilted trunks. The rest of the boots' owner was concealed by the thick fir trees. Grabbing a fir branch, he pulled along its length. Only two individual needles came off in his hand. "See? If it wasn't fresh I'd have a whole palm full." He held it out as the person peeked between the limbs.

She stroked his palm with her long finger as she picked up one loose needle. Her third finger sported a silver-banded family crest ring engraved with a giant curving G in the center.

"Nice Claddagh ring," he said.

She quickly snatched her hand back into the thickly nestled trees' obscurity. "What would you know about Claddaghs?"

"Only one thing, really," he answered. "I know who that one belongs to."

Luke started to his left around the tree stack and saw the boots quickly moving right. Turning, he watched them halt and start back left again. Tossing the trees to the ground, suddenly uncaring of breaking limbs, his only thought was getting through the evergreen maze to the woman behind them.

"Careful," she warned, "those are some very special trees."

"How would you know? You didn't even think

they were fresh."

"These are my trees. I'd know *them* anywhere," she said.

"Sara," he gasped, unable to keep it inside any longer. "I'd know that *hand* anywhere," he said. He clasped it firmly between both of his. His pulse tore at the flesh housing the veins his feverish blood raced through. Resisting the urge to pull Sara to his chest and cradle her to him, his body seemed perched on the edge of some unknown abyss. *What is she doing here? Surely it's by accident, yet…*

"Luke," she cried. "Forgive me. I'm stubborn, stupid, and—"

Luke didn't let her finish. Instinct-driven, he released her hand and clamped both his around her head, bringing her mouth to his. Covering her face with kisses—hungry rounds of nibbles at her cheek, chin, and ear lobes—he couldn't pull away from her. "I love you," he whispered.

Laughing, she returned his kisses with equal fervor. "Can we get out of here? I've got about an hour-and-a-half before I have to be at the office."

"Your dad is on break. But as soon as he returns, I'll…"

"Dad!" she squealed, running past Luke.

Over his shoulder, Luke saw Ben, arms spread, catching his daughter into an embrace.

"Get on outta here, you two." He motioned around the lot. "I've got this."

Beth jumped from the camper's step. "And I'm on hand to help."

Sara gestured between the three—Luke, Ben, and Beth. "You know this is really weird for me, right?"

Beth laid a hand on her dad's shoulder. "I sure hope so," she said. "How about you Dad?"

Looking mischievous, he tugged at his mouth's corner with a gloved fingertip. "Well, weird wasn't exactly the reaction we were going for, but if by weird you mean you're stunned, uncomfortable, surprised, I'd say you've pretty much summed it up."

Jerking her head toward the street, Beth spoke, "Go on."

Luke tugged her arm. "Come on, before they change their minds."

Chapter 28

Luke didn't ask where they were going. He'd made the trek the previous day, so he likely understood Sara was leading him back to her apartment.

There were too many questions to ask her family, so she'd asked none. But when she shut the door behind Luke, and threw the bolt, she knew it was time for some serious conversation. "I thought you came to New York to deliver a coat."

Luke looked shy and guilty. "That was only part of it. I really came to tell you I'm in love with you."

She wanted to believe it. He could have expressed his feelings for her over the phone…provided she'd answered his calls. "You came all this way to tell me that?" Sara knew there was more. His standing with hands in his pockets, verified it.

His face lost its mischievous expression. He made no move toward her. Though he appeared confused and shaken, he spoke softly, every word filled with emotion and honesty. "No. I came all this way to ask why you didn't say goodbye. And I wanted to apologize if I moved too quickly…or not quickly enough. I thought we were getting along great. And there was the project we were working on together. What happened?"

Sara could feel his sincerity, and knew this was a man in love with her. What made it even more special was she believed she loved him, too. Anybody willing to do for her what he had, certainly deserved it.

Still, something curled in her gut, her breath quickened. She felt claustrophobic, trapped like a butterfly caught by its wings. All the longing and urges to spend time with Luke dissipated once they were alone together discussing the topic of their relationship. Panic rose, bringing with it the urge to flee.

Marge McKay's voice filled her head. *"You just want to be left alone." No, Marge, I don't want to be alone.*

"What is it?" Luke asked. He reached for her and drew her into his chest. "Tell me what is wrong. What did I do? I can be a good listener."

Sara's heart wanted to give in to Luke. Her brain feared the outcome. She wrestled with her two opposing personality sides. *"Go home," Marge had said. "You'll end up like me." No Marge, I'm not like you.*

"What?" he asked, drawing her face back up to meet his.

"You didn't do anything wrong, Luke. It's me. I'm flawed. I have a lion's courage when it comes to my career or traveling the globe or talking to superstars. But when my heart is laid bare, I can't…I can't…" She couldn't even say it.

"It frightens you. You are scared of getting hurt. Sara, we all are. I'm so scared right now my knees could buckle."

"You're just saying that," she said.

He grabbed her hand and held it to his heart. His voice cracked when he spoke, reinforcing his nervous claim. "Do you feel how it's racing? I'm a total wreck. But I believe God brought us together and he will give me the courage to find out if this is true love."

Fear quickened her pulse. "I don't think I'm the right woman for you."

"Why?" he asked.

The small word communicated much confusion. Disgust would likely follow. With a deep breath for bravura, Sara spoke, "I don't think I can be happy coming in second to your job."

"My job?" His face was distorted, likely because of her selfishness.

She continued, "As a pastor you will be called away from dinners and movies and quiet evenings. I caught a future glimpse with you on my last evening in Bland when you couldn't make our date."

"And what do you see when you look into your alternate future without a man who loves you and wants to make a family with you?"

The air chilled. His question lingered between them, a frozen fissure. "That's not fair," she protested.

"It is totally fair. I want a whole life with someone, and I believe you are that person, Sara. I would never expect you to give up everything that makes you who you are, and I sincerely hope you don't require it from me. Besides, I wouldn't leave you behind. I'd take you with me. We'd be a team."

Her heart ached to believe him. She wanted to be part of his team, to be part of his world, but there were so many apparent road blocks. "I'm here. You're there. How would that work?"

"I thought we were working toward something together. I thought we were starting our own radio show. Now you seem to have closed that door and reopened this other. Let it go, Sara. Come with me.

Come back to Bland and give us a chance."

There was no point in not being totally honest with him now. "What if our idea doesn't work out? I will have given this up for nothing."

He took her hands in his, wrapping his palms around hers securely. "What if it does?"

For the first time, Sara allowed herself to envision the best instead of the worst. She imagined looking into his clear blue eyes for years to come and seeing their curly-haired children toddling around.

She turned an eager face up to him. She was afraid to go with him, but even more frightened to watch him leave without her. "I want to envision it working out. I want to believe you won't break my heart."

Tenderness dripped from him. "Is that what you're afraid of?"

"Yes. I'm afraid of being slammed to the curb if I open up and make myself totally vulnerable. My mother did enough of that to me before I became an adult. I don't want any more emotional trauma."

"So you nip love's bloom. You kill it before it can destroy you. But you're destroying your heart instead."

"So you do understand?"

"I just want to love you, Sara Jane. I know we haven't known each other for very long, but we did spend some concentrated time together when I got snowed in at your place. Why don't you let me try to show you how good a man's love can feel?"

The innuendo in his words shocked her. "Are you asking me to sleep with you?"

He laughed and shook his head. "I didn't come all this way just to ask you to have sex with me, Sara. I'm asking you to share your life with me; to share your dreams. And I'll lay down my life for you in doing all I can to make those dreams come true. I'm asking you to marry me."

Is it possible to believe someone can be this wonderful? Can it possibly happen to me? She was weakening, leaning toward his vividly-painted future. "If I could just believe it was true."

"Let me prove it. You don't have to say yes right now. Say, 'I'll think about it.' But come home with me." His palm cradled her cheek, his thumb caressing her lips as if willing them to speak the words he wanted to hear.

She leaned against his hand, loving the way it felt, the tenderness in his touch. Suddenly, Sara's heart broke open enough to let love's possibility into her life. *What if it works out? What if the outcome is wonderful and special? What if Luke Sterling is the right man for me?* "What if I say 'yes'?"

Luke smiled. "We can be home by tonight."

Home. The word sounded wonderful and horrifying at the same time. "No," she said. "Stay here until Christmas Eve. Let me show you my New York."

"Then will you marry me, Sara?"

His penetrating eyes sparkled with moisture as they searched hers, making it impossible to hide her fears and emotions from him. Offering him an out, a way to untangle his mistaken proposal, she asked, "Are you sure this is what you want? Maybe you're just tired."

"I am tired. And I am sure. I've never been more sure about anything in my life."

She thought about the time and effort and expense he had put into coming to Manhattan, with no safety net if she refused him. He'd orchestrated a peace treaty between her and Beth. He'd helped Beth and Ben figure out a way to make the money to pay for the coat. Only a man truly in love would do such things.

Luke dropped to one knee, looking up at her with an exhausted, but honest, gaze. "I told you I would follow the woman I loved if she ever ran away from me. I'm here now. So Sara Jane, I want to know one thing. Will you marry me?"

Her heart pounded. It thundered and thrashed in her chest, a wild beast. "Yes." She was crying through the words. "A million yeses."

He burst into a grin, the widest she had ever seen. "Do you want to plan a wedding at our church? Christmas Eve, maybe?"

"Christmas Eve sounds wonderful. But I want to get married here. I know just the place."

****

Sara expected Luke might protest having the ceremony in New York. Instead, he jumped right in and began to make phone calls. "We need to have our birth certificates overnight express mailed. We've both got driver's licenses, right?"

She nodded.

"We can get the marriage license right away, but we'll have to wait twenty-four hours to actually use it."

She was amazed at his efficiency and eagerness. "How do you know so much about the marriage laws in New York? I don't, and I live here."

"You may live here, but I have a few contacts, including a minister, here in New York. Unless there's someone you would rather use, I'll give him a call. We were at seminary together. He's who I've been staying with."

"No, that's perfect. Do you suppose it will matter to him where we get married?"

"I don't think so." Luke laughed. "But you are starting to worry me. Where is this mysterious place?"

****

The final day of interviews ticked away. Sara trimmed a few spare minutes off each one to be used to introduce Reverend Luke Sterling, to give him a platform to project his show. They recorded a spot in which she teased him mercilessly and he took it good naturedly. At the show's end, she invited listeners to follow her on social media to discover the station lucky enough to win the bid for his show. She ended with, "Good night, Marge McKay, wherever you are."

The *recording* light died. She was done for the year, possibly never to return to this job. A sad wave wafted over her at the thought. But as she glanced at the man sitting with her, she realized that sadness was nothing compared to the hole in her life if she allowed him to get away.

"Who is Marge McKay?" Luke asked.

"She's a Herald Angel," Sara said. "I'll tell you more about her later." She gathered her belongings. After a quick trip to the apartment to drop them off, she agreed to take him to the spot she desired for the ceremony.

Giving him time to absorb the sight of the massive Rockefeller Center tree once again, they continued across the square to the bench nobody ever seemed to sit upon except for her and the now-deceased Marge McKay.

It was there, in the tree's glow with the Herald Angels backing her up for support, she was able to talk about her short acquaintance with her homeless friend. She shared Marge's story and how her wisdom had played such a role in Sara's ability to see herself through Marge's eyes.

She hoped he wouldn't find her connection with the woman she barely knew as ridiculous and fanciful. "I don't think I would have had the courage to accept your proposal had it not been for Marge McKay."

He listened intently. "God sends us angels in many forms Sara. Maybe she was one of yours."

"That's why I want to get married right here. I want Marge to know I'm not alone and that I am going home."

"I feel like Marge knows it already," he said. He pulled her into his warm embrace. "But why not? I can't imagine a lovelier place."

His easy response surprised her. She had expected him to resist getting married anywhere outside a church. "Really? You don't mind?"

"God doesn't need four walls to attend a ceremony, Sara. I want our wedding to have meaning for you. If this place does, then I'm all in."

Sara searched Luke's face for even a single deceitful wrinkle, wondering if he could really be as wonderful as she found him to be.

The scene with Cade's determination to make their wedding so grand he wouldn't forget it played in her mind. When she had seen Luke walking through the church doors with Cade on that first day, she had thought them alike—two lumberjacks in similar attire with most-likely matching attitudes.

She had been wrong. Luke wasn't anything like Cade. Yes, they had both been athletes, large men with big hearts, handsome and smart—but the similarities ended there.

Luke had supreme confidence. He had a belief in something larger than himself that steered him toward choices and opened doors of opportunity he was wise enough to see. And he believed strongly enough in their love to follow her to New York, chance rejection, propose on one knee, and sit here beneath wire-and-light angels facing an enormous tree, accepting her faith in a homeless woman's words.

He believed in the commitments they would make to each other—not in the circumstances under which they were made. Somehow she knew he needed no special build-up to remember with absolute certainty every second of the day they would take their vows to each other. If it happened in a church, in a judge's chambers, or out here beneath the Herald Angels, it would always be—like her father's train-hopping Wyoming-bound stories—an adventure.

Sara could almost hear Marge's laughter. She looked beneath the bench, half-expecting to see her tiny feet jutting out, or the tassel-tailed toboggan dancing merrily on her head.

Luke's love washed over her. He had flown away from his town and church during the holidays to risk getting his heart broken. He was willing to make their wedding happen anywhere and any way that made her happy. "You'd have to love me to be so cooperative."

He kissed her on the forehead. "Of course I do. Now, I've got some plans to make and you've got some shopping to do, unless you already have something to wear to our wedding."

She felt her eyes bulging and her mouth forming a

giant surprised circle. "A wedding dress! I completely forgot. Oh my...where should I begin?"

He pointed up the stairs at the shops lining Fifth Avenue. "That looks like a great place to start."

"Beth! I'll get Beth to shop with me. I'll need another opinion."

Chapter 29

Luke was sitting in Pastor Jacob Henning's office, planning the ceremony, when he saw Sara's number pop up on his ringing phone. "Just a minute please," he said, winking. "It's my beautiful bride-to-be. Better take this."

From the moment he answered, her ebullient voice chattered on. "Oh Luke, you won't believe what I've found. Well, I can't tell you really, but after spending several hours trying on dresses and having no luck, Beth spotted a costume shop near the theater district. With help from a pair of the shop's seamstresses, the perfect ensemble has been procured."

"So Beth saved the day, huh?"

"Yes, she did. I'm so glad she's here, Luke. What a great day it's been. It feels like I have a sister, a real sister! Do you know what I mean?"

He could hear the enthusiasm in her voice, could sense her joy. She and Beth were getting along, bonding. Suddenly, realizing something else, he gasped. "Your dad, Sara. Has anyone checked on him? I've been making arrangements and you and Beth have been shopping, but what about Ben?"

Sara's wholesome laughter rattled the receiver and he held it an inch from his ear. "Don't worry. Beth and I stopped by twice to check on him, and Beth is there now. We took him a soft pretzel and then some Korean barbecue from a food truck. He was so excited. 'A food truck?' he asked, all amazed at the possibilities here."

She paused briefly before continuing to gush happiness. "Oh, yes, I almost forgot the reason I called. Beth and I are going out for dinner. But first we'll pick up a pizza for Dad, with some fancy ale one of the customers insisted he try, and take it to him, per his instructions. And that's another thing. Do you know Dad has made friends already? Yeah, they're coming back with little gifts for him. Unbelievable. He's been in New York for…what…a few days? And he already has more friends than I do. Isn't that amazing?"

Luke couldn't keep from chuckling. Having her family restored, a man who she knew loved her, a wedding to plan—all seemed to agree with Sara Goode. "Yes, Sara, it's amazing."

"Do you want to join us?"

Luke wanted to more than anything. But hearing how excited she was to be spending time with her only sibling, finding the connection previously eluding them, seemed a rare opportunity.

Beth's kids and husband were back in Virginia with Sadie, so he decided to give Sara one more gift. "I need to work out some more details to make our wedding come together. Why don't you and Beth have dinner, check on your dad afterward, and then you can call me later."

"What? You mean you aren't coming back to the apartment to spend the night?"

"I'm staying at the parsonage apartment tonight. I'm here right now with Jacob going over details. We'll be married before you know it. Then, I'm never leaving your side."

"Promise?"

"Promise," Luke agreed.

"I'll see you tomorrow, then," she said.

"Yes, Sara, and every day after."

Chapter 30

Sitting in her dark apartment after disconnecting with Luke, Sara realized she needed to make a few phone calls as well. She dialed her parents' familiar number. "Mom? I have something to tell you."

Her mother laughed. "You do? Something I don't already know?"

Sara couldn't help laughing as well. This was another rarity, laughing—without reservation or question as to what was funny—with her mother. "Well I don't know what you know, but let me tell you my news and then we can decide."

"Okay, shoot!"

"I'm getting married!"

"And who's the lucky man?" Her mother's question hung in the air across the miles.

"Why, Luke, of course. Who did you think?"

Another spurt of easy chuckling resounded through the phone. "I'm teasing. Your father's called, naturally. He's so excited about everything. Said he was eating food right off a truck and drinking some rare ale. I have no idea what he's talking about."

"See, I knew you guys would like New York if you ever gave it a chance. Now I'm not certain Dad is willing to leave."

"He most certainly is, Sara. He has to be home for Christmas, as does your handsome future husband."

"That's just it, Mother. We're getting married here, in New York, on Christmas Eve. You have to come. Get Thomas and the kids, and you guys can fly up here together."

"Oh, I can't Sara. You know that, honey. I'm on the hospitality committee for the Christmas Eve service. And a trip to see Santa Claus for the kids…with their mother gone, someone's got to do it. Goodness, Sara, I hope you appreciate what Beth has sacrificed for you, and…"

All hope was dashed. Her mother wasn't coming. Thomas wasn't coming. Darla and Benjamin weren't going to be there. This was the taint, the spoil. She should have known better, shouldn't have asked Luke to get married in New York. But it meant so much to her to do so.

Tears threatened, puddled, and pooled. She swallowed hard, and then harder, trying to force them down, keeping them at bay. "Mother, I'll be giving Bland the rest of my life. Can you please give Manhattan one night of yours?"

"I don't think so, Sara. Maybe we can skip it, I mean, Skype it, whatever that thing is where you see each other on the computer."

Sadie sounded so chipper. How could she be okay with missing her youngest daughter's wedding? And Beth was going to miss Christmas Eve with her husband and children because she had promised to be Sara's matron of honor, springing for another expense she likely couldn't afford.

"I suppose we could try, but it won't be the same." Sara heard the disappointment in her own voice, certain her mother would as well. "I thought you'd be happy with my decision to marry Luke."

"Oh, I am…happy. Luke's a great fellow," her mother agreed. "And, according to Daddy, it sounds like things are working out for you and Beth, too."

"Yes, we went shopping for my dress together. It was nice."

"Well, take lots of pictures so we can see it."

She sounded so calm and relaxed. If Sara didn't know her better, she would have thought her mother had started using sedatives. *Where are the lectures on honoring tradition?* "You're not upset we're getting married up here?"

"Not if that's what you want. But, you are coming home for Christmas?"

"Yes. We'll all be home just in time for Christmas."

"We'll see you then. Good luck." The phone clicked.

It was done. She was getting married and her mother didn't seem to care.

Sara dissected her mother's response over and over. Clearly this had something to do with the meticulously-planned, though-never-executed, first wedding. Perhaps this was her payback for the horrid experience of returning gifts, canceling catering, paying for venues and dresses and flowers and portraits that would never see the daylight. Her mother was resigned to forfeiting her role in this wedding now.

Sadie had sounded cajoling. She hadn't asked the expected questions. Was she sure? Had she thought it out, especially having known Luke for such a short time?

Sara bet her mother doubted the wedding would

actually take place. She was probably laughing right now, thinking her daughter would back out again.

Where had the warnings gone? This wasn't at all like her mother. There should have been at least a few diatribes issued on not breaking the pastor's heart. Something was definitely wrong with her mother.

****

The next two days rushed by. Sara barely had time to think about her mother's acceptance of her plans to marry Luke in New York. When she did, it was just a brief moment's flutter, a feeling something wasn't quite right.

It would pass and she would forget about it, until another still-time lapse coughed up her mother's voice in her head—she so sweetly giving her blessing without asking questions. Sara would shrug it off and another to-do list item would fill the gap.

"Dad's suit!" Sara screeched to Beth. They had just returned to the costume shop to find something for her only attendant. "He doesn't have one with him, does he?"

Her sister patted her arm. "Don't worry," she assured her. "I'm getting something for him to wear."

Beth twirled in a silvery flapper-style tea-length gown. Fringe fanned out in a circle around her. "It isn't Victorian like your gown, but…"

Sara could tell her sister liked the dress. It fitted her perfectly, accentuating her figure. "It's wonderful."

"This will work? You really like it?"

"Yes, and I'm going to buy it for you."

Her sister refused. "No, I'm buying my own dress." She pulled a few tens and twenties from her jeans' pocket, tree money she'd worked so hard alongside their dad to earn.

Its sight tugged at Sara's heart. She'd held her entire family to some expectations they hadn't signed on for. And now, Beth was trying to meet the obligation as best she could.

Pulling her lips to the side, Beth flipped through the jackets. "It is rather thin though. I'll need a coat."

With a growing smile, Sara said, "Come back to the apartment with me. I have the perfect thing."

Standing in her living room, Sara insisted Beth put the dress on one more time, just to make sure the jacket she was about to suggest would look right. "Just once more. We'll want to see them together."

Doing as she asked, Beth slipped the silver dress back on and waited for her sister to return.

Sara walked in with a garment bag protecting the pricey item it contained draped across her arm. "Try this." Taking a seat, she watched Beth tug the zipper down.

Her eyes bulged as they fell upon the winter-white designer coat. "Oh, no way," she exclaimed. "I'm never touching this expensive thing again."

Sara grinned at her sister's shocked face. "I insist. It will be perfect."

"No, no." She shook her head. "I can't afford to chance ruining your coat again."

Sara was thankful for the chance to spend time with her sister, which had only happened because Beth had come to New York to earn the money for the coat she was currently refusing. "But it isn't my coat, anymore." She pushed it back toward Beth. "It belongs to you."

After a few rounds pushing it back and forth,

though her voice maintained disbelief, Beth apparently realized Sara meant it. "You would give me this expensive coat?"

"Yes, it's my gift to you for being here for me, for being my matron of honor. I want you to have it."

Beth's hands shook as she caressed the coat's soft cashmere. "I've never owned anything this nice before."

Sara swiped at her eyes, trying to keep from crying, as she saw Beth in a new and precious light. "Well then, it's about time you did."

Hugging and crying, the sisters truly buried their long-standing feud. "You know, Mom only preferred me because Dad spoiled you rotten."

"Dad spoiled me rotten because Mother ruined you," Sara said.

"Sisters?" Beth asked, draped in the coat which had been such an enmity source between them.

"Sisters!" Sara declared. She had never been happier to give something away in her life, nor to receive a better gift than a loving sister.

Chapter 31

Luke had to laugh as he read the headlines on the New York social pages. *Sara's Surprises* had exploded on the Internet. The show's social media pages had become so popular she was trending in New York search engines.

People were talking about every aspect concerning her life. A local television news show interviewed her father and sister. And Ben was terrific. His voice had a great booming, God-like sound. A rival station even tried to hire him to compete with his daughter's lunch-time radio hours.

Though he played down the notion of becoming a radio personality, he clearly enjoyed the attention. And it was good for the tree-selling business. It took only the remainder of that day to completely sell out.

Beth was over the moon. Sara had been taking her all over Manhattan, shopping, sightseeing, and dining out. That was another headline—another fine quality chalked up to Sara as the press marveled at her ability to carve out so much time for her sister while planning a wedding.

With the intriguing and mysterious salutation to Marge McKay, her new venture in religious studies with her husband-to-be—*the well-spoken Reverend Luke Sterling* they called him—and the show's suspenseful aura had everyone musing.

Jacob had asked Luke if he felt sidelined by the attention Sara was giving her father and sister, or the press on the show's behalf. The truth was he was glad for it. Planning this wedding in the few short days before Christmas had been difficult.

Convincing his mother to fly in from Iowa had taken some doing. Having secured a hotel room for her for tonight and a second flight to Roanoke with them tomorrow, Luke was just on his way to pick her up at the airport.

As he waited at JFK, Luke listened to a discussion of Sara on another radio show. He had to laugh at hearing her life discussed so openly. She was now a celebrity like the ones she loved to interview.

"Do you think Sara Goode will take her husband's last name?"

"Why wouldn't she? His name is Sterling!"

"Sara Sterling certainly has a ring to it."

"Who is Marge McKay?"

"Maybe she introduced Sara to the pastor."

And so it went.

"Luke," someone called out. His head shot up from the phone he was using as a personal entertainment device. Rosemary Sterling's petite frame and silvery-white hair stood out, supermodel-style.

"Mom!" He ran to meet her, scooping her up. "I'm so excited you're here for the most important day of my life."

She patted him on the cheek. "You know what Mark Twain said. 'The two most important days of your life are the one when you're born and the one when you understand why.'" It was so like her. An English teacher, she often quoted her favorite authors, little quips from literature.

"So you *had* to be here for the second one, since you were for the first."

She waited until the taxi cab pulled away from the curb, the noise from traffic and horns shielding their privacy in the backseat, before asking questions. "Are you sure this woman is a good choice? You're a preacher, Luke. Your wife must be equally devoted. Can she do this? Is she the right person to be your wife?"

Luke had expected the inquisition. Any parent lacking knowledge about the person their child was bringing into the fold would be as curious and careful. He patted her reassuringly on the arm. "I'm certain."

"But you haven't known her very long, Luke."

"You know, I said that myself. And then I realized I had been hearing about Sara Goode since the day I first arrived in Bland. I've gotten to know her in layers—bit by bit, the good and the bad—over all those years. When I met her face-to-face, it was really as if finding someone I'd known for that many years. She was not a complete stranger."

Tears hit her cheek. "Sounds like your dad and me."

"Oh?"

They were pulling up in the theater district right off Times Square. The Marriott seemed like a good choice for his mom, given her love of the arts. And it was convenient for walking. Luke settled her in, before taking her to dinner, and returning her to the hotel.

She reached up and patted his face. "I'll tell you later."

He finally went to bed, satisfied all was done.

Tomorrow morning I'm marrying Sara Goode, and she'll never be alone again.

Do you hear that Marge? Oh, Lord, he was beginning to talk to Sara's angel now. His own angel still inhabited the earthly realm, but now Luke finally had a name to go with his gray eyes and serious face.

I'm marrying Sara in the morning! Thank you for your influence and wisdom. Good night, Marge McKay, wherever you are.

Chapter 32

Christmas Eve dawned clear, but by eight, storm clouds had started rolling in, dropping hood-like over the skyline. Weather forecasters were predicting a cold rain. But the temperature only had to drop a couple of degrees to make it snow.

The city loved snow at Christmas. Nothing set the town abuzz like the possibility of a good holiday snowfall. Sara could feel the excitement pulsating through her building's very ductwork. Or perhaps it was her own thrilling realization it was her wedding day.

She decided to let her hair do its own thing. If she tried to torture it into the straightened locks she loved, it would only frizz up in the damp air. Whether it rained or snowed, she didn't want to be fretting over her hair. Of course, her big, white top hat should help keep some of the moisture at bay.

She dressed carefully, aware every item was important. Sara wanted to look her best.

Luke kept saying he had everything arranged. He had bought her an exquisite faux fur muff, which she decided to use instead of a floral bouquet. They had purchased his ring—she would be using the family Claddagh—and she took it from its velvet box, held it up to the light, and watched it sparkle as only a brand new one could.

She supposed every argument, as well as time's passage, rubbed a little shine off wedding bands, just as it did with relationships. And no doubt, they would have their share. But Luke had a unique perspective that made her see disagreements in a new light.

For as long as she lived, she would remember the one simple question he asked which had changed her entire perspective. As she had fretted and feared getting involved, asking what would happen if their relationship didn't work out, he had asked what would happen if it did. That had tipped the scale in his favor.

It will work out, Luke Sterling, she mused. Laughing to herself, before placing the golden band back into its enclosure slit, she tucked the box into the long, white taffeta skirt's pocket. With the skirt's matching short jacket, cashmere shell, and top hat her sister had noticed in the costume shop, Sara appeared positively Victorian. Their outdoor wedding in Rockefeller Center would be perfect, especially if it snowed.

She opened the doors to her small balcony and stood on the ledge looking at the city as though she had never seen it before. It did look and feel different today. The gray overcast skies might have appeared foreboding—an omen, if she had believed in such things. Luckily, she didn't, although she feared a severe storm would threaten their flight home.

Luke needed to be home on Christmas Eve night for the children's play and the Christmas service. His parish depended on him.

Look at me, she thought, *already thinking like a preacher's wife.*

Sara shivered and looked across the horizon. Tiny

white dots danced in the air. At first they were few and far between. They could have been ashes from an outdoor fireplace. Sara continued to watch and realized it would not be raining on her wedding day. Like a swarm of white bees, it blew in from the southeast, the direction that always brought the most snow.

Her phone buzzed. "Good morning, my love."

It was still difficult to get used to having a man who loved her, especially as it had happened so quickly.

"Good morning to you, too." Luke's voice possessed a playful tone. "Do you still want to marry me today?"

She laughed. "Wild horses couldn't stop me now."

"Horses, huh? Interesting you should mention horses."

Luke was up to something. She could hear it lying just beneath his teasing words. "How so?"

"I'm sending one after you."

It took a moment for his words to sink in. *A horse? He's sending a horse?* "I'm not riding a horse through the city! Have you lost your mind?"

He burst into laughter. "No silly. You won't be riding it. The horse will be pulling a carriage. Regardless of the snow's depth, it should be able to get you to Rockefeller Center. There will be no excuses for you to stand me up."

His words startled her. There was the reality of her doing that to another man. She whispered into the phone, "I wouldn't do that to you...to us."

Ignoring, or not noticing, the change in her mood, Luke remained cheerful. "Nevertheless, a horse has been ordered. And you'll be alone in your splendor.

I've decided I want to stay with tradition and wait to see you. I'll watch as you descend the steps from Fifth Avenue through the Herald Angels and down to the square. Prometheus and the tree will be our backdrop."

Another panicked shock wave descended. "I'm supposed to ride through the city alone in a horse-drawn carriage?"

"You won't technically be alone. There's the driver, of course, and a photographer will be there to capture your last moments as a single woman."

He really had thought of everything. The necessity for a photographer had escaped her. "It sounds divine, Luke. I can hardly wait. I'm already dressed. So anytime you are ready, I am."

"My, oh my, for a bride who was quite reluctant only a few days ago, you now seem rather eager," he teased.

She peeked across the opposite building's rooftop, now nearly lost in winter weather's froth. "What can I say? I see no reason to hesitate. Besides, have you looked outside?"

"Snow?" He didn't sound surprised.

"And likely to be a large accumulation."

"Then the horse and carriage was more brilliant than I even thought."

"You really are special, Luke."

All the humor left his voice as he became sincere. "I just want our wedding day to be beautiful, and full of cherished memories, so you will have no regrets."

"I have no doubt it will be wonderful."

His voice radiated warmth. "I'll see you there. I love you, Sara."

"And I love you." It felt good in her soul to

exchange confessions of love. She suddenly felt full—blessed and whole. It was different from anything she had experienced before.

The snow fell harder and heavier, blurring the landscape, turning the buildings into impressionist paintings with the lights bending into streams and refracted slashes. It whitewashed the entire city, sticking to frozen roofs and statues and car tops.

A great peaceful feeling washed over her. The knowledge she was doing the right thing settled on her mind. She said a prayer, asking God to give her the strength and fortitude to be a good wife. She wanted that more than anything. Sara wanted a happy marriage and a peaceful home.

The door buzzer interrupted her serene thoughts. She pushed the intercom button. "Yes? Sara Goode speaking."

"Your carriage awaits Ms. Goode," the driver announced.

Sara looked into the mirror. "This is it," she whispered to herself. "I'll never be single again."

She hiked her gown up so as not to drag it along the steps. Two carriages sat at her building's front. The rear one had a photographer on board. He snapped her pictures as she exited the door and was helped by the driver into the first carriage. When sure she was comfortably settled, the horse was urged to move along, slowly pulling the carriage away from the curb.

The ride through the city was exquisite. It looked like a fairy land. Even the hats and caps of the people walking along the street were snow-topped.

Luke must have given instructions to take her through Central Park, as the horses clomped in unison into the joggers' and dog walkers' green space. The carriages paused on the bridge, by the ramble stone archway, and again by the lake in order for the photographer to hop down and snap several pictures.

People stared and waved and shouted congratulations. The entire city had become a setting, and all its inhabitants were participating as guests. Sara waved back, smiling broadly as she accepted their well wishes.

There was only one rub—an incessant consternation—as she realized her mother would not be there. Her sister had promised to rent something suitable for their father, but Sara had been so busy with Luke she hadn't checked to be sure. It didn't matter if he had on his work clothes and heavy gloves. At least he would be there.

They proceeded down Fifth Avenue, past St. Patrick's gothic spires and stained-glass windows. Sara couldn't get over how the snow made the city appear pristine, as if Luke had hired a baker to sugarcoat every inch. Christmas decorations popped with dazzling brilliance against the white backdrop as the carriage continued past the famous stores with their window dressings.

They pulled to a stop and the photographer approached, signaling with hand motions that she should remain seated until he was set up to catch her departing the coach.

Sara's heart began to drum wildly as she realized the moment had arrived. At the bottom of these few steps was a man she hadn't even known six weeks ago. Their attraction to each other had been instantaneous. Time slowed to a crawl as she started the descent in motion.

The carriage driver assisted her from the rig, steadying her as she stepped into the snow. At least she'd had the foresight to change into beige boots. Although not as attractive as her red-soled heels, they were much safer. The last thing she needed was to stumble and fall down the slippery steps.

The photographer snapped the shutter, directing her to look this way and that, stand taller, pull her shoulders up and back. She tired of his demands and started for the walkway. He raced ahead and landed at the bottom, camera pointed upward.

This is it Sara, she warned herself. Shoving both hands into the muff, she struck a pose at the top of the stairs. The Herald Angels seemed to turn her way, looking upward with their trumpets at the ready. Music came from somewhere. It was easy to imagine it coming from the brightly-lit wire angels in the Christmas snow.

Her gaze swept to the spot where the minister waited in a black suit and a clerical collar, his long stole wrapped like a scarf around his neck, an opened Bible resting in his hands. He looked up expectantly toward her, a thin smile etched across his face.

Luke stood at least a head taller, waiting anxiously to the minister's left. He could have been headed for a sports banquet, an athlete decked out for awards. His broad shoulders filled her vision's entire scope. She could easily make out the wide smile dimpling his cheeks. He shifted his weight in the snow as she approached.

People scurried about, exuding excitement as they raced to the stores for last minute gifts, expertly wrapped presents protruding from double-handled bags with the stores' names where they had been purchased displayed across the front. Ice skaters laughed as they circled the rink, making fresh figure eights in the newly fallen snow blanketing the frozen surface. Children played in the snow as their parents cajoled them to stay close to their watchful eyes.

None of this detracted from her day. Sara loved the bustle and the dreamy stares directed toward them. A young couple stopped a short distance from them and the woman laid her head against the man's shoulder. She pointed at Sara to be sure he noticed the unusual sight they obviously made to onlookers—the bride in her Victorian outfit, with the horses and their buggies lined up behind her—a fairy tale princess headed to the ball.

Life was moving ahead, but in this moment it had led them all into one shared experience, one communal event. It seemed to make up for the missing friends and family members who normally would have filled in the pews around the couple making their vows before God and assorted witnesses.

Sara tried to spot her father and sister. In the blur of snow, lights, and photography flashes, she only saw outlines. The couple to her left resembled her parents. The woman was too petite to be Beth. She squinted tightly, imagining it was them and not just her father and some random onlooker. She spotted Beth and someone conforming to Thomas's shape. *Benjamin and Darla should have been here*, she thought with dismay.

The absences at her wedding brought the one bit of sadness into her day. *If only they could have been here.* She felt the tears begin to pool and looked heavenward.

Help me, God, she prayed.

"Sara," a voice called out, followed by a chuckle. She looked around, expecting to see Marge McKay. Hands went up, floating skyward in waves.

"Auntie Sara!" a boy shouted.

Her father sprang up the stairs toward her in his own very dapper and fitted suit—the one with the pointed lapels he'd insisted on the last time they'd pulled him shopping. He held out his arm for her.

Sara broke into sobs. "Daddy," she cried, as he grabbed her tightly around the shoulders. "What have you done?"

Sara's mother grabbed her in an embrace, nearly knocking them both to the ground as she slid on the slippery surface of the stairs. "You look lovely, sweetheart."

Her mind wasn't forming the right questions, couldn't grasp the words from the air. "Mom? How? You?"

Her mother brushed her cheek with a soft, gloved hand. "Did you really think I would miss your wedding?"

"Why didn't you tell me you were coming?"

"I wanted to surprise you, honey."

Her dad stepped between them. "Are you two going to keep blubbering, or are we going to have a wedding?" He pulled back, holding his daughter out at arm's length. "By the way, you look absolutely gorgeous. Preacher Luke is a very lucky man." He winked at her.

He released her to first help his wife to the bottom of the steps to the position reserved for her, and then returned for his daughter. Sara accepted his arm and walked with her father to join the man who had just made her every wedding wish come true.

The minister started to speak when they reached the final step, but the rest of Sara's family raced forward. A round of hugs and introductions stalled the wedding as the snow continued to enfold them. It was a happy delay.

"You all came," Sara declared, encircling them into bear-hugs.

She threw her arms around Luke and showered him with kisses. "I can't believe you did all this for me. You have made me so happy…happier than I can express. I love you. I truly do."

She released him, and saw how wonderful her expression of delight at his efforts had made him feel. He practically beamed, emanating joy.

He gently pulled on her arm. "Sara, meet the other woman in my life, Rosemary Sterling, my mother." Luke motioned to the elegant, silver-haired lady standing near him.

Sara embraced her with a heartfelt hug. "You have raised a wonderful son, Mrs. Sterling. I can't tell you what it means to me that you have dropped everything to come to New York on short notice."

"I wouldn't have missed it for the world." She patted her soon-to-be daughter-in-law on the cheek. "I always knew when the right woman came along, Luke would be swept away."

"Look, Auntie Sara." Little Benjamin pointed to the skating rink. "We're going skating under the tree as soon as you finish getting married." It sounded like *maui'ied* in his little boy voice.

"Then we'd better get on with it," she declared.

"You're ready?" Pastor Hennings asked.

"Absolutely," she agreed, taking Luke's hand.

He nodded.

"Dearly beloved," the minister began. Silence fell over the square as if everyone there realized their great love and wanted to give them the proper reverence. Even the slush and scrape of blades cutting into the ice on the rink subsided. Small groups of people gathered around as if place holders, standing in for those who would have been there, if possible.

After a round of *I dos* and *I wills* the preacher pronounced them husband and wife to roaring applause and a cackle. Sara glanced behind her.

"One more thing, Preacher," she added.

"By all means," he replied.

"Goodnight, Marge McKay. I know you are here."

"Who is Marge McKay?" her family asked.

"I'll tell you later." She laughed. "Right now, I'm going home." She pointed to the carriage waiting to whisk the newlyweds away.

"See you at home," her parents called out as she and Luke raced between the Herald Angels. Skyward-pointing trumpets shone brightly against the freshly-fallen snow.

A word about the author…

Renee Canter Johnson is the author of *Acquisition, The Haunting of William Gray,* and *Behind the Mask. Herald Angels* is her fourth novel with The Wild Rose Press, and highlights a few of her favorite things: storytelling, romance, and Christmas in New York.

Renee has studied in France and Italy, and is a fellow at Noepe Center for Literary Arts on Martha's Vineyard, Massachusetts. She lives on a farm in North Carolina with her husband, Tony Johnson, and two very spoiled German shepherds named Hansel and Gretel.

Renee Johnson is a member of the North Carolina Writer's Network, Romance Writers of America, and She Writes. Her essays have appeared in *Bonjour Paris*, *Study Abroad*, and *Storyhouse*. Renee's blog for personal observations and photography is at http://writingfeemail.com. She focuses on the craft of writing at http://reneejohnsonwrites.com.

You can follow her on twitter at http://twitter.com/@writingfeemail and Facebook at http://www.facebook.com/renee.johnson..549436.